Try Not to Die
In Roswell and Beyond

Kevin David Anderson

Mark Tullius

Published by Vincere Press
65 Pine Ave., Ste 806
Long Beach, CA 90802

Try Not to Die: In Roswell and Beyond

Printed in the United States of America
First Edition

ISBN: 9781961740495
Library of Congress Control Number: 2025917109

Cover by Jun Ares

Try Not to Die
In Roswell and Beyond

Roswell New Mexico
August 19, 2019

It's not the lamest thing I've ever done with my parents, two confirmed sci-fi nerds of the highest order, but agreeing to spend my final weekend before I leave for college with them and my little brother in Roswell for the UFO Festival is definitely up there.

I don't even believe in aliens. I mean, I believe there is other life in the universe. We're not alone. You'd have to possess the intelligence of a Flat Earther to think otherwise. But I can't believe that beings with vastly superior knowledge travel across the galaxy to make crop circles, build pyramids, dissect cattle, play hide-and-seek with our military, and abduct village idiots in Kentucky or Alabama to perform highly invasive medical experiments, including sending a probe where no probe has gone before.

Unlike my family, I don't find any of the UFO lore credible, interesting, or even entertaining, but as we walk into the Invasion Station gift shop, one of many catering to alien nerdom, just a half mile from the convention center, none of that matters. What does matter is the replica sci-fi weapons in front of us, their elegant handles protruding from a display barrel. My younger brother, Wes, sees them too. We exchange grins and both know it's go time. It's like an alarm has gone off in our heads, screaming, *Immaturity Mode: Activate.*

Wes reaches the barrel first and selects his weapon. I move him out of the way by grabbing his backpack that he wears everywhere, and spin him into the center of the store, nearly knocking over a stack of Alien Desk lamps that I know project crop circles on the walls thanks to Mom buying one at Comic-

Con last year. Without much time to be picky, I grab one as well. We square off, eyeing each other like gunfighters. But we are not gunfighters, nor do we hold guns. We are knights, and although our plastic light-up swords may have been manufactured in China, when I look into my brother's eyes, it's easy to imagine our weapons were made in a galaxy far, far away ...

"I've been waiting for you, Dushe-be-wan," Wes says.

I try not to smile. "Good one." I depress the power button on my lightsaber engaging its kyber crystal, or triple-A batteries. It makes the familiar sound effect. "Give it up, Nerd-akin Dorkwalker. I have the high ground."

"You're a foot taller than me," Wes says. "You always have the high ground."

I return with my best Yoda. "Excuses you make. Die you shall."

I raise my weapon, ready to swing my battery-powered plastic laser sword of death when Mom steps between us.

"James, Wesley, stop this right now," she says. "You're both too old to act like this."

"I'm fourteen," Wes says with a laugh. "Statistically, this is exactly how I'm supposed to act."

Mom takes his sword and turns to me. "Can you please act your age?"

Before coming over to scold us, Mom had been trying on springy alien antennas, one of which flops over onto her forehead. I love her, but it's really hard to see her as an authority figure sometimes. I shrug, power down my implement of imaginary intergalactic death, and hand it over.

"Now, this is our first time in Roswell as a family," Mom says. "Please don't embarrass us."

I spy my father, who has tried on an alien mask, one of the Greys. He staggers like Frankenstein's monster while making beeping noises.

"Not sure that's possible, Mom," Wes mutters.

"We embarrass you?" I shout. Getting scolded for trying to have fun on a trip I didn't really want to go on releases the anger I've been holding. This summer, all I wanted to do was spend time with my friends who will be scattered across the country soon, and the rest of the time play video games. "We embarrass you?" I repeat. "We aren't the ones wearing pointed prosthetic ears!"

As soon as the words leave my mouth, I instantly regret it. The hurt is visible in my mother's eyes as she reaches up to cover one of her Vulcan ears she had worked so hard on. There is a Trekkie gathering this evening in the hotel lobby, and she had started her cosplay earlier in the afternoon. She looks like she is going to say something but turns away.

Wes steps close and lowers his voice. "James, that was not cool. You know how much they love this stuff."

I do know and I feel absolutely awful. Since before my brother was born, my parents had been taking me with them to fan conventions from *Star Trek* to *Lord of the Rings*. My favorite family picture from those early years with my parents is of us, without Wes, all dressed in Next Generation Federation outfits. I was in an infant-size onesie, posing with a Klingon, aka Uncle Kevin. Truth be told, I did enjoy it, for a while. But then I just grew out of it for the most part. About the time I became a gamer.

I'm about to apologize when my dad steps over, still wearing the mask. I don't know if he heard the whole exchange, but the alien façade on his face looks angry. The big bulging almond-shaped eyes seem to narrow. Not sure how that's possible, but they do. Instead of laying into me, he turns his back and puts his arm around Mom, who I hope is not crying.

Wes pulls on my arm. "Run away," he whispers.

I follow, mostly because it's the easiest thing to do. I don't have the words yet to tell her how bad I feel, but I know I will soon. I'll apologize in the car, where everyone can hear.

"Do you think there is a support group for children of Trekkies?" Wes asks.

"Man, I hope so."

Wes is a bit of a Trekkie as well, evident in his Starfleet backpack, which he is never too far from, as it contains his inhaler and EpiPen. Most of my family is firmly in Camp Trek, but not me. I'm the redheaded stepchild in the family. I'm a *Star Wars* fanboy to the core. If I'm being honest, I like them both, most geeks do, but I don't believe anyone can like them equally. Everyone's a little one way or the other, except for maybe Wes. He seems to be firmly stationed in the middle. He'd be comfortable with a lightsaber in one hand and a phaser in the other. It's probably because his real passion isn't Wars or Trek. It's much worse. It's Legos.

When my bookworm of a brother isn't nose deep in some boring pictureless novel, he is constructing something out of Legos. He spent all of last summer building a Death Star and Enterprise D out of the plastic construction blocks. He didn't see the sun for days. Mom set food in his room in the afternoon and checked on him in the evening to make sure he was eating. He's a little obsessed. If he could build a girlfriend out of Legos, he would. Sad but true.

Wes eyes the Lego section of the store and says, "Later, loser." My brother's Lego Quest on this trip can only be accomplished here in Roswell. He is hoping to score a limited series set of the 1947 Roswell incident. Regardless of how disinterested I seemed, Wes told me all about the famous alien crash landing. It's the main reason Roswell is a hotbed of alien folklore and nonsense. Supposedly in 1947, an alien ship crashed here. According to the story, not only does the U.S. military still have the spaceship secured away in a secret hangar, but they also have a couple of real E.T.s as well. The government explained away the whole incident as a rogue weather balloon, but that is no reason to let a good conspiracy theory die or deny Lego the opportunity to make money by selling limited series sets to UFO nerds.

I stand alone in the center aisle of the store. On one side of me is an assortment of alien delicacies. Alien Head sour candies, Alien Autopsy gummy pieces, Alien Probe Suckers that are straight up gross, flying saucer-shaped potato chips, and Alien Jerky—which I assume is beef. I hope it's beef. On the other side are games: Interstellar Tic-Tac-Toe; three-dimensional chess; Solar System Monopoly; Alien Operation, and Abduction: The Board Game, fun for the whole family.

I sigh and wonder if I should just go wait in the car. I turn toward the entrance, and before I take a single step, I see my brother outside the main window. At least I think it's my brother. The window is as clean as a dirt road, and Wes, if it is Wes, looks disheveled. The figure sees me looking at him and immediately ducks from sight. What the hell is Wes up to?

"Hey, Dork-Vader," says a voice right next to me.

I look over and see Wes. "How did you do that?"

Wes looks confused. "Do what?"

I turn around and look back out the window. "Were you just outside?"

"No, why?"

Go outside to investigate the would-be clone sighting of Wes.
Turn to page 225.

Stay inside, ponder the situation, continue browsing, and maybe insult Wes some more.
Turn to page 34.

I've got thirty seconds to convince my parents to leave with us. "This is so crazy," I tell Wes, heading towards their aisle. "We need a story."

"You don't think they'll buy the whole talking fish in your ear story?"

"Not helping," I say, still no idea what I'm going to tell them.

"I got this." Wes runs up to Mom and pulls on her arm. "We gotta go," he tells her. "James pissed himself."

That asshole. I spin around to the door so Mom can't see he's lying.

"Oh, honey," Mom says, putting a hand on my shoulder. "You haven't done that in years. Are you sure?"

I nod, cover my junk with both hands, and start plotting my brother's death. "Can we just go to the hotel?"

The front door opens in front of us. Two huge men in black suits, sunglasses, and bad haircuts block the exit, neither moving.

"M.I.B.," Mom mutters.

"Excuse me," I say to the suit on the right. "We were just leaving."

"Not yet," he says, taking a step inside and backing us up.

My mom steps in front, pushing me behind her. "My son had an accident. It's not his fault. He has his father's bladder."

He ignores her and reaches for my wrist. "We need you to come with us."

Mom slaps his hand. "Don't you dare touch my son."

"Outta the way, Ma'am," he says, pushing her to the side.

"Whoa, whoa, whoa," Dad says, running up, his voice muffled by the alien mask.

The one on the left goes for a holstered weapon. The other one grabs my wrist just as Dad arrives.

"Hey," he says pulling off the mask, his hair disobedient in all directions. Dad reaches for the man, I assume to get him to let go, but this ape's grip is fierce.

The agent brings out a sleek, futuristic device that looks like the toy guns and phasers in the next aisle over. But as he points it at my chest, I'm pretty sure it doesn't need triple-A batteries, or have prerecorded *pew, pew* sound effects.

"Outside," he demands. "All of you."

Mom grabs something off a shelf behind her, holds it over her head, and runs at the men. "Ahhh!" She hits the closest man right in the buzzcut with a 12-inch Predator action figure.

Unfazed by the assault, he turns and looks as if he is going to backhand her. I reach for his arm. Dad leaps on him and tries to grab his gun. The gun goes off. An explosion of light blinds me.

My eyes adjust, and Dad's on his knees, looking confused, picking up the pile of clothes Mom had just been in. She is gone.

"What did you do?" Dad screams at the men.

I feel arms around me as more black suits arrive. I aim low and slam my fist right into his nuts. His eyes go wide, and he bends forward, looking like he might puke. I take off running, see Wes standing still, and grab him as I go by.

We're barely to the Legos' aisle when a gun fires. My brother's grip on my hand disappears in an instant. I slow, look back, and see his clothes on the floor behind me. Then it's my turn.

The correct choice was to listen to the fish-shaped stowaway, grab Wes, and run out the back.

Turn to page 53.

"Let's just hang here for a while," I say. "We don't know what's out there."

Wes stands up. "Last I remember, we were over Nevada. Four thousand years ago, North America had indigenous people, a sea of bison, and probably the freshest air we have ever breathed."

I don't know why, but I think it's best if Wes and I stay put until we hear from Bob. To convince my brother to stick around, I activate the monitors and initiate a scan. "Let's see what we can find out while we're waiting." The overhead display comes alive with images and data, all of which capture Wes's attention.

"What does this one mean?" Wes points to stats readouts.

"That one is telling me that we're in about a meter of sand. Won't prevent us from exiting, but I bet it will hide the ship a bit."

"Who're we hiding from?" Wes asks, as he slides back in his chair.

"Well, let's find out." I deploy a probe that rises above us into the sky. I set the altitude for five meters. No need to draw attention to ourselves, even if it's just a mammoth out there. Could there be mammoths out there? I have no idea. I really did get into college by the skin of my teeth. I reach forward with both hands and manually expand the monitors.

The full-color images from the drone are projected onto the canopy as wide as possible. We seem to have landed in a sparse gully surrounded by sand dunes.

"Looks like Pismo Beach," Wes says.

"Is this what Nevada looks like ..."

"Wait," Wes says. "Over there."

Moving across a dune two hundred meters away is an odd being. It takes a second to realize it is not one odd being, but two. A man in a bright-colored tunic riding a horse. He is soon joined by another and another.

"I'm gonna get a closer look." I activate the probe's stealth mode. It doesn't make it invisible, just allows it to blend in like a chameleon so it's not easily noticed. I take it up another five meters and close the distance with the riders.

"I don't think we're in Nevada," Wes says

"Why?"

"No horses four thousand years ago."

"Sure there were. The Indians had horses."

"Native Americans. And they didn't have horses until the Spanish brought them over in the sixteenth century.

"Oh, yeah. I knew that," I lie. "So, where did ancient people use horses four thousand years ago?"

"Uhm, can you move the camera up a little bit?"

A wind whips around the probe and sand obscures the view for a moment. I nudge it another six meters higher. The screen flickers for a moment before resolving, and the vast expanse of the dune no longer blocks the view. What greets our eyes on the other side steals the breath right out of my lungs.

In the distance, shimmering in the heat haze, are structures unlike anything I've ever seen in a history video. Even from a kilometer away, I can see a flurry of activity around their bases. More structures dot the landscape, but two, and another colossal one half-built, dominate the horizon.

I raise a hand to my mouth, jaw agape. "Those can't be ..." I stammer, turning to Wes with wide eyes. "Are those ... pyramids?"

2543 BCE —Ancient Egypt, Fourth Dynasty, the Necropolis in North Africa.

"Okay," Bob says. "I've got good news and bad news."

"We're not in North America! We're in ancient Egypt!"

"Oh, so you already know the bad news," Bob says.

Wes puts his helmet on and lowers the mic. "So, not only are we in the wrong time, but we're on the wrong continent?"

"Yes, and I know that sounds bad, but there is a logical explanation."

I slump deep into my seat. "Let's hear it."

"When the Astral Fighter was damaged, we lost temporal fluxberries. Even the power cells were hochsenseeds."

"You're glitching again, but go on," I say.

"During a temporal jump, I am out of communication with the ship, and due to the stress of the time skip, you two were unconscious. The ship's onboard Heuristically Programmed Algorithmic Computer was forced to make decisions. With the destination date scrambled in the fight, it made the decision to take a temporal exit that had the statistical best chance of solving the ship's current problems."

"Okay, slow down," I say. "What problems?"

"In order to complete our mission, we need to fix the ship with replacement parts, and the best chance of securing those parts are here in North Africa at this time."

"Wait, so there are parts for this ship here?" Wes says. "In the ancient past?"

"Yes," Bob says.

Wes asks how that's possible.

"It's better I show you. I'm taking control of the probe."

The images on the screen abruptly change. The view is now higher and zooming in. There's a large, colorful statue with the body of a lion and the head of a man, donning a beard a good five meters in length. The tan and smooth features on the face and heavily made-up eyes are only dominated in presence by its gold and blue regal headdress.

"Is that the Sphinx?" Wes says.

"Can't be," I say. "It has a nose, and it's in color."

Wes looks at me. "You think they built it without a nose?"

"Would you both please look past the monumentalized ego statue," Bob says. "A few meters to the right. See it?"

I don't know why we didn't notice it at first. Maybe we were distracted by the Sphinx with a nose or the huge pyramids, not at all looking like the pictures I've seen. These are covered in white limestone glimmering in the sunlight, gold capstones on top like decorative hood ornaments perched on a pharaoh's chariot. But to the right of all that is something that looks about as out of place as a tauntaun in the desert.

"That's a spaceship," I say.

"Is it the Reptilians?" Wes asks.

The camera zooms in on a tall, ash-colored being, gaunt with a big head and almond-shaped eyes. "The Greys," Wes says.

"Correct," Bob says. "A real bunch of Zeta Reticulin berry-holes."

* * *

Bob explained why the Greys were here helping ancient humans build the pyramids, something I would have dismissed as BS just yesterday. How did he put it? It was a mix of a canine complex and galactic narcissism. The narcissism was the part where they felt the need to act like gods, experimenting and manipulating primitive species all over the galaxy. The canine thing was about the need to mark their territory. In this case, with massive pyramids humans wanted to build but didn't yet have the technology.

But the important part was that the Greys have been visiting Earth for a very long time, and at this particular time in ancient Egypt as they strut around the planet like untouchable gods, their security is relatively low. The parts we need are just a little petty theft away. The plan is simple. I will sneak aboard the Greys' ship, steal the parts, install them in the Astral Fighter, and jump forward to 1997, where I'm supposed to alter galactic history.

Bob calculates that I have a 34.7 percent chance of completing this successfully.

"So, there is like a seventy percent chance I'll fail?" I say to Bob after he lays everything out.

"Sixty-five point three," Wes corrects.

"Look, Bob. Can't you just zap us the parts we need from wherever you are?"

"Your location in history is too pastways back. There is not a solid temporal root near you to establish a landing plumstrudel."

I reach up to run my hands through my hair in frustration, but as fingers touch bare scalp, my hands fall away. "Well, can't do it without a landing plumstrudel."

"Precisely," Bob says. "And James, your choices are becoming more and more critical. Course reset may not be an option soon."

There it is again. The feeling that comes when Bob says something that causes the hair on the back of my neck to stand up, if I had hair. I look over at my brother. "Hey, Wes, I need a moment with Bob. Can you ..." I point to his helmet.

Wes sighs. "Fine." He removes the helmet so he can't hear Bob anymore.

I get up and walk to the rear compartment. It's cramped, not meant for hanging out, but far enough away to have a somewhat private conversation with the time-traveling alien speaking through a fish in my head.

"Bob. Earlier you said something like, we've never made it this far before. And once you said I never brought Wes. Have I ... I mean, have we done this before?"

"In a way. I have had to reset you a few times."

"Reset?"

"In your gamer lexicon it is referred to as respawning."

"Yeah, but that's what happens when a character is ... You mean, I've died before?"

"A few times. I have the ability to reset you. Send you back to the moment in which you made a terminal decision and give you a second chance to make a better choice."

"How many times?"

"Not important," Bob says.

"How many times?"

"Not enough to do damage."

"To what, the ship?"

"To your brain."

"Are you kidding me?"

"Relax. I am sure you are fine."

"How do you know?"

"Do you feel the need to wear your underwear on the outside of your clothes or write a personal manifesto?"

"What! No!"

"Then you are fine. I know this is confusing to your tiny …. Wait. Let me restart."

"You were going to be insulting, weren't you?"

"A bit, but I caught myself. I am trying to use terms you may understand and will not make me glitch. What we are attempting is both complex, and very simple. Moving through time is not what you understand it to be. In some ways, you have not even left Roswell. A version of you is still there, just like every time you respawn, you may meet a different version of me."

"Different Bobs?"

"Different, but the same. As I said, time travel is not what you understand it to be."

I run a hand over my bald head. "This is giving me a headache."

"Star Pilot, if successful, our actions will unleash a time quake, a ripple through the galaxy that will not shatter but mend, not destroy but unite, altering the dismal history that has afflicted trillions."

I look back at Wes, who is double-checking his pubic area and looking disappointed. "Well, that all sounds pretty good, I guess."

"Right now, you have a critical life or death choice to make."

"Which is?"

"Should you take Wes with you to steal the parts we need or leave him here safe in the ship?"

"That doesn't sound at all like life and death."

"My temporal fusion-melons and axle bloneberries indicate that it is."

I sigh deeply. "Why do some of these language glitches sound like interstellar fruit?"

"Uncertain. That is something to ponder."

Leaving Wes behind violates one of the rules for surviving a horror movie. Never separate. I don't believe we're in a horror movie, maybe a science fiction, time traveling, low-budget nightmare in which every other choice I make can get me killed, but I feel that the rule does apply.

I stagger back up to Wes, who swivels in his chair to look at me. He must have seen something on my face. "What's wrong? I mean besides the obvious."

"This adventure might be giving me brain damage."

"Oh, really. How would we notice?"

"Nice," I say. "Bob thinks we can sneak onto that ship. It's kind of insane."

"More insane than being stranded in 2543 B.C.?"

"Good point."

"How are we gonna get on that ship?" Wes asks.

"We'll figure it out as we go. We'll be creative. Use our improvising skills."

"Do we have those?"

"We'll *get* improvising skills."

Wes sighs and puts on his helmet. "Bob, this is Wes."

"Go ahead, Wes."

"If we are going to steal from aliens, I think it would make it a lot easier if I could communicate with you as well. If we get separated, I could get stranded. Or what if James dies. Then I'm really, really stranded."

I don't have the heart to tell him I have died already. Maybe both of us have.

"That's a good thought, Wes," Bob says.

"So, should I just keep the helmet on?"

"That would make you stand out amongst the locals, and the helmet range is only a few hundred meters from the ship."

"Is there another way?" I chime in.

"Two options," Bob says. "If you were in physical contact with your brother, say holding hands."

"Ewe," Wes says.

"Gross," I agree.

"You would be able to hear me but not talk back, and the level of glitching we're already experiencing via the temporal citrus-pastway would increase."

I swear Bob is just making up words.

"Okay, so what's the other idea?" Wes asks.

A tiny lid opens on the ship's command console, and reveals a small metallic box. It rises slightly with a mechanical hum. Wes picks up the box and gazes inside. "Oh, no."

"What?"

Wes holds it out to me. It's another Pisces Converter.

* * *

After twenty minutes of pacing about to psych himself up, Wes seems almost ready. He paces the same way when he has to take Robitussin or any other foul-tasting meds Mom thought we needed. Having already had an interstellar fish swim into my ear, I know it is way worse than any medicine.

"It's ready," I say. "It's all squishy." I want to add squirmy and alive, but Wes is already nervous enough. I bring it up to his ear.

"Wait," Wes says. "Does it hurt?"

"Uhm, hurt is not really the right word," I say, not wanting to lie. "It's more overwhelmingly unsettling, with intense tickling that is not at all funny, just deeply disturbing in a way that makes you think you might need therapy."

"Traumatizing," Wes says.

I snap my fingers and point at him. "Yes, that's the word. Traumatizing. Ready?"

"No," Wes says.

"You don't need to do this," I say. "This is totally optional."

"I don't mean to bud in," Bob says to me. "But my prognosticating algomelons suggest that the odds of overall success increase if he does. He has natural building skills and a highly developed sense of mechanics."

I tell Bob, "Shut your melons."

Looking at Wes squarely, I repeat, "You don't need to do this. If you want to know what's being said, we could just, you know, hold hands."

"Oh, yuck." Wes takes a deep breath, braces himself, and says, "Okay, I'm ready. Fish-me."

"On three," I say.

Wes nods.

"One, two ..." I begin, then quickly slap my cupped palm with the Pisces Converter over Wes's ear.

Wes's eyes go wide. I feel bad. Not horrible, just bad. He dances around a bit to unheard music that seems to have no rhythm, harmony, or any elements of musicality at all. He slaps his hands over his ears and sticks out his tongue as if hair was growing on it. "It's in my ear, so why do I taste it?"

"Yep, I remember that."

"Can you hear me, Wes?" Bob says.

"Yeah," Wes says. "Oh, man, when I had nightmares of an alien device probing me, it was never in my ear. It feels like it's swimming around in my brain."

"It's not swimming. Its tendrils are joining your inner–"

"No, no. Never mind," Wes says. "I'd rather not know."

"Good call," I say.

"Let's get to work." From overhead, a projector deploys rays of light between us. The light creates a three-dimensional map of the ancient city of Giza. Golden light bathes impossibly smooth pyramids, while the colorful Sphinx rests in their shadow like a guard dog. It is so unlike all the pictures of Egypt I've seen. I have to remind myself that the images in my head are in the future, and this version, one both familiar and alien, previously lost in time, is just outside the ship's door.

"What are these two lines?" Wes asks.

"I've calculated two routes to get to the Greys' ship," Bob says. "The Blue line takes you along the water, where you can take advantage of the rich vegetation. From there, you can move along this causeway, go around the pyramid, and come up on the ship from the rear."

"I didn't know the Nile River came that close to the pyramids," I say.

"It does not in your time. But back then, I mean now, the water flowed in many different branches. This one was used to bring the casting stones from a quarry on the other side of the Nile," Bob says.

"Huh," Wes says. "You learn something every day."

"Okay, how about the red one," I say.

"That route takes you right up the middle and into the religious center. It's more populated, but that could be an advantage. As long as you don't speak to anyone, you might get lost in the crowd and be able to make a beeline to the ship."

"Why can't we talk to anyone?" I ask. "With the fish in our ears, we should understand what they're saying, right?"

"Correct," Bob says. "But unless you speak ancient Egyptian or they have a Pisces Converter in their ear, they won't understand you."

"Ah, no chitchatting," I say. "Good safety tip."

"Hold up," Wes says. "Assuming we get that far and make it inside the ship, how do we find the parts we need, or even know what they look like?"

Over at the command counsel, the same lid that popped up to reveal Wes's fish opens again. This time, two metallic boxes emerge.

"I don't care how important it is. I'm not sticking anything else in my body," Wes says.

"No, these are info units. They have maps, the ship's layout, and specs for the parts we need," Bob says. "They go on your wrists."

"On the outside of the wrist, right?" Wes says.

"If you prefer, yes."

"I do," Wes says.

"Well, all that is left is to pick a route. Red or Blue? Bob, is this one of those critical life or death things?"

"Do you really want to know?"

I sigh. "Not really."

"What're you guys talking about?" Wes asks.

Take the Blue route along the water, and use the cover of vegetation. Plan to enter the ship from the rear, but not in a creepy alien probey kind of way.

Turn to page 110.

Take the Red route, head up the city center, keep my head down—don't talk to anybody, like a teen on their smartphone, and board the ship from the front.

Turn to page 121.

Wes grunts and bangs around inside the ship while I keep an eye on the flat expanse of the desert from the ship's open hatch. The Greys searching the area are going to discover our trail sooner rather than later. Wes needs more time, and I know exactly how to give it to him. I shut the hatch.

Stepping over Wes, I slide into my seat and bump his knees.

"What're you doing?" he says.

"Cool, Star Pilot stuff."

"Doubtful. You're supposed to be keeping a look out."

"Less criticizing, more kumquat installing."

"Please stay focused, Wes," Bob says. "Stems must align perfectly with the Rind endocarp, or you will have a misfire in the pulp-drupe."

"Boy, if I had a nickel for every time I've heard that," I mumble to myself as I fire up a small display to enable the probes. If I do this right, I can send the Greys hunting in the wrong direction. By the time they figure out they're on a wild goose chase, we will have boldly gone somewhere else.

"Bob, after Lego-boy is done, how long until we can take off?"

"A complete Honeyflex powerup should take just a few minutes. What are you doing, Star Pilot?"

I load a probe into the bay and arm the weapons system. My plan is to rise fast and fire a quick burst to get their attention. "Remember Level 13 when it became necessary to disguise Star Pilot's location by projecting a false image of an Astral Fighter?"

"Yes," Bob says. "The decoy solution. But if—"

"Bob," Wes says. "Am I doing this right? The top isn't aligning, and the honey-thingy isn't fluxing."

With Bob and Wes busy, I initiate my plan. On a small monitor, I can see the nearest Grey platform. If I maneuver the probe fast, it should lead them away, but where? I decide to lead them toward the uncompleted pyramid. There is lots of activity on the ground, which should add to the confusion.

"I'm detecting a slight power surge," Bob says. "James, have you activated systems?"

"You guys keep kumquating." I launch the probe, and it rockets straight up at full speed. I give it a few seconds for its signal to reach the Greys, then open fire with the pulsar guns. A grin spreads across my face as I watch tracer fire streak across the night sky. I then take the probe low along the sand, going wide around the search parties and rising behind them. I open fire again, shooting a small burst into the sand and flying away as the Greys return fire and give chase. I level the probe off and move straight at the uncompleted pyramid. On the monitor, I can see all the platforms pursuing. It's working.

"Did you launch a probe?" Bob asks.

"Yes. I was feeling a little useless, so I'm leading the Greys away from us. Give you guys some more time."

"You created a large energy signal! Power down!"

"But it's working. All the hovering platforms are moving away. What's the problem?"

"They aren't the only ones looking for you."

A sinking feeling weighs me down in my seat. I forgot about the big ship. "Do you think they could locate us from our power signature."

"Incoming!" Bob shouts.

"I take that as a yes."

"There are four, no five, no seven inbounds targeting your location."

I adjust the monitors in time to see all seven missiles moving through the sky, coming right at us.

"Are shields available?"

"Negative," Bob says.

"Can we deploy counter measures?"

"If they were not under a meter of sand."

"How about thrusters?"

"Inoperable during the kumquat alignment process."

I throw my hands up. "What's available?"

"The cleaning bot."

"How can that help us?"

"It cannot," Bob says. "I was just answering your question."

Wes sits up on the floor. "What the frak is going on. What's incoming?"

I point to the screen. Text flashes—*Impact in six seconds*.

Wes glowers at me. "Dude, you had one job! Keep a look out."

Impact in four seconds.

"Sorry. I hate feeling useless."

"Oh, I see," Wes says. "Do you feel better now?"

Impact in two seconds.

I sigh. "Not so much."

Impact.

The correct choice was to ready a probe for launch. If discovered before the Astral fighter can lift off it could be used to hold off the Greys long enough to get in the air.

Turn to page 195.

I take the fighter vertical, slamming Broken Neck into the rear of the cabin.

"Wes!" I hand him the spatula. "Wipe the puke off your chin and figure this out."

Wes grasps the weapon. "Bob said, no. He outlined several very descriptive reasons why."

"Bob also said you had a knack for figuring things out. So figure it out."

Wes turns the thing over in his hands and brings it very near his face.

I hoped he would just point and shoot, not sniff the thing. "What're you doing?"

Wes doesn't answer, and I can't watch him anymore. Broken Neck crawls on all fours to his own spatula, black eyes narrow, angry, determined. I bank hard. The two dead Greys tumble across the floor like loose luggage, but Broken Neck maintains a grasp on where he was.

Frak!

The proximity alarm sounds again. I turn forward and see nothing but black. I'm confused until I notice the moon's crescent-shaped reflection shimmering on the water in front of us. We are diving straight at the Nile. The ship doesn't have enough room to avoid contact with the water. I make a snap decision. Having seen it go on and off, I know where the control is to activate the environmental stabilizers. I hit it just in time.

We dive into the water, an impact that might have snapped our necks with the stabilizers off. Wes unbuckles his harness and stands. I hope he knows what he's doing because I don't have time to help. I'm busy reconfiguring the ship for the new environment as we submerge. I glance over my shoulder and see the stabilizers have allowed the Grey to stand and grab his spatula. He's a second away from firing when Wes aims his weapon. I don't see what button he pushes, but he yells, "Everte Statum!"

From the tip of Wes's spatula comes a yellow pulse of light. It hits the Grey with a force that knocks him back into the rear bulkhead. The Grey slides down from the wall and falls to its knobby knees. It looks as if it might collapse, but it raises its weapon.

Wes turns his spatula sideways, spins something on it, and shouts, "Protogo!"

The Grey fires. A thin blue laser strikes Wes, but he is unmoved. His spatula is deflecting the beam of light with some force field I can't see. It ricochets up over my head, and I hunch over. Wes steps forward and aims his weapon.

The Grey is visibly upset. "Insolent Hew-mon!"

"Expulso!" Wes shouts, returning fire.

A searing, red beam erupts from the weapon, engulfing the Grey's head. Its body convulses violently, a grotesque puppet show before its head explodes in a spray of gore. The alien's soft gooey, Grey-matter, which looks like cotton candy, redecorates the ship's interior. I get some in my mouth.

I spit pinkish goo out and look up at Wes. He is splattered in goo, but even so, he looks confident, cool even. Something I will never tell him.

I wipe my mouth. "Were you shouting Harry Potter spells?"

Wes lowers his wand. "Just for mental motivation. I memorized all eighty or so." He turns to me. "You know, in case magic turned out to be real."

"Wow, cool brag, weirdo."

There is a loud thud on our hull.

Wes moves back to his seat. "What was that?"

I check the monitors. "Crocodile, I think."

"Why are we hitting ..." Wes's sentence drowns out as he gazes forward, clearly realizing where we are. "Are we? No, we can't be."

"Yes, we can," I say, grinning. "You're in de-Nile."

"Really? Jungle Cruise puns?"

"Come on. When am I ever gonna get to use that again?"

"Status report," Bob says.

"Well, I think I'm hilarious, the ship is now a submarine, and Wes might be a wizard."

"I simply do not have the energy to figure out what that means. I'm getting some odd reading from the plumpercott matrix."

I look up and notice the blue switch, which I still don't know what it does, is fried. "Yeah, one of the Greys got off a shot in here and did some damage. Is it gonna affect the time jump?"

"I don't know," Bob says. "Can you get some—"

Alarms fire off again.

"Now what?" I check the monitors.

"The Greys' ship has fired more projectiles," Bob says.

"Jeez, they're really holding on to their anger," I say as Wes straps in. I wonder if they can target us in the water, but I get a quick answer as the six projectiles submerge and torpedo our way.

Frak.

We break the surface and I hit the thrusters. One got lost in the water, but five projectiles emerge and move to pursue. I barely escaped two. I know I can't get away from five.

"Bob, can we jump?"

"We were set until our uninvited guest threw our weight off. I need to make adjustments."

I look at the monitor, watching them close the gap. Six seconds to impact.

"Wait until the final moment, then go," Bob says.

I look over at Wes. He is scared. I am too. But we've been through this before. We can do it. I put my fingertips on the switch above my head. Three seconds till impact.

Wes gives me a nod, and I take a deep breath. Two seconds, one. I pull the switch.

* * *

I honestly do not know which is worse, going back in time four thousand years or going forward, but both feel like being run over by a herd of banthas. I look over at Wes. He's already got his helmet off, running a hand over his grey, bald head.

"Were you hoping it'd grow back?" I say.

Wes shrugs. "A little. Are we in 1997?"

I look up at the time console, eyeing the display. There are no numbers. Everything is shut down. "No idea."

Except for the pink goo, Wes's vomit, and the dead alien bodies, everything seems all right. The cleaning bot emerges from the back, breaking the stillness in the ship, and slurps up the pink slime. The sound is unsettling, like an over-sugared toddler sucking the final remnants of a cotton candy Slushie.

"Hey, Bob, you there?" I say, looking out the front canopy. The terrain looks desert-like, but not ancient Egyptian desert. There are rocks of various sizes, scattered vegetation, and cacti.

"I think we're in North America." Wes points out the window. "There's a flapjack prickly pear."

"A what?"

"North American cactus."

"Oh, for a second there, I thought *you* were glitching."

"I'm going outside."

I don't think that is a fantastic idea, but there doesn't seem to be anyone around. I follow Wes to the hatch and hit the controls. The door opens, revealing the same exact terrain that's in front of the ship. The sand is hot and rocky, and we walk a few steps, cautiously trying not to cut our feet. When we're a good five meters away, we look around, both of us turning in circles.

The Astral Fighter is a wreck. At least two gaping tears run the length of the hull, evidence of a brutal landing. Skid marks stretch back further than I can see, confirming the rough impact. I'm grateful we were asleep through it. Chunks of metal litter the landscape, and I realize the Greys' hovering platforms must have been attached during the jump. Pieces are scattered across our landing path, and most of one is still attached to the ship. Another, unfamiliar material, highly reflective, sways ominously in the wind.

"James, Wes, come in."

"Bob, where've you been?" I ask.

"Do you have any idea how challenging it is to establish contact with a point that has moved four thousand years in time?"

"No."

"Well, it takes a minute."

"Fine. Where are we? Is this 1997?"

"Data from the Heuristically Programmed Algorithmic Computer is coming in. As it did before, it took over as soon as communication and your consciousness were lost. It reports that the target programmed into the Honey-flux seeds was achieved."

"Then why do I have a bad feeling?" Wes picks up one of the pieces of reflective material. "I think this is from a—"

"A what?" I say.

"A weather balloon. Bob, we're in New Mexico, aren't we?"

"Yes, I can confirm that."

"About a hundred kilometers outside of Roswell," Wes says, like it's a fact.

"Geographical location confirmed," Bob says.

"Did you have time to make your adjustments before we jumped?" Wes asks, his voice rising.

"Negative. I was on the last calculation when you jumped."

Something catches Wes's eyes behind me. I turn and see an old pickup truck heading our way on a dirt road.

"W.W. 'Mac' Brazel," Wes mumbles.

"Friend of yours?" I say.

"We need to get back inside." Wes walks past me toward the ship. "Now!"

I raise my hands. "Why?"

"Bob, I'm guessing the destination was off a little," Wes says, stepping inside.

I follow him in.

"You arrived at the set target, but I was attempting to adjust it when I ran out of time. So, yes, we are a little off."

"Off what?" I say. "Will someone tell me what is going on?"

Wes closes the hatch, then steps over to the time controls. "I'm guessing we're off by about fifty years." He pounds the console with his fist. The system lights up and numbers appear. The destination screen reads 1947.

"Correct. If I had just another second—"

"We wouldn't be on Brazel's ranch in 1947 in a crashed spaceship." Wes runs a hand over his grey head. "Oh, boy."

"What?" I shout.

"Remember the Roswell incident?" Wes says.

"The one from your Lego set?"

"It's us."

"What?"

"*We* are the Roswell incident."

The weight of it hits me. I slump into the pilot chair. "That's fraked up."

July 7, 1947, 100 kilometers northwest of Roswell, New Mexico

Five minutes later, I'm still stunned, sitting in silence as Bob relays the rest of the information. The time jump was successful based on where Bob had enough time to recalculate. But it was exactly fifty years shy of where, or when, we needed to be. When our jump completed, Wes and I were unconscious like before. The Astral Fighter would have been able to land safely, but it collided with a weather balloon. The same weather balloon the U.S. Military will use in a few days to explain away the Roswell flying saucer incident.

"So, now what?" Wes says. "Can we jump again?"

"You could, but it would be pointless," Bob says.

"Why?"

"The ships too damaged," I say, looking at the reports on the monitors. "Even if it could fly, and that's a big if, there're several large breaches in the hull, making it hard to dogfight in space."

Wes slumps in his seat. "Is there any good news?"

"The 1940s and '50s were a very nice time in America," Bob says.

Wes sits up. "Is that a joke? Are you suggesting we stay here, in the past?"

"Not forever. Just until I can figure out a new plan," Bob says. "I can probably get a new Astral Fighter to you in less than ten Earth years."

I shake my head. This isn't happening. Why did I agree to go to Roswell with my parents? In a month, I'd have been off to college, doing normal stuff, like a normal person. Dorm parties, drinking, meeting girls, maybe catching an STD. Normal stuff. But no, I'm stuck in 1947, bald, and painted grey. I don't even think they have video games in 1947, do they? This can't get any worse.

Three loud thuds boom from the other side of the hatch. "All right, you goddamn Martians. You come out of there."

I roll my eyes. "Frak me."

"Brazel," Wes says.

"What?"

"The guy who owns the land we crashed on."

"Get your green asses out here before I start shootin'. Y'all ain't startin' a war of the worlds on my watch, you alien sonsabitches."

Wes stands up and grabs his spatula. "I'll deal with this."

"What're you gonna do?"

Wes opens the hatch, then steps away from the opening. He waves his hand, encouraging me to move so I'm not seen.

I peer outside and see a lone figure: a tall man with a receding hairline, his jeans held up by suspenders. He cradles a shotgun, its barrel not aimed at the ship, which is good because his hands are trembling.

"Come on out of there or I'll..."

Wes steps out from around the corner and aims the spatula. A wave of distortion like ripples in a pond emanates from the end. I think Wes says, "Stupefy," but I'm not sure.

Brazel goes stiff, like a petrified tree, and falls over. He doesn't put his hands out to brace his fall, so I assume he can't. He lands straight back, shotgun bouncing off his belly.

"Did you kill him?"

"No." Wes looks at the spatula. "I don't think so. You know, I'm pretty sure I'm communicating with this device mentally. When I imagine what I want it to do, and the spells help, I instinctively know what button to hit."

I step out of the ship. Brazel is still breathing. Just stunned. I gesture to the alien spatula. "Since you're one with the spatula, we should probably take it with us when we go. Could come in handy."

Wes looks at the weapon then back at me. "Are you saying that we're really staying here for a decade?"

"It's better than ancient Egypt. At least we speak the language."

"Language?" Wes points the spatula at the unconscious rancher. "I don't speak angry gun-toting 1940s New Mexico Redneck. Do you?"

I raise my hands. "Not fluently, no."

Wes waves the spatula like it's a laser pointer. "We're stuck here, in New Mexico. They don't even have Legos yet. And what if we run into our grandparents or something. Or what if we *are* our grandparents."

"What? How would that even work?"

Wes continues gesturing with the alien weapon. "I don't know!"

A light flashes on the weapon. I duck as the small hill behind me explodes. I stand slowly as dust and debris drift down all around us. "If you're gonna rant, will you please holster your wand."

"Meatsacks!"

"What?" we say in unison.

"By all estimations, temporal fusion-melons calculate that your best option is to blend in for a few years until I can get you a new ship."

"Wait," I say. "I don't understand. You are this time-manipulating being. Why can't you just bring us a new ship like a few yesterdays ago, and park it over on the other side of the hill Wes just blew up?"

"I can't."

"Why the hell not? They did it in those old *Bill and Ted* movies."

"Because your crash landing here in 1947 created a major event. One that is already rearranging the course of human and Reptilian history. New temporal vines must take root, and budding axel blondberries must germinate to sprout stability."

I throw my hands in the air. "Oh, blah, blah, blah, frakty-fruit basket!" I slump down in the dirt.

"I am sorry. I cannot get near you for a few years without tearing a hole down the center of our universe," Bob says. "But—"

"But what?" Wes says.

"There is more than one way to time travel."

I pick up a rock and toss it. "We're listening."

"You could be put in a prolonged stasis. Hibernation."

Wes meets my confused gaze. "You want us to go to sleep for ten years?"

"No," Bob says. "Fifty years."

"Fifty?" I shout.

Wes asks if it's safe.

"It has risks," Bob says. "Many things can go wrong."

I ask where we will be sleeping. "Who will be watching us?"

"Like I said, many risks, but if you do not want the safe option–"

"Which one was the safe option?"

Brazel stirs, moaning softly. Wes steps forward, grabs the shotgun, and throws it into some prickly vegetation. I crawl over and dig in his pockets for his truck keys. I find them on a leather keychain with stained letters that read *Eat what you can, and can what you can't.* I stand and show the keys to Wes. "What do you want to do?"

"I want to go back in time a few days and convince Mom and Dad to take us to Disney World instead."

I shake the keys. "Not an option."

Grab supplies and jump into Brazel's pickup truck. Look for a place to lay low for a few years until the interstellar, time-traveling fern can get us a new ship, jump forward to 1997, and save the galaxy. Easy Peasy.
Turn to page 91.

Roll the dice and sleep our way to 1997 with no idea how we will be taken care of while we are in stasis, who will be watching over us, and when we might wake up, if at all.
Turn to page 95.

I look over my shoulder at the Sleestaks, wondering which I'd rather be caught by: the cosplaying lizard people or the M.I.B. At least in those cheesy Will Smith movies, the black suit guys' main mission is to protect humanity from the aliens. That makes them the best option.

"C'mon, back to the store," I say to Wes.

He hesitates. "Why?"

"We're better off with humans. They're the good guys, right?" I point back at the Lizardman sporting a Stetson. "I've no idea what chance we'll have with Tex-Rex back there."

"I don't know. You're not basing this logic on those M.I.B. movies are you?"

"No," I say, sounding offended. "Not entirely. A little. C'mon, let's do this."

"You're putting our lives in the hands of the Fresh Prince?"

"On three," I whisper, pointing to the store. I count with my fingers.

"Status report?" Bob says as I'm down to one.

I ignore Bob and hit the ground running, pushing Wes in front of me. The Sleestaks are behind us, yelling at us to freeze.

"Go! Go! Go!" I yell, my eyes focused on the men in black running our way, raising their weapons.

Explosions erupt behind us as laser beams and energy pulses fly by. A searing fire rips through my knee, and I fall to the ground, my palms tearing open on the gravel.

"Holy crap," Wes says. He picks up my cauterized lower leg and shows it to me.

I must be in shock. The pain isn't registering as the beams and blasts fly through the air.

Wes tries to fix my leg, pushing on it, trying to reconnect it. He clearly wants to snap it back together.

"Dude, I'm not a Lego figure."

It still doesn't hurt, but it doesn't look good. A horror show rated somewhere between PG-13 and R.

Wes drops my leg and tries to pull me up. "Come on, we got—"

A blazing blue laser slices through Wes's neck. Still clutching my hand, he collapses on me. His head slides off his shoulders and thuds face first on the ground. It rolls just out of reach, leaving a streak of gore that is definitely rated R.

I hug Wes tighter than I've ever hugged anyone in my life. "I'm so sorry," I say, crying, as laser beams and pulses fly overhead. It's just a matter of time before one of—

Try again. Turn to page 57.

"It's just … I thought I saw … you might have a clone," I stammer.

"Cool," Wes says. "Think I could convince him to take P.E. for me?"

"I'm serious," I say.

"Me too. I really hate P.E."

I shake my head. "I don't know what I was thinking. No one would want more than one of you. I thought you were looking at Roswell Legos."

"I did, found the ones I wanted. A real collectors set. In a few years, it's gonna be worth—"

"Don't care. Sorry I asked."

"Anyway, when I went to pay for it, the guy at the counter took my Lego set and handed this to me, then said, 'Your brother will like this.'" Wes holds out a familiar fish-shaped trinket.

My eyes go wide. "He said I would like this?"

"No, wait. That's not what he said. It was more like, you'd know what to do with it. After a few seconds, I realized he wasn't going to ring me up until I brought it to you, so here I am."

I take it from Wes and turn it over in my palm. Its fish-shaped form is cool and smooth against my skin, smaller than my thumb, barely five centimeters long. Despite its metallic sheen, it lacks the expected weight of metal. My fingers trace the outline, snagging slightly on the raised ridges that mimic fins. But it's the symmetrical rows of pinprick holes on either side that truly capture my attention. Located where gills would be on a real fish, these tiny openings bear an uncanny resemblance to a miniature microphone or speaker. I recognize it and grin. "This is incredible," I say, more to myself than to Wes.

"What?"

"It took a second because it's never on the screen very long. It's from my favorite game, *Star Pilot*."

Wes rolls his eyes. "Oh, gamer crap." He turns away and looks at the sci-fi stuff on the table in front of him, picking up a *Star Trek* phaser replica.

"But how did the guy know I'd like it?"

"James, isn't it obvious?" Wes jabs my belly with the phaser, reminding me what I'm wearing, the newest *Final Star Pilot* T-shirt I got at GameCon. *Final Star Pilot* is supposedly the last chapter in the epic game series. The game in which the last of the Star Pilots rally at a point to defend the planet from the Progenitor Armada. Only the best of the best Star Pilots would be allowed to advance to the final battle. I had spent the last year making sure I was going to be one of them. And I was. I'd gotten an advance copy a week ago, and late last night after two Monster Energy drinks, I finished it.

"You're a walking, talking, gamer-nerd." Wes says.

"And you're an undersized shaved Wookie."

Wes chuckles. "So what is it supposed to do, and why does it look like a fish?"

"Well, in the game, it is a living creature, and it helps with communication. The Star Pilots come from different parts of the galaxy and don't use the same language. I know it does other stuff." I turn it over again in my hands. "But they never really show how it's used."

"Sounds lame."

"Your face is lame."

"What're you supposed to do with it?"

I bring it a little closer to my face and remember in the *Star Pilot's* opening cut-scene, newly recruited characters held the device to their ear. I don't imagine myself doing that, but then I hear something. Distant whispering, too faint to be distinguishable. I look around for the source.

Wes looks confused. "What is that?"

"You hear it too?"

Wes nods. "Like a distant echo."

We look down at the replica device from the game. "I think it's coming from ..." I trail off as I bring the item close to my ear. The closer it gets, the louder the whisper. Only an inch away, I can distinguish a single voice, not whispering, yelling. Distant yelling, like from down a long, echoing passageway. I turn the device like a radio dial trying to tune in the voice. It gets clearer, but understanding is just out of reach.

I look at Wes. "Who gave this to you?"

"I told you."

"Point him out."

Wes looks around. "He was just over there, behind the counter but ..."

I scan the store. My parents are on the other side looking at Area 51 T-Shirts. There are a half dozen people all looking as eccentric as my parents, but I don't see any employees. Then I catch movement in the back. A tall man moving toward a door stops and looks back. Our eyes meet. He raises an eyebrow, thick and bushy.

"That's him," Wes says looking at the same man. "Oh, damn. He's taking my Legos."

"Hey," I say, holding up the device from *Star Pilot*. "Why did ..."

The man opens a door marked 'Employees Only,' and leaves.

"That was strange," Wes says.

"And familiar."

Wes turns to me. "What?"

"Did he remind you of anyone?"

Wes shrugs. "Does he look like one of your lame Final Pilot characters?"

"No. I think we know him."

"Really?"

"Remember the cosplayer Mom and Dad sometimes hang out with at cons?"

"Uncle Kevin, the Klingon? Think his character name was quHow ... something."

"Yeah, I think it's him. Take away the prosthetic makeup, platform shoes, ridiculous costume and what's left?"

"A Lego-stealing Trekkie nerd, living with his mom, who goes to all the same cons our parents do. If that was Uncle Kevin, what's he doing in Roswell, and why wouldn't he say hi to Mom and Dad?"

I shrug. "All good questions. He's probably here for the same alien convention, and maybe he didn't see them or something."

"We've never seen him without his cosplay costume," Wes says. "Sure it's him?"

"I'm not positive. Just a feeling." The device in my hand starts squawking again. I bring it back up to my ear, holding it a few inches away. Even as I do, I can feel it changing. The fish-shaped object, which initially felt solid, begins to soften. It could just be my imagination, but it feels lighter. I want to bring it in front of my eyes to take a look, but the voice emanating from it is becoming clearer. I hold it closer to my ear as it changes in my fingertips. It's not just soft, but squishy like a gummy bear.

I can distinguish some of the words, and I bring it closer, touching the device to my ear. The device moves on its own, and it leaps from my grasp, diving into my ear. I try to get a hold of it. The tail slaps my fingers away as it slides its way in.

"Oh, frak!"

It slithers halfway into my ear, and I seize it by the tip of its tail. I pull but it does not budge. It's now gooey, slimy, and holding onto it becomes impossible. There's an unsettling sensation as it disappears into my ear. Its slimy presence vibrates through me all the way down to my toes.

"No, no, no," I scream, grabbing hold of my whole ear, thinking I might need to tear it off.

"Relax!" a voice shouts. The voice is so clear and vibrant, it sounds as if it's coming from inside my head.

I stop squirming for a moment as the thing wiggles further into my ear and wraps itself around a part of my anatomy I can't name. It's so gross. It's like when snot goes down the wrong pipe and you swallow it, but this is someone else's snot, and in my ear.

"Pilot, I am reaching out to you from the Solar year 45-4127. Your unique skills are needed. Billions of lives are at stake. I know this is confusing, but you must get out of there right now," the voice says. "You have less than a minute."

The voice is synthetic, a militant whisper marching in from another world, lacking any discernible gender. "Who the hell is this?" I say out loud.

"No time for introductions. Don't go out the front; move to the back."

"What did you do to my ear?" I turn in a circle. "And where are you?"

Wes grabs my arm. "Who're you talking to?"

I look at Wes. "That thing went all slimy and into my ear."

Wes steps back. "For real?"

"And now it is talking inside my head."

"Nasty. What's it saying?"

"If you don't get moving it's all over," the voice says. "Forty-five seconds."

"What's all over?" I question the voice.

"Everything. The skills you demonstrated in the game are needed, but you must go now!"

"It says we have forty seconds to get out of here," I say to Wes.

"What? Why?"

I look over at Mom and Dad on the other side of the store. "What about my parents?"

"You can't help them. They have served their purpose, but you are the Star Pilot. You must survive. Thirty seconds."

"It's saying we have to go out the back, now," I say to Wes.

Wes looks over at our parents. "What about them?"

I don't know what to do. With the clock ticking, I'm rooted to the spot.

"Hurry," the voice says. "They. Are. Coming!"

Listen to the fish-shaped stowaway making itself at home in my head while thrusting what can only be described as an alien tongue down my ear—all without buying me dinner—uproot myself from the floor, grab Wes, and run out the back.

Turn to page 53.

Without mentioning how my ear has been violated—something I'll need to work out later in therapy—come up with a decent story to tell my parents that will convince them to leave with me and Wes.

Turn to page 6.

Who in their right mind thinks returning to a *War of the Worlds* gun battle is a good idea? Not this motherfraker, that's for sure. "Police station," I tell Uncle Kevin. "Hit it!"

He shouts, "Qapla'!" and accelerates.

"Didn't fish-guy say not to go to there?" Wes says.

"Going back to the Camaro is suicide. We'll get shot at the Not So O.K. Corral."

He nods and checks the rear window while Uncle Kevin blasts down the street at a very unsafe speed, shouting, "There are no old warriors!"

Wes doesn't look thrilled at Uncle Kevin's battle cry.

"The police station is compromised!" Bob reminds us.

"Well, so is that parking lot," I say.

"It is your only chance of survival. You must get to the transport."

"Relax, fish-guy. They aren't even following us."

Wes clears his throat, and nods behind us. "Do you ever get tired of being wrong?"

"Oh great," I say, looking out the back window where two Men in Black vehicles, one police car, and the spacecraft sphere are chasing and firing weapons at each other.

"Full speed ahead!" Wes tells Uncle Kevin, pointing at the station at the end of the block on the left side of the street.

Uncle Kevin grunts and guns it. "Victory is ours!"

It looks like we'll reach the parking lot before any vehicles catch up, but what then? Jump out, screaming for help?

Uncle Kevin barely slows to make the turn, our tires screeching as he whips the wheel. Between grinding teeth he says, "It is a good day to die."

We're nearly there, but the sphere accelerates to warp speed and slams into our side, sending us tumbling over and over and slamming to a stop.

Oh frak, everything hurts. My head throbs like a Talosian's, and I must have brain damage because I just used a *Star Trek* reference. I'm blind from the blood leaking from a gash on my forehead.

Wes moans and starts crying, the panic rising in his voice when he calls my name and shakes my shoulder.

"I'm okay." I wipe blood from my eyes, coughing on the smoke.

"Quy'QoQuj!" Wes yells. "Wake up! The car's on fire."

Uncle Kevin moans. "It is a good day to—"

"Stop saying that!" Wes shouts.

I clear my eyes and see we're completely fraked. Both doors on the driver side have been smashed in, and the passenger doors are blocked by the brick building we're up against.

Uncle Kevin is slumped over the steering wheel, and a fire rages in the engine compartment and down by his feet. "I am ready to join my fellow warriors in Sto'Vo'Kor," he mumbles.

"Bob! We need help!"

"I'm afraid I can't stop what's going to happen next."

"What's gonna happen next?" I shout.

"You will burn to death, of course," Bob says. "It will be exceedingly painful for all of you."

"How is that helpful!" I scream as Uncle Kevin's lower half ignites in bright orange flames.

"It is not, but there is good news."

"What?"

"We will meet again, Star Pilot. You journey is not yet at an end."

Uncle Kevin's hair catches fire. He screams, "Sto'Vo'Kor!"

"You're an asshole, Bob!" I shout as the flames move our way with the sharp, acrid smell of Uncle Kevin's charred flesh.

I look at my terrified little brother. He knows as well as I do, we are about to burn to death. I grab his hand. "I'm sorry."

We both scream as our skin cooks and blisters. We swallow flames, searing our lungs, silencing our painful cries.

The correct answer was to try to save our pickles by returning to the transport. Turn to page 58.

I glance back down the corridor. The Greys look much angrier than the last time I checked and are ten meters away. They'll be on us in seconds.

"The hatch is almost completely open," Wes says.

"Let's go." I grab him by the elbow and push him ahead of me, so he doesn't see what I'm about to do. I'm not moving very fast because I want the Greys to close the gap a little.

I tear open the Lego box and grab several of the clear bags filled with Lego pieces. The Greys' naked footfalls are right behind me. I rip holes in the bags with my teeth and toss handfuls of pieces behind me. Hundreds of tiny pieces bounce on the alien floor a second before the yelps of alien pain fill the corridor. I turn around and grin as several aliens have collapsed, holding their feet, hard-edged Lego pieces, manufactured on Earth four thousand years from now, protruding from weak, Grey skin.

I'll never forget my dad's howls of pain as he snuck downstairs for a midnight snack, only to be foiled by one of Wes's Lego landscapes set adrift in the kitchen. The Greys are not faring any better. In moments, the entire detail is either hopping on one bare no-toed Grey foot or writhing on the floor, Legos deeply embedded.

Wes looks over his shoulder as he runs.

"Keep going," I shout, quickening my pace. "To the hatch."

Wes keeps moving but also keeps looking behind him. It's clear he's trying to figure out what has happened to our Grey pursuers.

"Wes, look out!" I call.

Wes refocuses. He runs past the hovering platform, and Tutface reaches for him.

Frak!

Tutface hooks his fingers into the hanging loop of Wes's backpack. Wes attempts to shake it off, but before he does, I'm there. Without breaking stride, I plow into the man. I've never tackled anyone before, but it feels pretty cool. At least until I hit the floor. I land on top of him to the sound of a bone crack. Thankfully not mine. Tutface screams and grabs his chest as I roll off him. I think I broke his ribs. Didn't mean to.

The Grey that's with him has pulled out some device, from where I don't know, and is bringing it to bare. Could be a gun, could be a salad mixer—I have no idea. In my rush to get back up, I stagger, like, well, like a guy who has never tackled anyone before then tried to get up real fast. I careen into the Grey, my shoulder knocking his arm and the device skyward. Without much planning or waiting to plant my feet, I swing my fist at his face. I am way off balance and miss the face but connect with his skinny neck. His head falls back with a sickening snap, and his body drops to the deck. The device falls into my other hand, and somehow, my pinky loops inside a part of it. The Grey remains sprawled on the deck, unmoving. I think I killed it. Really didn't mean to do that.

The object in my hand resembles a kitchen tool you'd make pancakes with, yet it's far more bedazzled with incomprehensible, and likely unnecessary, technology. Imagine if Tesla designed a solar-powered spatula that inexplicably streamed Netflix. If it's a weapon, maybe it will help. If it's not, maybe I'll use it to make breakfast.

"James, come on," Wes says.

He stands at the open hatch, which I hope still leads to the ground. The ship has shaken so much in the last few minutes, it isn't hard to imagine we might've lifted off. The sound of bare feet grabs my attention, and I whirl around. A small group of Greys are heading my way, moving to intercept me before I reach the hatch. They might succeed, but I still have my armory of plastic incapacitators. I run across the deck toward my brother, who watches in horror as I unleash the remaining Lego pieces on the Greys. Their howls and looks of anguish as they fall one by one, is mirrored on Wes's face.

"You A-hole!" Wes screams.

"Desperate times, man," I say as I reach Wes and gaze down into the opening. I can't see the ground, but there are lights on the ramp illuminating the walkway. While we've been stealing spaceship parts, night has fallen.

"You said you'd take care of it," Wes says. "I trusted you."

"I said I'd take care of the Lego box, and I did. The box is fine. Here." I hand it to him and, without asking, remove his backpack. "Come on."

We head down the ramp and Wes tosses the box. "Worst. Brother. Ever!"

Ignoring Wes's justified but ill-timed rant, I unzip the backpack and pull out the long cloak-like garments Bob made for us. "Throw this on. We need to blend."

We don't bother with our shoes, and our bare, grey-painted feet touch the soil. Judging by the warmth of the ground, the sun didn't go down too long ago. I glance behind to see if anyone is following. There isn't. Not yet.

Fewer people are traveling along the thoroughfare, but enough to try and get lost amongst them. That feels like the obvious thing to do. I look over and see the convoy of two-ton stones still moving as it had before. Illumination glistens in front of each stone, almost like headlights, making them look even more like a convoy of trucks.

"This way," I say as Wes pulls on his cloak. We pull our hoodies up and cover our bald, grey heads.

Don't mean to fall back on a *Star Pilot* scenario, but on level 33, I maneuvered my fighter low and concealed the ship behind a wall that ran on the outside of an enemy fortress. The gunners searched for me in the main corridor, while I slipped away around the outside. That might work here as well.

Wes seems to know what I have in mind and doesn't argue when he sees the direction I'm running. He might be too scared to argue, or just mentally busy plotting my death over the Lego thing, but either way, he tucks in behind me, and we make it to the far side of the convoy of massive blocks.

Just as we make it behind the convoy, multiple flying balconies emerge from the hatch of the ship. They spread out in different directions, forming a search pattern. Several zip off toward the river, a few fly up and over the ship. I duck down low as one skims over the thoroughfare. The beam pauses over one particular person for a few beats, then it moves to the next group of ancient Egyptian pedestrians.

"Status Report!" Bob shouts so loud in my head, I find it hard to believe the Reptilian stone movers I'm walking past can't hear.

"Running for our lives," I reply. "Where the frak have you been?"

"I think a gamma-melon leak interfered with comms for a bit. Did the Greys' vessel take some damage?"

A huge explosion, peppered with mooing sounds, comes from the ship. The hatch begins to close while Greys, humans, and at least a dozen cows emerge. Some plummet to the ground, but most of the bovine run straight into the air, levitating, then begin to go up, and up.

"Ah, maybe a scratch or two," I say.

"Holy cow," Wes says, eyes locked on the weightless cattle.

"Oh, my analysis is coming in," Bob says. "You did more than scratch it. It is leaking all kinds of volatile radiation. You two need to get some distance from that ship."

"That is the current plan, Bob." I say. "We're using the giant blocks as cover."

"Are they searching for you?"

"Yep, they're scanning people on the road."

"Stay close to those stones," Bob says. "The tech used to alter the block's weight has the same matrix as the kumquat nods we stole."

"*We* stole?" Wes says. "I don't see you here running for your life."

"I am there in spirit," Bob says.

"Yeah," I say, "like an omnipotent, animal spirit guide."

Above us, a hovering balcony casts its scanning beam just ahead, covering two stone movers.

"I take offense at that," Bob says.

Wes and I stop moving, waiting for the beam to move on. "Which part, omnipotent?"

"No, the animal association. My species has evolved beyond meat."

"It was just a metaphor," I explain.

"Actually, it was a simile," Wes says.

"God, I hate both of you," I say as the beam snaps off, and the hovering balcony moves on. We have about a hundred meters to the end of the convoy, and then our cover is gone. I hope the darkness will be enough to conceal our long journey back.

"So, Bob," Wes says. "You're not a being like us, with muscles, flesh, and blood?"

"Not at all," Bob says with a bit of superiority in his voice.

"Then what kind of life form are you?" Wes asks.

"I am more what you might call a planted-based life form."

Wes and I both stop, unable to absorb Bob's words and walk at the same time.

"You mean," I say, "you're like a fern or a flower?"

"A fern? A flower?" Bob shouts. "I am a plant that has superior intelligence, an extensive life span, and the ability to transcend space, time, and dimensions."

"Okay," I say. "Don't get your vines in a knot."

"Touchy," Wes whispers.

"My scans say you are halfway back to the ship," Bob says.

I gaze down at my info unit. It displays a map back to the ship, which is good. Not sure we'd be able to find it in the moonlight alone.

"I will send the kumquat installation instructions to your info units."

"Sounds good," I say as we reach the end of the convoy. There's just enough moonlight to light the ground ahead of us, but also enough to see two thieves scurrying away. I look at Wes. "I think we'll have to run for it from here. Can you hang?"

Wes pulls out his inhaler and takes a hit. "What choice do I have?"

"None," I say as an annoyingly perplexing thought rifles through my mind. "Hey, Bob, can I ask you something about your species? It's gonna nag me if I don't."

"Is it an irrelevant, unintelligent, meatsack kind of question?"

"Probably."

"Go ahead."

"If one of your kind were to eat another of your kind, would that make them a cannibal or a vegetarian?"

Wes shakes his head. "You are a meatsack."

We start the final leg of our escape at a light jog. So light, in fact, a power-walking Grey could easily catch us. But that's all the energy we have. I just hope it's enough.

* * *

It feels like our journey back to the Astral Fighter takes forever with Wes's wheezing, and my paranoia causing me to look over our shoulders every other second. My info unit reads that it took just twenty minutes, but we are exhausted when we get back. I want to change back into our own clothes, but we are low on energy and time.

Although the Greys didn't follow us back to the ship, I can see them in the distance, searching. It's only a matter of time before they pick up our trail. I want to be way gone by then, and I can tell Wes does too. After a minute of respite, he pulls up the installation instructions, gets Bob on the line, and goes to work.

I can hear them talking: put this here, reconfigure that there. It's very boring, and I try to tune them out while I keep a lookout. I stand at our half-open hatch, twirling the alien spatula while scanning the direction we'd come. Even from this distance, the moonlight shining off the limestone covering the pyramids is mesmerizing. So mesmerizing, I almost miss the Greys on a hovering platform, less than a kilometer away. They have several beams of light scanning the ground. They haven't found our trail, but if they keep moving in the same direction, they soon will.

"How's it going?" I ask.

"Just one more kumquat node to insert," Bob says. "Your brother really has an aptitude for this. Very glad we brought him this time."

"This time?" Wes says.

"Never mind," Bob and I say in unison. I look back at the platforms in the distance, which don't seem all that distant now.

"Hey, Bob." I tap the spatula to my chin. "Does this Astral Fighter have the kind of probes we got in the upgrade in level 19?"

"With the pulsar guns? Of course. There are five probes in the bay."

Hmmm.

Ready a probe for launch. If discovered before the Astral fighter can lift off, it could be used to hold off the Greys long enough to get in the air.
Turn to page 195.

Launch a probe, and send it towards the Greys that are searching, hopefully sending them on a wild goose chase before their search discovers the Astral Fighter half buried in the sand.
Turn to page 19.

"The killing baby Hitler plan seems like a long shot," I say. "Bob doesn't sound convinced it would work, and honestly, I don't really understand it. I much prefer a straight-up fight—just me and two other highly skilled Star Pilots from planets unknown."

Wes sits hunched, his face a mask of concentration. "Like I said, it's your call, Star Pilot."

"Red-Five, what's your status?" Red-Four repeats.

I respond and try to sound cool and calm, but inside, I'm shaking like a frightened child. "Red-Five enroute. We're coming to join the party."

Wes takes in the incredible number of enemy Scale Runners on the scope. "I haven't been to a lot of parties, but this one looks terrible."

I take in the ships massing ahead of us, and my stomach tightens. "Agreed. Let's divert all power from nonessential systems to forward shields: Artificial gravity, environmental regulators, life support."

"Life support?" Wes says and stops what he's doing to look over at me. I can see in his eyes he now realizes our reality. When life support becomes nonessential ... He takes a deep breath and says, "Aye-Aye, Captain."

I chuckle. "It's just one Aye. We're not pirates."

"Definitely not, 'cause that would be way more fun."

"With so much of your ship's power dedicated to shielding, our connection may be broken," Bob says.

Suits me fine. He's not much help in a fight anyway. "Understood, Bob."

"Good luck, Star Pilot." While Bob's voice fades away, a cascade of green energy envelops the ship as the shields deflect a barrage of plasma fire.

"We've got company," Wes says.

Just like Reptilians, they get my attention in front and try to hit our flank. It does little damage, but it really pisses me off. I bank hard just as Wes finishes the power adjustment. Two seconds after our shield absorbs their attack, we're nose to nose, and I open up our railguns at point-blank range. At least twenty Scale Runners are torn to shreds, Reptilian bodies floating in our exhaust. I grin.

"Fantastic flying, Red-Five!" Red-Four says. "What's your rendezvous ETA with Red-One?"

"About six—"

The comms crackle with static, followed by a burst of distress. "I'm hit!" Red-One shouts. "Surrounded. Can't see. Engine down. Re—" The transmission cuts off, replaced with a chilling silence.

I take a deep breath.

"Up to us, Red-Five," Red-Four's voice chimes in, calm and steady. "Got a plan?"

I did have a plan, and it was terrible. "Turn to mark 3,4, and let's go straight at them."

"Then what?"

"You take the hundred on the left, and I'll take the hundred on the right."

Red-Four's alien chuckle is a kind of low-pitched dolphin sound. "I love this plan."

"Me too."

"Do I get to vote?" Wes asks. "'Cause I'm not a fan."

A moment later, Red-Four's on the main viewport, a flash of red light as it takes out a dozen Scale Runners with a short-distance omni torpedo. I break off from him to advance on my targets with no idea what the Star Pilot looks like, just that he fights like a giant Orca surrounded by sharks. He howls into his comms as he fires into the mass of enemy ships. "Stay sharp, Red-Five. And try not to die!"

"That's the plan." I take a deep breath and focus on the battle ahead. The odds are ridiculous. Two Astral Fighters against more than 300 enemy fighters, and we're charging straight at them.

"Stay sharp," I say to myself. "Remember your training."

"I've had exactly zero hours of training! I know math is not your thing, but that equals no training."

"I know," I say under my breath with a grin. "But I have." Hours and hours.

I weave through the hail of fire, feeling so in tune with the ship, almost a part of it. Then, when the enemy hesitates, the kind of calculated pause to assess what they've hit, I open up with everything, full spread torpedoes, pulse cannons, railguns. There are so many targets, it's nearly impossible to miss. One Scale Runner after another explodes in a fiery inferno of twisted metal and green-tinged blood. There's so much debris, we're in danger of being eliminated in a collision.

I break off the attack as a new wave of Scale Runners swoops in, their sharp, needle-like snouts glinting above us. We clear the debris, then without hesitation, accelerate in a 90-degree turn and rush straight at them.

"There're so many," Wes yells, his hands a blur over the shield controls. The ship shudders under the barrage of enemy fire, alarms blaring. The main viewport lights up with distant explosions. Red-Four, a brilliant star of fire and fury, collides with an enemy fighter, and in a flash of blinding light, it's gone.

In the span of a moment, we are alone.

"They're boxing us in," Wes yells.

Proximity alarms sound with missiles closing in from every direction. The viewscreen's a sea of green, red, and blue as enemy fighters surround us. No escape.

I take a deep breath and feel a profound sense of peace. I look at Wes, who doesn't seem as peaceful. He looks angry. Ready to keep fighting. I want to say, 'Love you, bro,' but it isn't time yet. If he still has a little fight in him, so do I.

He stares at the scope and eyes the main Talon Cruiser, the one we think has all the Progenitors on it. "I have an idea."

"A good one?"

He shakes his head. "Not at all. Do you remember the movie *Midway* and its depiction of the Battle of Okinawa?"

"I don't think this is the time for movie trivia?" I hit the thrusts and evade missiles. "Wait, is that the one where Woody Harrelson is an Admiral?"

"Yes."

"Terrible casting."

"I know, right, but do you remember what the Japanese pilots did?"

I look over and see him pointing at the Talon Cruiser.

Oh, crap. He wants us to go Kamikaze on those scaly assholes. "Screw it. Why not?"

Wes's eyes narrow into a slow, fierce grin that spreads across his face. "Hoping you'd say that," Wes says, a look of pure defiance in his eyes.

I don't know where this burst of courage came from, but I am very proud to be Wes's brother right now. A single tear runs down my cheek as I engage full thrust. I take the weapons offline and reroute the remaining power to the engines. The Astral Fighter shoots forward for one last time, a streak of red light piercing the darkness.

"I'm glad I got to do this with you, Wes."

He smiles. "I'd much rather we went to a Lego convention together, but this is good too."

"Love you, bro."

"Love you."

A barrage of enemy fire rains down on us as we skim the cruiser's outer hull. Our shields flicker as they near exhaustion, but they hold. The Scale Runners swarm to pursue, but they hadn't anticipated the sudden direction change and fall behind.

I open up comms to hail the enemy and broadcast a final shout of defiance. "Hey, Progenitors!" I look over at Wes, and we both shout, "UP YOURS!!!"

The Astral Fighter slams into the command deck of the Talon Cruiser in a brilliant flash of light and sound, a supernova of energy and fire.

The correct choice was to utilize Plan B.
Turn to page 230.

"If I do what you say, will my parents be alright?" I say out loud to the voice in my head.

"Uhm, define all right."

"Like, not be hurt, or killed."

"If you get moving, there is a very good chance they will not only be okay, but they will never suspect anything has happened."

I look at Wes, wishing he could hear the conversation in my head.

"You have less than ten seconds before they see you."

"Frak!" I say and grab my brother's hand. Wes offers no resistance as I pull him toward the back.

"We're really going to listen to the fish-thing talking in your head?" Wes asks.

"Yep." We go through the door Uncle Kevin went through. I immediately run into a stack of boxes, which start to tip. I let go of Wes and I grab them, keeping them from falling.

Wes glances back. "Who're those guys?"

There are two big men in black suits, both with the same nine-dollar haircut, standing next to Mom and Dad. One grabs Dad by the arm.

I want to help, but the voice in my head is insistent. "Keep moving."

"Fine," I say and pull Wes by the shoulder.

"What about Mom and Dad?" Wes asks as we move through the souvenir store's storage room.

"The fish-guy says they'll be okay."

"And how does he know that?"

"Good question."

"Because they don't really want them," the voice answers.

"Okay," I say. "Who do they want?"

"You. Now go out the back door and stay low."

We reach the back door and hit the push bar. My brother and I stay low. Not sure why, but we tuck behind a dumpster. "Hey, fish-guy. Now what?"

"You must find the transport. To your eyes, it will look like a yellow 1977 Chevy Camaro with a black detailing strip up the hood."

"What're we supposed to be doing now?" Wes asks.

"Looking for an old yellow Camaro."

"I don't know what a Camaro looks like."

"Like Bumblebee."

"Oh, why didn't you say so?" Wes points across the parking lot. "How about that one?"

I follow his finger and see the back half of a yellow muscle car eighty feet away, parked behind a black brick building. "That could be it. Let's go."

"Fish-guy, we're moving to the car," I say. "Is that where you are?"

"No."

"Well, I assume you're not actually in my head, correct?" I ask, hurrying through the parking lot.

"Correct. Remember to stay low."

I hadn't remembered, so I hunker down as we move. Wes does as well. "Then where are you?"

"It's hard to explain."

"I'm smarter than I look."

"Doubtful."

"What's that supposed to mean?"

"Look, I can try to tell you, but you would not understand."

"Try me," I insist.

"I am situated within a multi-expansive rift exhibiting spatiotemporal anomalies, existing at the hypothetical event horizon of the universe's nascent singularity."

I stop and unhunch a little. "Sooo ... not in Roswell."

"No. Not in Roswell."

"Can you at least tell me your name? I don't want to keep calling you fish-guy."

"You may call me Bob."

"Bob?"

"Whose Bob?" Wes says.

I keep forgetting he is only hearing half the conversation. "Fish-guy is Bob."

"That sounds made up."

"Yeah, neither of us believe your name is Bob," I say. "That's like a telemarketer's name."

"My real name is BoH-Bento Seven'takesch Busmuzzel-bartfast Melondrift the Third."

"Bob it is then," I say.

We are nearly to the Camero when a bolt of turquoise light erupts from a vacant parking space. It ascends skyward, disappearing into the clouds. Wes sees it too and we both stop. The light vanishes as abruptly as it appeared, leaving in its wake two figures standing in the empty parking spot. They step forward as if emerging from a door. Less than five meters away, they turn, and that's when I see them. Not the silly human costume they are wearing, but the real them. Scaly, humanoid, with the eyes of snakes.

I'm afraid and drop down behind a Prius. Wes hunkers down next to me. In a hushed tone I say, "Bob, are there such things as lizard people?"

"They do not call themselves that, but yes. Why do you ask?"

"Two of them just arrived. They look like humans on the outside, but I can see what they really are."

Wes tugs on my shirt sleeve. "What do you mean they *look* human?"

We both gaze back. Although I can see their true faces, Wes can only see their attempts at human cosplay. One is dressed like an urban cowboy, the other clad in dark leather like a biker.

"Well, that is both good and bad," Bob says.

"How so?"

"Good because that indicates that the Pisces Converter in your ear is functional. It does more than act as a temporal communicator and translator."

"And the bad is?"

"The Reptilians are hunting you as well."

"Anyone not hunting us?"

Bob ignores my question. "I have carefully planned your exit, but you must get to the Camero."

"Any suggestions on how we do that?"

"Carefully," Bob says.

"That's not helpful." I peer out to see if they have moved. Not only have they moved, but they've split up. The biker is heading to the Camaro. The cowboy is on a search pattern that will likely bring him toward us. If we don't get moving, it will walk right up to us.

"Those aren't people?" Wes says.

I shake my head. "The fish in my ear lets me see their real faces."

"What do they look like?"

"A less cuddly version of a Sleestak."

"Yikes. What does Bob say?"

"He says he can get us out if we can get over there."

"Where?"

"Bumblebee."

"Maybe we can circle around the parking lot by heading back to the store," Wes suggests.

I think it's a good idea, until several of the men in dark suits that took Mom and Dad burst out the store's back door.

"Frak, now what?"

Head towards the men in dark suits. At least they're human, and I might have a better chance amongst my own kind.
Turn to page 32.

Screw this. When am I ever going to have a talking-fish-guy in my head again? We need to listen to him and get to that Camaro.
Turn to page 228.

Slide under the Prius and hide, hoping that the Men in Black and the Reptilians are like most people on Earth and find nothing alluring about a Prius.
Turn to page 113.

"We need to go back," I say, not at all confidently.

"Back where?" Wes asks.

"To the Camaro."

"That's a terrible idea."

"Wes is right," Uncle Kevin says. "The police station is just a few blocks away."

Inside my head, Bob shouts, "They have infiltrated the police!"

"Who?"

"Reptilians."

"Bob says there are bad guys at the police station."

"Okay," Wes says. "So not the police station, but why back to the parking lot with the shooting and the exploding?"

"If you don't get to the transport, they will catch you and put you somewhere out of my reach," Bob says. "When that happens, it is all over, not just for you, but possibly your whole galaxy."

"Hey," I say to Bob. "That's a lot of pressure."

Wes nudges my arm. "What's he saying?"

"He's being super intense right now."

"Even if we went back," Wes says, "how would we get through the M.I.B. guys and the Sleestaks, not to mention all the weapons fire?"

"Uh," Uncle Kevin says gazing into the rearview mirror. "I don't think they are fighting in the parking lot anymore."

Wes and I turn around and look out the back window. It seems the carnage we escaped in the parking lot is following us. At least three cars are on our tail: two black sedans and one police car, lights flashing. There is a fourth vehicle, but I can't call it a car. Cars tend to move on the ground. This thing isn't restricted to the pavement. Its spherical shape and pinpoint lights move between the cars, zigzagging like nothing I've ever seen before.

"Jeez, aren't we the popular ones?" Wes says.

Uncle Kevin accelerates. "I can try to put some distance between us."

I keep my gaze aimed backward, hoping Uncle Kevin can lose them. All four vehicles accelerate, with one black sedan so close to our bumper I can see the driver's veins bulging across his forehead just under his terrible haircut. On the upside, as hell bent as they are to catch us, they also seem determined their opponents don't. They continue fighting one another as we speed through the streets of Roswell.

The police car rams the car behind us. A man in black leans out the passenger window with a bizarre-looking gun. He doesn't fire at the police car bumping them, but at the spherical whatever it is hovering in the rear. It darts and zips along the sidewalk, avoiding the attack. The streets of Roswell blur into a chaotic tapestry of neon and asphalt as the chase descends into a speeding demolition derby.

"This is gotta be a dream," Wes says. "This is what happens when I stay up past my bedtime, eat too much pizza, and fall asleep watching the SyFy channel."

How I wish Wes were right. I'd give anything right now to wake up on the couch, with a stomachache, and see that wide-eyed crazy-haired guy, Giorgio what's-his-name, on TV gazing back at me, saying, *I'm not saying it's aliens, but it's aliens.*"

Suddenly, there are cars ahead of us, tourists clogging up the main road. Uncle Kevin grips the steering wheel tighter, his knuckles turning white. With a guttural Klingon yell of "Hold on," he turns the wheel sharply. The electric car lurches, its tires screeching in protest as it swerves onto the sidewalk. Pedestrians caught completely unaware, scatter. A group of teenagers, wearing matching novelty antennae, narrowly avoid becoming hood ornaments. They dive into the open doorway of a shop emblazoned with a giant, neon green-lettered marque that reads *ALIEN ZONE.*

The black sedan, hot on our tail, tries to follow, but the space is tight. Uncle Kevin yanks the wheel, sending us fishtailing back onto the street. The sedan's driver, probably still glued to our bumper, doesn't see the hulking lamppost looming ahead. There is a bone-jarring crunch as they slam right into it. The impact sends the entire post shuddering, the alien-head-shaped globe on top exploding in a shower of glass. I twist in my seat, heart hammering, just as the globe's painted black, almond-shaped eyes rain down.

"Uncle Kevin, we need to go back," I say. "If they're all following us that means the parking lot is clear for the moment."

"They'll just follow us back there," Wes says.

"Yes, but if we can get some distance, maybe Uncle Kevin can drive by and slow down just enough for us to jump out."

"When did we become stuntmen? Assuming we don't break every bone in our body, then what?"

"Uncle Kevin accelerates, leading them away, and we find the transport."

"The what?"

"Bumblebee." I lean into the front seat. "What do you say, Uncle Ke ... I mean, quy'QoQuj?"

Uncle Kevin lets out a laughing growl. "As I said before, it is a good day to die."

"I'm not a big fan of you saying that," Wes says.

Uncle Kevin, or rather, quy'QoQuj, spins the wheel, sending our car into a high-speed whirlwind. Downtown Roswell swirls by as we leap off the street and into the unexpected haven of a McDonald's parking lot. This being Roswell, it isn't your typical golden arches establishment. This one is a full-on spaceship replica, complete with a bulbous metallic body, rows of neon-lined windows, and a tilted conical roof that gleams silver in the afternoon sun. Wes, momentarily forgetting the tense situation, can't help but gape out the window at the spectacle. Meanwhile, quy'QoQuj makes a U-turn so tight the back tires fight for traction. We narrowly miss the looming green drive-through sign, with a *whoosh* of wind that carries the faint scent of greasy fries and nuggets.

"Jeez, that was McClose," Wes says.

I wasn't positive, but it seems Uncle Kevin is driving with not just confidence but a plan. We exit the parking lot just as our pursuers enter. Their attempt to all change directions at the same time causes them to career into one another. Even the flying whatever-it-is smashes into the metal facade of the interstellar fast-food building. I can't see it, but I imagine the flying orb buzzing around the space-age playland as kids full of Happy Meals dive for cover.

We drive into an alley that takes us along the back wall of the Roswell Museum. I keep looking back to see if we have pursuers, but Uncle Kevin makes one sharp turn after another. If they are still on our tail, they are at least a hundred meters back, which should give Wes and me enough time to jump out *Mission Impossible* style.

"Hey, Bob," I say. "We're nearly back. What are we supposed to do when we get there?"

"Excellent," he replies. "Jump inside and look for the stairs."

"Wait, are we still talking about the yellow Camaro?"

"Ten seconds," Uncle Kevin says. "I can't see them behind us. We may have time to actually stop."

"Good," Wes says. "My tuck and roll skills are terrible."

"Bob, you might be glitching again. Did you say stairs?"

Before Bob answers, Uncle Kevin hits the brakes and says, "Go, go!"

I fling open my door, and it hits a parked car.

Wes grabs the unopened box of Legos and holds it up. "Can I have this?"

"Wes, come on," I say.

Uncle Kevin nods, and my brother sticks it in his backpack.

We jump out as fast as we can. Even though we've stopped, I still manage to tumble. I use the SUV my door hit to keep from landing on the pavement. Wes doesn't fare much better, resting on the bumper of a VW.

I slam the door shut and look at Uncle Kevin as he prepares to speed away. He gives me a nod, puts a fist to his chest, and says, "Qapla!"

Wes stands straight and returns with a hardy, "Qapla."

I remain slumped. "Gesundheit."

Quy'QoQuj, aka Uncle Kevin, accelerates out of the parking lot. Turning onto the street, two black sedans, I can't tell from where, fall in line behind him. Sirens blare in the distance, and I hope with Uncle Kevin's tinted windows it will be a little while before anyone realizes we aren't in the backseat anymore.

I look at Wes. "Come on." The Camaro is a few spots over, and we move quickly. I try the door handle, but it's locked. I peer in the window and see another problem.

Wes looks at me. "Now what?"

I shrug. "Hey, Bob. The car is locked, and I can't drive a stick. What should we–"

"Find the butt," Bob interrupts.

"Ah ..."

"What did he say?" Wes says.

I hold up a finger. "Bob, what was that? I think you're glitching again."

"Go to the Camaro's butt. You should see the stairs."

Wes must see the confusion on my face because he steps closer and says, "What?"

"Bob wants us to find Bumblebee's butt."

"His butt?"

"Bob, we're a little unclear on the whole butt-finding thing?"

"Switching to manual translations," Bob says. Unpleasant static begins popping between my ears, then it tapers off. "Backside, rear end, bottom, bootie, caboose ... Is that any clearer?"

"Not so much. Kind of worse actually."

"Okay, manual translations are ineffective. Switching back."

"Do you think he means the trunk?" Wes says.

I snap my fingers. "Trunk."

"Yes, trunk," Bob says. "I was so close."

"Were you?" I say as we step over to the rear of the muscle car.

Wes explores the trunk with his fingers. "It's locked."

"Hey, Bob. The trunk is locked."

"Not for you. I synced the Camaro facade to your DNA before you arrived."

"Okay … Not sure what that means."

"Hold your hand over the trunk and concentrate."

"On what?"

"Scantily clad females of your species."

"Really?"

"No!" Bob shouts. "Concentrate on opening the trunk. See the lock in your mind. Will it to release."

"Hey, I'm new at this. Why couldn't you just put a key under the wheel well?"

"Please, hurry. I am detecting hostiles in the vicinity."

Wes asks what's going on.

"Bob is now being a sarcastic dick."

"I can hear you," Bob says.

"I'm aware."

I take a deep breath and say to Wes, "Bob wants me to try something." I hold my hand over the trunk. I don't touch it, but I can feel the warmth emanating from the metal. I have no idea what a 1977 Camaro trunk locking mechanism looks like, but I imagine it anyway. A few beats go by, and I feel pretty silly, and then there is a soft click. The trunk lid rises an inch and touches my hand.

"Freaky," Wes says. "For a second there, you looked like that guy from the Matrix, only way less cool."

I frown. "Thanks."

"What is your status?" Bob says.

"Your Jedi mind-thingy worked."

"Great," Bob says. "Now get in."

"The trunk?"

"Yes. Do you see the stairs?"

I throw the trunk all the way open and start to say *what stairs*, but the words get stuck in my throat as my brother and I gaze into the classic car's rear compartment.

"How is that possible?" Wes asks.

I wipe my eyes and blink several times, hoping that when I am done, I will be staring at a completely normal interior compartment of a 1977 Camaro's trunk.

No such luck. All we can see is the top of a spiral staircase plunging at least ten feet into an abyss of darkness, beyond the reach of the afternoon sun.

Wes and I crouch down together and peer under the car. The undercarriage looks normal. I wave my hand over the pavement under the car, expecting to touch something I can't see. But there is nothing. *How?*

We stand in unison, gazing into the compartment.

"Bumblebee's butt is way bigger on the inside," Wes says.

"What is your status?" Bob says.

"Perplexed," I reply.

"Crap," Wes says, then grabs my shirt and pulls it down. We lower back into a crouch.

"What?" I whisper.

Wes points toward the front of the Camaro. I take a peek but keep low. The strange flying sphere is circling the parking lot. A yellow conical-shaped light moves across the parked cars. I've seen enough science fiction movies to know it's scanning, most likely for us.

"Warning," Bob says. "I'm detecting a hostile in your immediate area."

I roll my eyes and whisper, "Thanks for the update, Bob."

A rear door of the building opens behind us, and a blonde teenager in an apron steps out from one of the stores. A sign above the door says *Employee Entrance. Hangar 18 Confections: You won't believe what's inside.* The teenager props the door open and rolls out a garbage can. She moves out into the parking lot with the refuse and heads toward a dumpster smelling of tauntaun innards.

Wes points at the open door. "We can make it."

Run into the confection store seeking safety and maybe a sweat or two. I did skip breakfast and am a bit peckish.
Turn to page 117.

Stick with the plan and jump into Bumblebee's butt!
Turn to page 79.

I scan their name tags. The older of the two, Carter, seems to be in charge. He didn't wait for Bob to answer when he asked to see the Visitor's Badge. He just moved in. His partner, Skully, looks on edge and has already unshouldered his weapon.

"What do you think?" Skully says.

Carter's eyes move over our badges. "Looks about as genuine as a three-dollar bill."

Uncle Bob steps forward. "Gentlemen, I have assured you I have clearance …"

Before Bob finishes, Carter unholsters his side arm and, without even looking at him, aims the handgun at Uncle Bob's face. "Call it in, Skully."

After lowering his rifle, Skully reaches over and activates his CB attached below his left shoulder. "This is patrol 89."

"Go ahead, patrol."

"We have encountered possible trespassers. Lt. Randle is here with two teens claiming to be his nephews."

There is no response. Skully looks over at Carter, who steps back and joins him. Carter switches hands with his gun and reaches over to use his walkie. "Patrol 89, holding for orders."

The mechanical grind of the elevator noticeably slows, and with a jolt, it stops.

The MPs exchange glances. "That's odd," Skully says, looking nervous.

Carter scoffs. "What, that an elevator as old as our grandparents stopped?" He steps over to the control panel and presses buttons. "We're halfway between level one and the surface."

"Oh, gawd," Skully says, sweat on his forehead. "This is my nightmare."

Carter turns around. "Keep it together, private. Remember your training."

"Training didn't cover dangling over a quarter-mile shaft built more than a half century ago by contractors with the lowest bid."

I smile. "When *I'm* tense, I take deep breaths."

Skully takes my advice and sucks in a deep breath as the elevator creaks under the strain of decades of use. After several breaths, Skully says, "It's not working." He bends forward. "My balls are receding into my body."

Carter hits the emergency call button. "More soldiering, less ball talk."

Wes removes his backpack. "I have an inhaler. Would you like to try?"

Skully nods. "Yes, please."

Carter whips around. "Do not open that backpack, young man. And you," he turns to Skully, "stop engaging!" Carter talks into his walkie. "Patrol 89, standing by for orders."

A voice comes back over the walkie. Clearly a different voice than before. "Patrol 89, you are clear to terminate."

Carter and Skully exchange horrified glances. "This is Patrol 89, repeat instructions."

"You are clear to terminate. Artifacts must not reach the surface."

Carter says, "I have two teens and Lt. Randle, not artifacts."

Skully suddenly stands up straight. "It's them. Remember the last security update? It said the aliens were shapeshifters. They can appear human."

"What security update?"

"It was a unit e-mail."

Carter rolls his eyes. "Who reads emails anymore?"

"Trust me," I say, "we are not aliens."

"Well, he is," Wes says, pointing at Uncle Bob.

I glower at Wes. "Stop helping." I look back at the MPs. "Okay, yes, he is kinda an alien. There is this living plant controlling him from far away. It's a whole thing. But my brother and I are very, very human."

Scully raises his weapon, aims at my face. "That's exactly what an alien would say."

"Patrol 89. Are the artifacts terminated?"

"No, we are holding."

There is no reply.

"Carter, don't look into their eyes," Skully says. "They have mind control powers."

"What?"

"It was in the e-mail."

"Jesus."

The two-ton freight elevator vibrates. We plummet. My stomach shoots into my throat as if we just plunged over the peak of a roller coaster drop. But there's no safety bar to hold us in place. We're weightless, our feet leaving the floor. I look at my brother, floating next to me, and reach for his hand, seeing my own fear mirrored on his face.

"We're in freefall!" Carter shouts, dropping his weapon to grab hold of the wall. "Cable must have snapped."

"Bullshit!" Scully says. "They're killing us all."

"What?"

"They won't let them leave!" Scully yells. "And we're expendable!"

"No, we're not!" Carter's ass floats higher than his head. "Where do you get this stuff?"

"It was in the e-mail!"

The correct choice was to be our authentic selves. Start acting like spoiled brats. Act so horrible that not even MPs on a high security base would question our authenticity.

Turn to page 216.

In level eighteen of *Star Pilot,* a Locknar Syndicate smash-freighter offered to escort rebel Astral Fighters through an amorphous ice field by opening its massive bay doors. Every fighter that flew inside was killed, and their ships stripped for parts. My distrustful nature had sent a wave of suspicion crashing through my body when I played that level, allowing me to avoid an embarrassing virtual death. I feel the same wave now.

"We're gonna find another way out." I scan the interior of the hanger. The walls are reinforced with heavy materials, lots of steel, lots of concrete, but the roof is thin by comparison.

"Which way?" Wes says.

I activate the internal stabilizers and rotate the ship. "Up."

"I was afraid you were gonna say that." Wes reaches for the control in front of him. "Forward shield to max."

I hit the thrusters, and we ascend with terrifying speed. The roof rushes toward us, and I have to fight the instinct to evade. The internal struggle lasts only a moment as the Astral Fighter explodes through the hangar. Our view changes to the inky blackness of the Nevada night sky. I glance at the rearview monitor and see the hanger, with its new skylight ceiling, and Area 51 fall away into the distance.

Scans indicate that they had fired some conventional artillery our way, but our rapid ascent renders their attack useless.

"Hey, meatsacks. Did you just punch through a structure?"

"Ah, little bit," I say.

"You are not in a smash-freighter," Bob scolds. "That ship has been patched together with inadequate indigenous materials guided by as much science as I could download into the brains of what passes for engineers on your planet."

"There are a lot of insults in there," I say as I decelerate and level off the ship. "And you said the ship was good to go."

"I did not expect you to fly through walls."

"Technically, it was a roof," Wes says.

"My readings indicate structural integrity is down eleven percent. And the Greys' platform I used to patch a breach in the hull has become dislodged."

"How bad?" I ask, checking internal scans.

"Cabin atmosphere and life support are stable, for now," Bob says in a tone that feels like a warning. "I did not have time to make the ship perfect."

"You had fifty years," I say.

"From your point of view, not mine."

"What?"

Bob grunts. "I am not going to try to explain bloom dilation of temporal grapeseed and pedalsprout fields to you. But that does remind me of something. I did have time to find an answer to your query."

"What query?"

"You wanted to know why the Pisces Converter's language glitches were sounding like, how did you put it, 'interstellar fruit.'"

I throw up my hands. "That was like four thousand years ago. Literally."

"Does that mean you are no longer interested?"

"I'm interested," Wes chimes in.

"The Pisces Convertors have been struggling to find vocabulary to translate concepts and technology that do not exist in your world, especially those related to future-casting and time-traversing."

"We already figured that out," I say.

"If I may continue. Using my species as a framework, it attempted to find plant-based vocabulary in your language that would bridge somewhat of an understanding. It settled on fruits and vegetables as a common thread to base its translation. Obviously, it was a misstep, as it does not work."

"I so don't care," I say.

"I thought it was interesting, Bob," Wes says.

"You would. Okay, Bob, what's the plan?"

"I'm sending your ship coordinates. Level off at 8,000 kilometers and activate your heads-up display."

I tap the control. The heads-up display illuminates the interior of the canopy in front of us. Wes and I take in the images. I know my brother doesn't recognize any of this, but it's all familiar to me. Schematics fill the display, including armament stats on the Reptilians' main fighter, the Scale Runner. They're sleek, maneuverable, and cold-blooded as can be. But we're in luck. Since this was intended as a first-contact mission for them to reconnect with their hybrid descendants on Earth, their approach will be diplomatic.

"I don't expect Scale Runners to be deployed until after our attack begins," Bob says.

"What're we attacking?" Wes says.

The display changes, and the Scale Runner schematic is replaced by an image that makes my heart sink. It's a massive V-shaped ship that I know from the final boss level in *Star Pilot*. I died eight times before finally defeating it.

"I estimate there will be three Talon Cruisers."

"Three? The *Star Pilot* game only had one to defeat."

"And that is the same scenario here. The one that matters will be in the rear, positioned in orbit. It's the command ship. All the Progenitors orchestrating Plan 9 are onboard."

The view on our heads-up display shifts from the schematic of the V-shaped Talon Cruiser to a live feed. Bob has tapped into military satellites, and the display shows two cruisers entering Earth's atmosphere. Their descent trajectory will take them over Arizona in seven minutes.

New information lights up my screen. The U.S. military has scrambled A-10 warthogs to investigate unusual movement. Not in the sky, but on the ground. Somewhere in Nevada, strange vehicles have emerged from underground. I know what's happening. The strange vehicles are the indigenous Reptilians. They must have received communications from the Progenitors and are moving to greet them. Phase two of Plan 9 is happening now. And my brother and I are right in the middle of it.

My hands are shaking. "This is impossible," I say, more to myself.

"Star Pilot, I know what lies before you seems overwhelming. But like your brother, who has the gift of mechanical instinct that defies explanation, you have the gift of a Star Pilot. You are one in a billion. Ten billion to be exact."

I take a deep breath. "So, I'm special."

"Do not let it unduly inflate your ego. Like your brother, you are an anomaly."

"That does not feel special."

"It is not supposed to," Bob says. "Now change course to rendezvous with the other Star Pilots."

"Other Star Pilots? Didn't you just say I was the only one?"

"I said you are one in ten billion. Do you have any idea what the population of the galaxy is? There are eight billion small-brained bipeds on your planet alone. Do the math."

"Math really isn't James's strong point, Bob," Wes says.

"I don't like either of you," I say. "Changing course."

* * *

On the edge of space, we met up with the four other Star Pilots, all flying Astral Fighters. Compared to their pristine vessels, our craft looks like a relic salvaged from a demolition derby. As in the game, each pilot has a Pisces Converter nestled in whatever orifice gives access to the brain, allowing for direct, cross-species communication.

They had all just arrived from different parts of the galaxy, and none had prior experience with the others. Before Wes and I arrived, the small group had enough time to adopt call signs. The group designation was Red Squadron, and as the latecomers, Wes and I were dubbed Red-Five.

Now, Red-Three nominates herself squadron leader, and since we only have minutes to start our attack, no one argues. "Intel from my handler indicates that the command ship is maintaining orbit above your planet's largest continent," she says.

"Hi, Red-Five here. Did you say handler?"

"Yeah, a plant person that recruits you to become a Star Pilot."

"Bob," Wes says. "They all have Bobs." He looks over at me. "Feeling less special?"

"With every passing second."

"Cut the chatter Red-Five," the squad leader says. "Reds One and Two with me. Reds Four and Five, I want you to approach from the dark side of the planet and attack the command ship from behind. Target the communication tower and engines. The rest of us will engage in a frontal assault and draw its fire."

"How long do you think we'll last against their guns?" Red-Two asks.

"Long enough for one run," Red-Three says. "We'll pull away fast, and hopefully the Scale Runners will follow us."

This is a terrible plan. They won't last thirty seconds once the fighters are launched.

I want to say something, but Red-One says, "When will we know if we need to plant Death Blossom?"

"Only as a last resort. My handler advised there are too many unknowns," Red-Three says. "Now get into position. We attack in two minutes. Good luck, Star Pilots."

Feeling as if I'd slept through a school lecture, I switch off my mic. "Bob, what are they talking about? Death Bottom?"

"Death Blossom," Bob says. "It's a plan B that me and the other Bobs came up with after I relayed Wes's concerns about finding a more permanent solution to the Progenitors' lust for conquest. Death Blossom was conceived while you were in stasis. It's unstable, unpredictable, and highly illegal amongst my kind. It is not an option."

I bring the ship in line with Red-Four and hit the thrusters, taking us to the nightside of Earth.

"Bob, you got one minute before five Astral Fighters are gonna take on a Talon Cruiser, and I can't imagine how many Scale Runners. I'm smart enough to know the odds are not in our favor. So cut the crap. What's plan B?"

* * *

Bob explains it, and even though the Pisces Converter went into glitch-overdrive, Wes and I get the gist. Hidden in each Astral Fighter is a terrible, morally questionable weapon that has never been used. Death Blossom is a low yield Temporal Bomb that Bob and his cohorts have genetically coded to obliterate not only the main Reptilian Progenitors orchestrating Plan 9 but will create some kind of time-quake that will erase them and their families from galactic history going back at least ten generations, back beyond Plan 9's conception.

"It's the baby Hitler dilemma," Wes says.

I turn to my brother. "Okay, pretend I don't know what you're talking about."

Wes rolls his overly book-read eyes. "If you could go back in time and kill baby Hitler, and prevent World War II, the holocaust, all that death, would you?"

I shrug. "Why is the question about killing a baby? Can't I go back and run Hitler over as a middle-schooler. Most tweens piss me off anyway."

"That's not the point."

"It is irrelevant. The time-quake created by Death Blossom would be highly unstable, making eddy-berry rootwaves throughout the galaxy. Besides, you two would not survive the explosion. You would both be dead."

"You mean like dead and respawnable or dead-dead?"

"The latter I believe. Unless—"

Red-Four's voice comes through the com. "Red-Five, the others are starting their run. Should we engage?"

I turn on my mic. "Negative. The plan was that we hold until they launch their fighters and pursue the others. It shouldn't be long." I flick the mic back off. "Bob, you said unless. Unless what?"

"You could survive the explosion if you were in it."

"In it," I repeat. "Like ground zero?"

"I could program Death Blossom to activate the plumpercott matrix on your ship to return to your point of origin upon detonation."

"Scale Runners have been launched," Red-Four says. "Prepare to engage."

"Bob, how long do you need to program the bomb?" I say.

"A few minutes, but I will not let it come to that."

I peer out and see Red-Four's shatterpoint cannons deploying, targeting the communication tower. I switch on a targeting beam and lock onto the tower as well.

I look over at Wes. "Are you ready?"

"No."

"Me either. Hey, Bob, my brother is a little nervous. Do have anything encouraging to say?"

"On my world we have a motivational phrase used to inspire a successful outcome."

"Which is?"

"Try not to die," Bob says.

I groan.

"Worst. Pep talk. Ever," Wes says.

"Star Pilots have engaged the Scale Runners," Red-Four says.

"Let's do this," I say.

We emerge from the dark side of Earth, weapons locked on the Talon Cruiser's communication tower. Through my headset, I can hear the battle raging on the other side of the ship. Our scans indicate the Reptilian fighters are pursuing the other Star Pilots, so we open fire.

The tower takes several direct hits, and I turn my weapons onto the starboard engine. Red-Four breaks off to the port side, and I lose sight of him as the tower explodes. This doesn't make the cruiser any less formidable, but it will handicap their communication.

I'm about to release a spread of Sundiver Missiles when Red-Three shouts over the comms. "Red-Two is down. Repeat: Red-Two is down. I've taken heavy damage, lost navigation, shields down fifty percent."

"This is Red-One, in pursuit of Scale Runner squadron. I'll try to draw them away from you."

I fire the missiles, then dive under the cruiser. I can't see if any of them hit their target. I move into position to start a strafing run on the cruiser's deck. I open up with the starfire cannons, not bothering to aim. There is no need. The target is everywhere.

"Wes, check if our missiles hit their engine."

Wes examines his heads-up display and scrolls back. "I don't think so. None of ours and none of Red-Fours. There's some kind of shielding around the engines. Nothing got through."

"Frak."

"Red-Three is down," Red-one says over the comms. "I'm assuming command. Regroup on my position. We'll concentrate our fire."

I pull up, assuming a ninety-degree angle from the cruiser. I check our rear scans, hoping to see that we've done some damage to the massive ship.

Wes looks at the same images I do and shakes his head. "Besides the tower, we've barely scratched it."

"Red-Five, enemy fighters heading our way," Red-Four says. "Coming in point three-five."

I bank the ship and hit the thrusters.

"You're heading straight at them," Wes says. "Why?"

"We can't run away from our problems, little brother."

"We could try!"

* * *

My words are more strategy than life lesson, but I think they work both ways. In level 39 of *Star Pilot*, I learned that Scale Runners are practically blind when approached head-on; most of their scanned data is peripheral.

Wes sits back, watching in terror as I eliminate sixteen enemy fighters before a single one manages to get a shot off at us.

Red-Four calls out to us. "I'm heading out to rendezvous with Red-One."

I had punched a hole through the wall of Scale Runners and could easily regroup with the other Star Pilots. I start to make the course correction, but hesitate. I turn my mic off. "Bob, how accurate did you recreate the Talon Cruisers in the game you used to recruit me and the other Star Pilots?"

"It is one of their most closely guarded vessels. We had to extrapolate its design from earlier models. We may have been a bit off."

My screen lights up with new signals. Both of the other Talon Cruisers have sent more fighters our way. Hundreds. "Bob, when you and the other Bobs came up with this whole plan, how many Star Pilots did you expect to find?"

Bob remains silent for a moment. "Our initial estimates were very encouraging. We expected to find at least two hundred or more."

I sigh. "I'd have loved to be in that battle, but this ... I mean, what are we doing?"

"We have to try, Star Pilot. When we stop trying, hope is lost."

There's a point in every video game where the player realizes all the available options are bad. A no-win scenario in which escape is impossible, defeat is inevitable. Trekkies call it The Kobayashi Maru, and it feels like we're there. I look over at Wes.

"What?" he says.

"We can rejoin the others and fight on, and maybe ..."

"Or?"

"Try to kill baby Hitler."

"Red-Five, what's your status?"

"You mean Plan B." Wes takes a deep breath. "It's your call, Star Pilot."

Like a Catholic girl on the morning after the prom, I decide to utilize Plan B.
Turn to page 230.

Summon my courage and regroup with Red Squadron, then finish the assault on the Talon Cruiser in a battle so spectacular they will be talking about it in the next *Try Not to Die* book.
Turn to page 49.

"Wes, no. We need to get inside." I push the trunk lid all the way open.

Wes shakes his head. "There's obviously some kind of weird spatial Doctor Who-type anomaly going on in there."

"And?"

"We don't know what it could do to us. It could smash our atoms together or stretch us beyond our ability to physically … you know, stretch. We could end up looking like Plastic Man, or Mr. Fantastic, uh Elastic Girl, or Elongating Man."

"We get stretchy superpowers, cool. Wait. There's an Elongating Man?"

Wes throws his hands up. "I don't know, probably."

"You're overthinking this."

I stand up hoping that if I jump in first, Wes will follow. Before I can get in, the alien sphere hovers over the hood of the Camaro. The debate is over. We no longer have time to run to the candy store's back entrance. The yellow scanning beam turns our way. I grab Wes by his Starfleet backpack and yank him up. "Get in Bumblebee's butt! Now!"

Wes must see the floating orb because he hops in without arguing. I follow and somehow manage to close the trunk lid behind me. It didn't look like it from the outside, but there is at least a meter drop to the floor. Neither of us are prepared for it. It's like stepping off the stairs onto the floor, only to realize there are a few more steps. We tumble to the hard surface one on top of the other.

"Get off me!" Wes shouts.

I sit up and roll over. I don't get to my feet, because in my mind, I'm inside a car's trunk. The total darkness does nothing to help my mind catch up. Reaching out to where I remember the staircase being, my fingers touch the spiral railing. I feel something more, and it's hard to explain. It's as if the railing is reaching out to me and offering a hand. I grip the railing and the stairs light up. Each step illuminates from underneath a soft white hue. The steps come alive from top to bottom, and I see

Wes next to me looking like a kid watching the Christmas tree come alive with light for the first time.

"Did ... did you do that?" he asks.

"I don't know. Are you okay?"

"I think so ... I mean..." Wes goes silent for a moment and puts a hand on his stomach.

"Oh, jeez." He quickly turns away from me, and a second later I am extremely grateful. Without the preamble of a dry heave, Wes projectile vomits for at least a meter. It looks like Mom's homemade breakfast burrito. Big chunks—Wes never chews his food. I'm so glad I skipped breakfast today.

I put a hand on Wes's shoulder as he heaves one final time.

"Hey, just a bit of a warning," Bob says.

"Not now, Bob," I say as Wes turns back to me. "Better?"

He nods and wipes his lower lip. "That was fun."

"I need to let you know before you get inside that the spatial displacement may cause some nausea, "Bob says.

I roll my eyes. "Thanks, Bob."

Wes pulls some napkins from his backpack and works on the refried bean-colored liquid on his lips. "What did Bob say?"

I grin. "He wanted to know if you developed any superpowers."

"Is projectile vomiting a superpower?"

"Not a good one," I say as I stand. "Bob really said that there might be some nausea."

Wes gives me a thumbs up. "Roger that." He gets up, slowly, wobbles a bit.

I help steady him and am about to ask if he wants to sit back down when, from out of the darkness, something streaks across the floor. It moves with purpose, doesn't seem interested in us, and heads straight for the lumpy vomit. It reminds me of a remote-controlled mini-skateboard, only big enough for one foot, carrying a tiny city of metallic structures on the top.

"Hey, Bob, got a status update for you. We're inside, Wes hurled, and there is a ... I want to say mini-robot, playing in the vomit."

"Not playing. Working," Bob says. "You are in a self-cleaning environment."

I tell Wes, "This place cleans itself."

Wes finishes wiping his lip. "Cleans itself, huh." He crumples up the napkin and tosses it to the floor.

The cleaning bot stops slurping up barf for a moment, while a focused energy beam projects from a tiny aperture. It envelops Wes's soiled napkin, then gently levitates it within the beam, drawing it toward an intake port. As the napkin nears, a hatch hisses open, and sucks it inside. The hatch seals with a soft *thunk*, and the bot gets back to work.

"Wow," I say. "I know what to get Mom for Christmas."

"My reading says, you are stationary," Bob reports. "Can you resume moving?"

I sigh. "Always so pushy, this guy."

"I can hear you."

"I'm aware. Look, I think it's time you answer like nine hundred of my questions."

"It will not take them long to locate you two. You need to resume moving."

"No. We're not going anywhere until you tell me what is going on."

"There is no time for a huge info dump right now."

"Info-what? Are you glitching?"

The room we are in, and room doesn't seem to be the right word because there are no visible walls, just darkness all around, jolts a little. Wes grabs the railing.

"Just tell me why this is happening," I say.

"Which part?" Bob says.

"Any of this!"

The room jolts again, much more violently, and Wes and I bump into each other. I ask him if he's okay.

He nods, and I can see the color coming back to his face.

"They have found the transport," Bob says.

"Is that what the shaking is?"

"Shaking? They must be attempting to breach."

"Breach is bad, right?"

"Yes!" Bob shouts. "You need to get airborne."

"What's Bob saying?" Wes asks.

At this point, I'm pretty sure we need to head down the stairs, but I'm really getting tired of Bob barking orders at me, especially when I have no idea why any of this is happening.

"You are still stationary," Bob says. "Listen, how about I answer questions as you move?"

Seems like a good compromise. "Fine." I look at Wes. "We're going down."

"Really?" Wes says.

The room shakes again, and we both hold onto the railing. The sound of metal bending echoes from far away.

"We can't stay here."

Wes looks down the stairs that simply make no sense in our minds. "After you."

Cautiously, I step down. I take several more and feel pretty confident we won't tumble into darkness. "Okay, questions," I say. "Those lizard people up there, they're aliens, right?"

"Yes and no," Bob says. "Parts of their DNA are alien."

"How does that happen?"

"It is difficult to summarize several millennia of galactic history."

"Try," I say as I gaze as far down as the steps' lights allow. I keep expecting to see something different, but the steps just keep spiraling down.

"Eons ago, on the far rim of the galaxy, the Progenitors, the oldest Reptilian species known to exist, embarked on a campaign of conquest. Their initial attempts were conventional—terraforming alien worlds, encountering other species, and then ruthlessly subjugating or eradicating any that dared to stand in their path. This brutal campaign of expansion across the stars was their first step toward galactic domination."

"Okay, Darth Vader, Emperor type stuff," I say. "I'm with you so far."

"The Progenitors, driven by an insatiable hunger for conquest, launched eight separate campaigns to subjugate the galaxy. Each time, they nearly achieved their goal, their relentless advance halted only by the desperate resistance of a burgeoning galactic alliance. After their eighth and final defeat, the once-mighty Progenitors were shattered, their empire crumbling. They were forced to retreat to the obscurity of their ancestral home, a distant corner of the galaxy not far from the fledgling human civilization on Earth."

"Okay, so happy ending. The good guys win," I say. "How are they here?"

"I'm not finished. Defeated, the Progenitors' ambition remained undiminished. They devised a new strategy—Plan Nine—an insidious scheme of genetic infiltration. Instead of brute force, they would subtly manipulate life across the galaxy. Covertly, they would dispatch emissaries to emerging worlds, seeding them with their own DNA, merging it with cold-blooded species. On Earth, this meant discreetly altering the evolutionary path of prehistoric reptiles, creating aberrant hybrids, their progeny destined to serve the Progenitors' long-term agenda. Plan Nine was initiated across countless worlds."

"How does merging with Earth's ancient lizards help them?"

"Still not finished. Over countless millennia, these hybrid species would evolve, grow in intelligence, shaped by their respective worlds. When the time deemed right, the Progenitors, the architects of their existence, would re-establish contact."

"Why?"

"To guide them to the next phase of Plan Nine."

"Which is?"

"To take over the galaxy, planet by planet, from within."

"Oh, man, Galactic History is a bad B-movie," I say. "Okay, terrible plot aside, what does any of this have to do with me?"

Suddenly, the stairs end, and we step into a compartment the size of a suburban teenager's bedroom, with metallic walls—walls that are not stationary. They're moving or reshaping. "Bob, something is happening here."

"Nothing is happening. Your eyes are just adjusting to the reality I need you to be in."

"That clears things up," I say, watching the room slowly transform into a large cockpit. Not just any cockpit, but one I recognize.

"You are in a point of multiple locations. I'm simply stripping away the locations we do not need at the moment," Bob explains. "Like peeling back layers. Your primitive ocular units will interpret this from their limited experiences as a rapid environmental change."

"Sounds like there is an insult in there somewhere, but I think I understand." A chair takes shape next to me, or according to Bob, reveals itself as other locations are removed. I've seen this chair before. It's a Star Pilot's chair.

Behind us, a distant female voice descends. "Wes. James."

My brother turns around, looking back up the stairs. "Mom, is that you?"

"Yes, sweetie. Wes, is James with you?"

Wes puts his foot on the first step. "Yeah, he's here. Are you and Dad alright?"

"Yes, we're fine. But you two need to come back up here. I think you're in danger."

Wes looks back at me. I step to the stairs and holler up. "Why do you think that, Mom?"

"Well, there are some officials up here that say someone might be trying to abduct you."

Wes takes another step up. I put a hand on his Starfleet backpack. "Wait." I lean over the stairs and look up. "Mom."

"Yes, hun."

"When's my birthday?"

"Why it's June third, two-thousand-one."

Wes meets my gaze. "She got it right. It's Mom."

"James, the people up here said that someone may try to put something in your ear. You shouldn't listen to them. They're dangerous."

I believe it's my mom, and conclude that the being calling itself Bob, the one that put a live interstellar fish in my ear, is the real bad guy. We need to head up the stairs.
Turn to page 165.

I'm 90% sure it's Mom but we need to investigate a bit more before abandoning Bob and his bizarre take on galactic history.
Turn to page 179.

Reluctantly, I give Wes a nod. I expect him to start moving one way or another but to my surprise, he reaches up and seizes the car's rear passenger door handle.

"What're you doing?" I say as debris clinks on the dumpster behind us.

Wes doesn't answer. Continuing to crouch, he opens the door and hops inside the back seat. As he does, he motions me to follow. I carefully jump in behind him and shut the door. The car smells new, clean, and with the door closed, the sounds of fighting are muffled.

"Why did you lead us in here?"

"We can drive away," Wes says.

"Do you know how to hotwire an electric car? Can anybody hotwire one?"

Wes grins. "Don't need to." He points to the driver's seat while he sits up.

I rise to a seated position and see the back of a man sitting in the driver's seat. I don't need to see his face to know it's the guy from the store. The same one I am almost positive is my parent's Trekkie friend, Uncle Kevin.

He seems to be just sitting there, not moving. He's in his late-forties, olive skin, clean-shaven, and when he hangs out with my parents, he is very animated, always ready for a Klingon-sized battle. But not now. I don't know if it's the war being waged outside the windshield that has petrified him or if it's something else, but he just sits there, staring. Dazed.

Careful not to scare him, I rest my hand on his shoulder and say, "Hey."

He turns around slowly and doesn't at all seem surprised to find people sitting in the back of his car. He stares at us and tilts his head. Confusion covers his face like Klingon cosplay prosthetics. There's a flash of recognition and he says, "Hey, aren't you Richard and Crystie's kids?"

"Yes, yes," I say. "Uncle Kevin, it is you."

He smiles, turns around further and takes us both in. "Do you guys know what I'm doing here?"

"What are *you* doing here?" I say. "Don't you remember?"

He shakes his head.

"You met Wes in the store, gave him the Pisces fish-thing, which by the way, jumped into my ear, thank you very much."

"I have no idea what you're talking about," Uncle Kevin says. "I remember I checked into the hotel at the Roswell convention center. Put my bags in my room ... next thing I know I'm walking to my car in this parking lot with this box of Legos." He looks out the window behind me. "Are we ... Am I, still in Roswell?"

Just in front of our car, a man in a black suit dives for cover as another blue light bursts from the pavement. The man in the suit turns and fires, striking the figures that tried to emerge from the light. Uncle Kevin turns back forward. He points out the windshield. "And, qaStaH nuq jay?"

"What?" I say.

"He said, 'What the hell is going on?'" Wes pipes in.

I turn to him. "You speak Klingon?"

"Don't you?"

"No, I took Spanish like a normal person." I turn back to Uncle Kevin. "Can you get us out of here?"

"I don't know," he says.

I look at Wes, who shrugs. I decide to phone a friend. "Hey, Bob, can you hear me?"

"Yes, I can hear you. Are you at the yellow vehicle?"

"Uh, working on it. Listen, did you do something to the guy that brought the fish-thing to my brother? He seems very confused, and can't remember how he got here."

"A few days ago, I borrowed him," Bob says.

"Borrowed?"

"I had every intention of returning him."

"Dude, people aren't library books. So, you hijacked him? Why? Was it to bring me the fish thing?"

"Pisces Convertor."

"Whatever," I say. "Wait, if you need my skills, like you said, why didn't you just hijack me?"

"Symbiotic control would not give me access to your skills as a pilot. In any case, I did not identify you until you finished the game, which you did during the last night cycle. I am not going to explain the fundamentals of Psychohistory, but I did know that you or someone like you would be in Roswell at this time. I borrowed someone that I knew would also be in Roswell. And he was highly susceptible, almost as if he'd been borrowed before."

"How did you know Uncle Kevin would be in Roswell?"

"Instagram. Facebook. X. Your species isn't really good with hiding your lifestyles."

"That's fair."

"You want to know what he had for breakfast? He posted eight pictures of it."

"No." I look over at Wes. "Bob is kind of a dick. And a kidnapper."

Wes points to Uncle Kevin. "Is that why he seems a bit out of it?"

I nod. "Yeah."

Uncle Kevin looks scared, and I understand. He doesn't know what's going on, where he is, or how he got here. But we don't have time to sort any of that out. It's time for action, and I need to tap into Uncle Kevin's courage.

"Are those Men in Black?" Uncle Kevin says.

"Uhm, probably," I say. "Look, Uncle Kevin, you've known my family for a long time. Heck, I think I thought you were our real uncle until I was fifteen."

Uncle Kevin smiles and looks a little less scared.

"But we don't need Uncle Kevin right now," I say. "I need ... what's your Klingon name?"

Without hesitation, he says, "Quy'QoQuj, son of Qoquy'QIrgh of house ghorghmeq."

"Of course it is. We need *that* guy. And we need him now."

Uncle Kevin looks beyond his hood. The battle between two disagreeable species fills his windshield. It's slight but I notice a change in him. He takes a deep breath and sits up a little taller. Reaching into his shirt pocket, he pulls out a pair of aviator glasses and puts them on. "Where to?" he says, his voice much more confident.

The car rocks as something explodes next to us. Even with the doors and windows up, I can feel the heat.

"Anyplace but here," Wes screams.

Uncle Kevin grins. "It is a good day to die," he says in a voice I barely recognize.

Wes sits way up. "Is it?"

The dashboard lights up. Uncle Kevin grips the wheels. "Hold on." We lurch forward, a surge of power throwing us back against our seats. Before I can even buckle up, Uncle Kevin spins the wheel, sending us fishtailing across the asphalt. I slam against the door, Wes tumbling into me with a grunt. The designated exit fades into the distance as Uncle Kevin veers wildly towards the sidewalk. With a sickening crunch, we launch over the curb, the e-car's adaptive suspension groaning in protest.

We touch down on 5th Street. I imagine sparks dancing behind us as Uncle Kevin straightens us out, narrowly avoids oncoming traffic, and heads toward the Convention Center.

"What is your status?" Bob asks, echoing inside my head.

"Hard to say, Bob. Is fleeing for our lives a status?"

"My indicators say you are moving away from the transport."

"Transport? You mean the Camaro?"

"Yes, the Camaro," Bob says. "Look, this is no time for you to break wind."

"What?"

"Breaking wind. You need to stop."

"You know that means farting, right?"

"Farthing?" Bob says. "No, I mean to take a break, go sightseeing, linger off course."

"Then why—"

"The Pisces Convertor is not a perfect being. It makes mistakes, and with all this excitement, it gets glitchy."

"Glitchy!"

Uncle Kevin accelerates, and I tumble back into my seat as Wes grabs my arm. "What's glitchy?"

I look at Wes. "The fish thing in my ear. Apparently, it translates as well as Google."

"Nice," Wes says.

"I think we're being followed," Uncle Kevin says. "We should probably head to the police station. We're not too far."

"No!" Bob shouts inside my head. "You need to get back to the transport. Your pickles depend on it."

"What?"

"Sorry, glitching again. I mean lives!"

Try to save our pickles by returning to the transport.
Turn to page 58.

Go with Uncle Kevin's suggestion, a forty-year-old man who still lives with his mom, and head to the police station.
Turn to page 40.

Before Wes can finish his sigh, I decide for both of us. "I can't sleep for fifty years. No way. I'll go crazy if I'm stuck with my thoughts for more than a minute."

"I don't blame you," Wes says. "I can't imagine being stuck with your thoughts ever."

"Maybe we do insults after we get out of here."

"How?" he asks, staring at the damaged spaceship.

I hold the truck keys in front of him and give it a little shake. "Grab anything you want from the ship."

"If this is your decision, I need you to hide a few things," Bob says.

"On it," Wes says, heading into the ship.

I go to Brazel's pickup, which looks about as reliable as a stormtrooper's aim. The truck's features consist of an ignition switch and a manual stick shift, a bad beginning for our new adventure. I start the truck, blocking the memory of my one attempt at driving a car with a manual transmission.

Wes throws open the passenger door and tosses in his backpack. "Sorry it took so long. Bob had me ditch the weapons, and he said he'd be out of contact for a while."

"You know I can hear him too," I say, waiting for him to close the door. "I think we should go to the closest town, which I assume is Roswell."

"It's not," Wes says. "It's Corona? Go south."

"Seriously? Roswell isn't the closest town in the Roswell incident."

"Did you not read anything about the Roswell crash?"

"Might of, if I knew I *was* the Roswell crash." I gently put the relic of a truck in gear, take my foot off the clutch, and give it some gas. We lurch forward and the truck dies. I'd let the clutch out too quickly.

Wes looks ahead of us. "I think we have to go a little farther than this."

"Ha, ha. Do you want to drive?"

Wes sits back and shakes his head. "Are you sure you can do this? Remember when Grandpa tried to show you how to drive a stick?"

"Can we stay positive, please?" I snap. "And Grandma walks just fine now."

"With a cane," Wes mumbles as I run through my checklist again.

Foot on brake and clutch. Start truck, ease into gear. Slowly take foot off ... We roll forward, rocking side to side as the truck picks up speed. We drive onto a dirt road as I find second gear. There is some grinding, but we don't stall. I look over at Wes, hoping for some brotherly encouragement.

Wes folds his arms. "Great work, Star Pilot."

We cruse silently for a while. It takes most of my consideration to remember when to shift and what pedal to push.

When I can no longer see the Astral Fighter in the rearview mirror, I say, "Okay. It's 1947. What should we do first?" A grin curls up the side of my brother's face. I ask, "What? What are you thinking?"

"Well, besides the obvious, find Corona, de-alien our look, secure some shelter and a means to live. But after that, I thought it would be fun to find Gene Rodenberry. In 1947, he's in his mid-twenties."

"*Star Trek* guy. Why?"

Wes chuckles. "Kind of a gift for Mom and Dad. I think I could convince him not to let Shatner take the helm of *Star Trek V.*"

I laugh. "I think that'd be a gift to everyone. Hey!" I snap my fingers. "How old is Lucus in '47?"

Wes considers for a second. "About three or four."

"Damn. I have a few tweaks for him."

"Phantom Menace?"

"Specifically, no Jar-Jar."

"Right!"

"So annoying. So racist."

While trying to shift, I brake instead of putting the clutch in and accidentally kill the engine. As we drift to a stop, the truck leans to one side. "Damn. I know what I did. I think I'm getting better."

"How'd you come to that conclusion?"

"Shut up, Wesley." I open the door and step out.

"Are we walking?"

"No, I want to check the tires. Might have a flat." One of the front tires looks good, but the other is low. It might have a slow leak, or it might just need air. I'm about to check the back when Wes gets out of the truck.

"Do you hear that?" he says.

"Hear what?"

A distant hum answers. I turn around, my gaze instinctively drawn to the sky. Squinting into the sunlight, I try to make out whatever is approaching. As the high frequency whistle nears, recognition sparks. It's the sound of a plane, and anyone who has ever been to an airshow or played countless hours of *World of Warplanes* knows that signature sound.

"It's a P-51," I say. "What the frak is it doing out here?"

"Probably from the SAC base at Roswell."

"What?"

"Strategic Air Command."

"Is that like the Air Force?" I say as the vintage fighter nears.

"It will be. Right now, it's an Army Air Base where Major Marcel is stationed?"

"Am I supposed to know who that is?"

Wes rolls his eyes.

The P-51 passes overhead, and the sound vibrates through my body. As it goes by, it dips its wing to allow the pilot a view of us on the ground. I feel like waving, but remember we look like invaders from Mars.

"Do you think he saw us?" Wes says.

I don't need to answer as the fighter is banking around. "Back in the truck," I tell him.

We jump back in, slam the doors, and I get the engine started first try. We start rolling, and I force it into second gear. The only sound above the grinding of the gears is the hum of the P-51's Rolls-Royce Merlin V-12 engine.

"Do you see it!" I shout.

Wes looks over both shoulders, then straight back. "It's coming in right behind us."

I check the rearview mirror and see the warplane pull out of a dive, and level off just above the ground. It's preparing for a low-level pass, a strafing run. I look for cover, a place to protect us from the six .50 caliber machine guns. There is nothing but New Mexico sand and cacti.

Best I can do is turn hard just before it fires, but before I do, my foot slips off the clutch as I try to shift. The engine sputters. I attempt to get it under control as the P-51 fires.

Rounds strike the truck bed with the sickening sound of metal tearing as bullets rip through the vehicle. Glass explodes from the rear window, and the dashboard disintegrates. The cab is bathed in crimson as thirteen-millimeter-long bullets moving at nine hundred meters per second tear our bodies apart.

The correct choice was to roll the dice and sleep your way to 1997 with no idea how you will be taken care of while you are in stasis, no idea who will be watching over you, and no idea when you might wake up, if at all.

Turn to page 95.

Wes sighs. "I don't want to spend years in a world without Legos."

"Really? That's where the line is for you? You can't get by on Lincoln Logs for a while?"

"What about you? You think I want to spend the next few years watching you go through video game withdrawals?"

"Okay, that's fair." I drop the keys next to Brazel. "Alright Bob, we're doing the long sleep thing. What do we need to do?"

"Get back in the ship and secure the hatch."

Without saying a word, Wes and I walk our grey-painted butts back inside. I tap the hatch's control, and as I listen to the clicks and thuds of the latching mechanism engage, I wonder if it's for the last time.

"Will this door keep them out?" I ask.

"For a time," Bob says. "When they do get in, they will be unable to touch you."

I want to ask why or how, but the compartment behind me begins to transform. The side walls slide apart, and two shelves unfold and drop down. It takes a moment for the realization to sink in: the shelves are roughly our size. They don't look comfortable, like a Murphy bed designed by a mortician.

I step over the ship-cleaning bot, who is still slurping up its meal of the Grey's brain goo. I take a closer look at the spot I'm supposed to spend the next fifty years. "I have a lot of questions, Bob."

"Asking a bunch of questions you won't understand the answers to is pointless," Bob says.

"I hope you're referring to your translating space fish's glitches and not calling me dumb."

Bob doesn't answer.

"Just tell me we're not going to wake up as old men?"

"I cannot slow aging completely, but I can impede the process dramatically."

Bob's answer does not make me feel great. If I ever do see my parents again, will they recognize me, or expect me to have grandchildren?

"The technology for your stasis is Atari," Bob says, probably sensing he hadn't assured me. "It does not get better."

"Is that supposed to mean something to us?" Wes asks, sitting on one of the shelves.

"The Atarians were one of the first species to master intergalactic travel, putting themselves in stasis for centuries, just to explore the universe."

I slump down on the other cold, uncomfortable shelf. "Fascinating."

"I feel there is a catch coming," Wes says.

"The Atari are long gone, but their technology is still used throughout the universe, mostly because it's highly adaptable to other species, and easy to insert."

"There it is," Wes says, jumping off the shelf. "I'm out."

Two panels, one on each side of the shelf, slide open, revealing a pair of tiny, pod-like devices attached to slender handles. Each pair emerges from the wall on a retractable platform. I reach over and pick up one like a lollipop. "And where will we be inserting these?"

"For your species, the optimal placement for the stasis Pomseeds is the nasal passages."

Wes exhales. "Thank God. Okay, I'm back in."

"James, I'll walk you through the instructions to put Wes in stasis. Please pay attention. You will have to do the same procedure on yourself."

"I get to stick these in my brother's nose?"

"Yes. Then your own."

I smile. "One more thing crossed off the bucket list."

Wes gives me a weird look. "You have shoving something up your brother's nose on your bucket list?"

I shrug, smiling. "Don't you?"

He scowls at me, then takes off his cloak. Moving to the shelf, I can see his hands shaking. I step next to him. "I'm sorry your brother's an insensitive meatsack."

"You really are." Wes smiles, then lays down. "But you're the only brother I have."

I lean over him with the Pomseed in hand.

His eyes focus on it. "Do you think we'll wake up from this?"

I know this is one of those times when the older brother is supposed to reassure the younger one by saying everything is going to be all right. But I am as terrified as he clearly is, and a horrible liar to boot. Besides, he is too intelligent to fall for any false hope, even if it were meant to be comforting.

"I really don't know, Wes. But we've made it this far. What're the odds of that?"

Wes gives me a nervous smile.

"I could calculate the odds, if you are interested," Bob says.

"Shut up, Bob." I hold up the Pomseed.

"See you in fifty years."

"Not if I see you first."

* * *

Wes didn't enjoy the process. Neither did I. It was simple enough, insert the stasis Pomseed into one nostril, gently rotate it against the front part of the nasal passage for DNA processing and stem-rooting. Repeat this process in the other nostril. Fun stuff.

When I finished with Wes's second nostril, his eyes closed and the lollipop handles detached from the inserted Pomseeds. A mucusy ooze seeped from his nose, spreading across his face like a Halloween mask, and expanded. Within seconds, it enveloped his entire body, even underneath. At first, it was like looking through frosted glass, but as the ooze crystallized, it became transparent. I could see my brother, preserved within.

I'd imagined it would be cold, like frozen food, but I was wrong. I placed my hand on his chest, touching his new, protective casing. It was warm, like sunbaked sand, and as hard and impenetrable as diamond.

"Bob, is he okay?"

"He is, James."

I turn away and look at the other shelf. "Okay, my turn."

"You need to stow a few things first." A hole opens in the floor. "Put the Greys' weapons in there. No need to give your species that technology."

"Good call." I take off my cloak and fetch the spatulas. I deposit the Greys' weapons under our clothes at the bottom of Wes's backpack and toss it into the hole. I look at our uninvited passengers. "What about them?"

"Leave them where they are. If your military has their bodies, perhaps they will not spend much energy trying to access yours."

I nudge one alien's limp leg with my foot. "What will happen to them?"

"Most likely, they will be dissected over the next few years, each part examined and cataloged. Your species does enjoy cataloging."

I glance over at Broken Neck's headless form, imagining men and women standing around trying to figure out what happened to its head. "Sorry guys, it looks like it's alien autopsies for you." Which makes me wonder. "Bob, that won't happen to us, right?"

"The technology to breach your Pomseed cocoons will not exist on your planet for a century or more."

I move to the shelf and sit down. "Feels like we're cutting it kind of close."

"It is not. The Pomseeds are primed and already sprouting. Whenever you are ready, Star Pilot."

I grab a stasis lollipop and lie down. My hands are shaking, and it's hard to imagine sticking this thing up my nose and twisting. Twice. But I do it. As I twist the second one along the front part of my nasal passage, it suddenly becomes hard to breathe. The sensation of drowning seizes me for a terrifying second, then nothing.

March 13, 1997, Nevada, Somewhere in Area 51

I sit up fast, electricity pulsing through me. "Surrender, Dorothy!" I scream.

"James!" Wes shouts, putting his hands on my shoulders. "You're alright."

I'm dazed, but the fog is thinning. A man I kind of recognize stands next to Wes, but my vision is too unfocussed to identify him. I run my hand over my face. "Oh, man I was having the weirdest dream." I lower my hand and look at Wes. "You were there ..." I look over at the familiar man. "And you were there ... I think."

Wes steps back and lets me get a better look at the man. I do know him, but the last time I saw him, he looked a bit different. "Uncle Kevin?"

Wes smiles. "Not just Uncle Kevin. Go ahead, say something."

A much younger Uncle Kevin than I have ever known, raises a hand and gives a little wave. "Hello, Meatsack."

"Bob? Holy crap on a crop circle."

"Nice to see you too," Uncle Bob says.

"Remember Bob said Uncle Kevin was highly susceptible to being borrowed?" Wes says. "Almost sounding as if he'd been borrowed before?"

"Kind of," I say, running a hand over my head, long fingernails raking my hair.

"Turns out, he had been borrowed before. By Bob," Wes says. "So, you're not going to be talking in our heads anymore?"

"While I borrow the use of your Uncle Kevin, I will utilize a Pisces Converter I have with me and communicate with his vocal units. Otherwise, there would be a painful reverberation in your tiny primitive skulls."

More of me wakes up, just catching Bob's insults. "Oh, my God, I have hair." I take Wes in. He has three inches of uncut, unstyled hair covering his head. I hold my hands in serious need of a manicure up to my face. "And we're not grey anymore."

"I was able to slow your aging to under five months. Not bad considering you have been in stasis for fifty years."

My eyes widen. "So, we made it to 1997?"

Young Uncle Bob nods, grinning. Wes clearly seems to be a few steps ahead of me.

I look at Bob. "You woke him up first?"

Wes turns to Uncle Bob. "Yeah, why was that?"

"Having never brought a human out of stasis, there was a 24.66% chance that I might botch the first one, and at this stage, the Star Pilot is necessary to complete the mission."

Wes points to himself. "I'm not necessary?"

"If you do not like my answers, do not ask questions."

I shake my head. "Fifty years later, you're still a dick, Bob."

"I am practical," Uncle Bob says, pulling my street clothes from Wes's backpack. He tosses them into my nude lap. "Get dressed."

As Wes and I put on our 2019 outfits, Uncle Bob updates us. After the crash, our ship was transported to an undisclosed Air Force base in the Nevada desert. Once they finally gained access, Wes, I, and the deceased Greys were moved half a kilometer underground, where we've remained for the past fifty years. Since they were unable to penetrate our stasis cocoons, we've mostly remained undisturbed in a low-security section for decades.

Uncle Bob pauses his history lesson long enough to hand us Tardis-blue canvas slip-on shoes. They don't go with anything we're wearing, but it beats being barefoot. He moves to the open doorway and peers into the hallway as I take in our surroundings. We're in a concrete-walled room with a single, massive observation window. On the other side, there are seats and computer consoles, likely used by technicians and scientists who specialize in aliens. Clearly my brother and I have been studied.

"They moved you here to this high-security area two years ago," Uncle Bob says. "After a breach."

Wes slips his shoes on. "What kind of breach?"

He hands us baseball caps and visitors' badges to hang around our necks. "In 1995, alien autopsy footage found its way off the base."

"The Greys' bodies?" Wes says, putting on his badge.

Uncle Bob nods and peeks out the hall again. "The footage was turned into a documentary."

"I saw that on YouTube," Wes says. "Narrated by Johnathan Franks."

"M.I.B. was able to get the film dubbed a hoax, but after that, security for all Roswell artifacts increased dramatically. That is when your Uncle Kevin comes in."

Uncle Kevin is wearing some kind of uniform. Military. His name tag reads *Lt. Kevin Randle.*

"Your Uncle Kevin is a First Lieutenant in the Air Force, working high-level security in Area 51. He's an expert in digital and high-tech security. For the last two years until the end of his military service, which starts today, he was in charge of two human artifacts believed to be from the future. You two."

"The end of his military service starts today," Wes says, sliding on his backpack. "Why was it the end?"

"My temporal fusion-melons indicate it is for what he is about to do."

"Which is?" Wes asks.

"Help two human artifacts steal a spaceship from Area 51."

* * *

We move down a hallway decorated with portraits of people in uniform: former base commanders, presidents, lots of well-dressed white men. My brother and I stay close to Uncle Bob, ready to play along with whatever ploy he uses to get us out of here.

"Try to keep your faces hidden," Uncle Bob whispers, his eyes darting around the corridor.

I am about to ask why, but then I remember my brother and I have been in a clear cocoon, sleeping in this place for fifty years. They know what we look like. I reach up and pull the brim of my hat down.

"Does everybody know our faces?" Wes asks.

Uncle Bob shakes his head. "Just the old timers, the key scientist, and those on Uncle Kevin's detail." He pauses to peek around a corner. "None of the surface security will know your faces. They do not have clearance."

"Surface?" Wes asks. "Where are we?"

"Half a kilometer underground. There are two ways up," Uncle Bob says. "The main elevator and the cargo elevator. We'll try the main one."

A sudden, sharp alarm blares through the base. Red lights flash, and the sound of heavy boots echoes down the hall.

"What was that?" I whisper, my heart pounding.

"They know you are missing," Uncle Bob says, his voice urgent. "I really underestimated that. We need to move fast."

He guides us through a series of unmarked doors, each one more imposing than the last. We finally slip into a maintenance tunnel, the air heavy with the scent of oil and metal. The tunnel is narrow and dimly lit, forcing us to crouch to avoid scraping our heads on the low ceiling. It doesn't take a tactician to see this was not Bob's plan A.

"We will take the service elevator," Uncle Bob says.

I ask, "How much further?"

Before Uncle Bob answers, we emerge into a vast chamber. Men and women move about, some snapping salutes at Uncle

Bob as we pass. He leads us directly to a freight elevator, easily large enough to hold a fighter jet. We step inside, and Uncle Bob swipes a security card at the control panel, then punches a code into the keypad. The massive doors begin to close, but before they do, two large men run inside. They have different uniforms than Uncle Bob. Darker, with armbands marked MP.

I look over at Uncle Bob, and even though an alien fern from the other side of I don't know where is controlling his features, I can tell he's nervous. The MPs eye us suspiciously.

"Take your nephews to work day," Uncle Bob says as the doors close, muffling the alarms.

The massive elevator starts ascending to the groans of fifty-year-old gears and pulleys in dire need of maintenance. One of the MPs, who hasn't taken his eyes off me, steps closer. "Lt. Randle, is it?"

Uncle Bob nods. "Yes, Artifact Security, Level Blue."

"Yeah, I've not been to that section, but I've been here near two years now, and I swear I've never even seen a Visitor Badge." He moves closer while his partner unshoulders his rifle. "Do you mind if I take a peek?"

The disbelieving look in his eyes tells me we're caught. That much is clear. What's not clear is what to do next. We have only seconds to react.

Be our authentic selves. Start acting like spoiled brats. Act so horrible that not even MPs on a high-security base would question our authenticity.
Turn to page 216.

Realize that Bob has had fifty years to plan this. Trust that he can talk our way out of this.
Turn to page 66.

The Astral Fighter thrums, a low, deep vibration that resonates inside my bones. Then, a sensation unlike any I have ever known—a nightmarish dissociation. It seems my body has shattered, my tissues, skin, muscles, organs, all wrenched apart from the skeletal frame. The sensation lasts a moment, or maybe forever. Hard to tell. It's difficult to put into words, but at some point, my physical body doesn't matter anymore, and everything that I am, my mind, consciousness, or soul is everywhere all at once. I do know that whatever I'm experiencing is incomprehensible, and my mind shuts down. Everything goes black.

My eyes pop open with an electric jolt. "Holy frak."

"James," Bob says, sounding a little surprised. "Thank the whole-menannah you are still with me."

I sit up very straight. "Ah, yeah. That was the plan, right?"

I take in my surroundings. The ship is powered down, lights flash, indicating damaged areas. I look over at my brother. Not awake yet. He's breathing, so alive. I check myself, run my hands over my torso. I have the distinct memory of not being a part of my torso, so the examination feels valid. I'm okay.

"I'm running a bio scan," Bob says.

"Did you call me a meatsack?"

"Yes, I apologize. I was flustered."

"I'm not a hundred percent sure, but that seems racist."

"It is derogatory. It is a term my kind sometimes uses amongst ourselves. I am trying to be better."

"Are we dead?" Wes asks while stirring.

"No, your vital signs are strong," Bob says.

"It was rhetorical, Bob." Wes reaches his fingers up under the edge of his helmet. "My head itches. What did I miss?"

"Well, we traveled in time, and Bob is kind of a racist."

"I am working on myself," Bob says.

Looking beyond my control panel, I notice something odd. "Hey, Bob. I can't see anything outside. The canopy is covered in … sand. Think we landed on the beach or in the desert. Do you know where we are?"

"I am checking on that. I sort of lost you when you jumped."

"Lost us?" Wes says.

"Lost is the wrong word," Bob says. "Unable to find your current location."

"That sounds like lost," I say.

"Semantics. Let us begin by activating your temporal squash-nutts. Above you is a bank of buttons."

I look up. The fish is glitching hard, but I see the buttons. "One bank of buttons is over my head and one's closer to Wes."

"It is the one over your head. Look for the button with a symbol that looks like melons."

"What?"

"Manually searching synonyms. Hooters, bosoms, sweater puppies. Any of this helping?"

"Not particularly …"

"How about milk-secreting glandular organs."

"I think he means breasts," Wes says, then points to a button with a symbol that looks like a curvy number three laying on its back.

"Ah." I hit the symbol, and the panel hums to life, each button a firefly waking up.

"My head is so itchy." Wes flips up his microphone. "I'm taking this helmet off."

"Sorry for the confusion," Bob says. "My species does not possess any lactating organs nor the words to describe them."

"Well, that sucks for you. Your ladies must look terrible in a bikini," I say. "Now what's next?"

"Can you tell me what the destination numbers read?"

Remembering what screen that was, I look at the flashing number. It does not look like a date at all. There is even a negative in front of the first digit. "I think it's messed up, Bob. It doesn't …" My words trail off as I eye Wes without his helmet.

My brother sets the helmet down, scratching his bare scalp with both hands. He smiles with relief as he scratches away the itching. His sense of relief must be overpowering because his fingertips are not registering what my eyes are seeing.

"Hey, Bob," I whisper into my mic. "Do you know why my brother's hair is gone?" He's not just bald up top, but his eyebrows have been abducted as well.

"His hair?" Bob says. "No, it is quite impossible."

"Why would I make that up?"

"That only occurs when traveling a millennia or more."

Wes's expression suddenly changes. He stops scratching and starts exploring the top of his head.

"Tell me exactly what the display reads," Bob says.

No longer needing to whisper, I say, "It starts with a negative two, followed by five, four, three." I glance at Wes. He looks like he is about to cry or scream, or both.

"What the hell!" Wes shouts.

"No, no, no," Bob cries. "This cannot be. This is not ... no, no, no!" I have no idea what Bob looks like, but I imagine an alien toddler throwing a tantrum.

One of Wes's hands migrates down to his absent eyebrows. "Oh my God!"

I lean close to Wes. "Calm down. You're okay."

"Don't tell me to calm down," Wes snaps. "I look like Professor X, the teen years!"

"It's just hair," I say. "And not to be a Marvel nazi, but I think adolescent Professor X had hair."

Wes faces me. "Really? Now's a good time to nit-pick my Marvel references?"

"It'll grow back."

"Oh, yeah. How do you know?" Suddenly Wes's anger fades slightly, and the beginning of a smirk emerges. "Hey, big brother. Does your head itch a little?"

My head does itch. Oh, frak. I pull my helmet off, and run a hand over my bare scalp.

"Ha, ha," Wes says.

"Oh, man."

"Don't worry," Wes says. "It'll grow back."

I scowl at him. "Hey, Bob, would you please explain why we lost our hair."

"Yes, I can explain. Complete hair disintegration is a side effect of temporal jumps."

"Why didn't you mention it?" I say. "We could have, you know, mentally prepared."

"Wait," Wes says. "Did he say *complete* hair loss?"

"There was no need to mention it because it was not supposed to occur. Your planned jump should have taken you back to 1997. Short trips such as that would not have produced any hair loss."

Wes sits up in his seat and unzips his fly. "Oh, man. I just got those."

I look at Wes. "Really?"

Wes sadly nods.

Damn.

"So then why are my brother and I baby-butt-smooth all over?"

"Because you went back a bit further than intended."

I look up at the numbers on the destination screen. Four digits beginning with a negative.

"Your display was calibrated to your current Gregorian calendar for your understanding."

Wes asks what Bob's saying.

"I don't know, something about Gregory's calendar and going back too far."

Wes puts his helmet back on to join the conversation. "What was that about too far, Bob?"

"The readout on the destination display is correct. It should show the present time according to your calendar."

Wes joins me gazing at the display. "Does that mean we're in the year twenty-five forty-three, B.C.?"

"Correct. You have traveled approximately 4.5 thousand years into your past."

"What the hell, Bob?" I shout. "Our parents haven't even been born yet."

"Are you kidding?" Wes shouts. "Our grandparents' grandparents' grandparents' grandparents' grandparents haven't been born yet."

"Okay, okay, I get it. It's a really long time. So, are there like dinosaurs out there?"

Wes throws his hands in the air. "Oh, my God. How did you get into college?"

I glare at Wes. "There were no time travel questions on the fraken entrance exams!"

"Good thing!"

"Will you two meatsacks please stifle-berry!"

"Hey!" I shout in return.

"Sorry, that was out of line," Bob says. "Give me a few moments to figure this out."

"I don't know," Wes says. "We gave you permission to take us back a few decades, and you took us back four and a half millennia."

I don't know what it sounds like when Bob sighs, but I feel that he has.

"I deserve that," Bob says. "Let me investigate. Stay inside the ship. Be right back."

There's a strange sound that feels like Bob just hung up a phone from the 1980s.

"Did he just hang up on us?" Wes says. "Did he just freaking ... ahhhrrgh."

"No, sounded more like he put us on hold," I say, hoping that that is the more accurate analogy.

Wes takes off his harness, then his helmet. "Let's go take a look outside. I need fresh air and a walk."

"What are you, a dog?"

Stay inside and give Bob a minute.
Turn to page 8.

Join Wes in storming outside in a humanoid huff and explore the situation on our own like a couple of ungrateful meatsacks.
Turn to page 202.

I'm not about to tell Wes I'm picking the Blue route because it's my favorite color. I nudge his shoulder. "B for Boys, right?"

"That's your reasoning?"

"Well, that and it's Africa-hot out there. Call me crazy, but in my limited experience, river water is cooler than blazing sand."

Wes nods. "That, I can accept. Blue it is."

"Decision made," Bob says. "Let's get you situated and looking like a local."

"You have instant tan spray? I'm guessing we'd win the award for being the palest people they've ever seen."

"Your apparel," Bob says, like he's speaking to a toddler. "Open the locker on port side. The matter fabricator created authentic clothing to help you blend in."

Wes goes to the locker and pulls out two brown hooded robes, both appearing well worn. "You just made this?" he asks, poking his finger through a small hole in one of the hoods.

"Yes, the matter fabricator is capable of synthesizing clothing from pure energy."

I slip the cloak over my shorts and shirt and hope no one asks me to disrobe. "Couldn't make a complete outfit, I guess."

"The fabricator requires a great deal of energy," Bob says. "We need to conserve. The cloaks will suffice."

I grumble. Captain Kirk wouldn't send a landing party out with half a costume. I lift my foot. "I'm betting ancient Egyptians don't have these kinds of sandals."

"So we don't get close enough for them to notice," Wes says, sounding like he's had his fill of my whining. He dons his hood. "Are we doing this or not?"

We exit the ship and streamline it to the closest point of the river because the sand burns, these sandals suck, there are fraking aliens all around, and we're two teenagers lost somewhere in time.

Wes slides the reeds out of the way and steps into the water. "Excellent cover."

I follow his lead and bunch up my cloak so it doesn't get soaked, the water reaching up to the bottom of my shorts. Wes is right about the cover. With the vegetation on both sides of the river, we don't have to worry about being spotted.

It's nice finally making a good call. Feeling like a real leader, I check my wrist display. "Straight ahead," I tell Wes. "A couple curves, but leads us right there."

"Status report," Bob says.

"Wading through the Nile on the lookout for babies floating by in baskets."

"Why in the world would you be looking for that?" Bob asks.

Wes chuckles and tells Bob to ignore me.

"I wish that were an option," he says.

"What's up, Bob-O?" I ask as we wade further down the river.

"I've reanalyzed the situation and determined that the risks of your path on the water's edge outweigh the benefits."

"Little late for that, Bob. We're knee-deep at the moment, but hidden," I say, waving my arm around us like Bob can see what I'm gesturing at. "Wasn't that the point of this route?"

"If Bob has new data, we should hear him out," Wes says. "What risks?

"Well, going from smallest to biggest, there are parasites. Specifically, Schistosomiasis. Parasitic worms that burrow into your skin, then lay eggs, which migrate to your organs, liver, intestines—"

"Okay," I say, cutting him off and changing my path, closer to land.

"Then there are the brain-eating amoeba," Bob adds.

Wes moves closer to the land as well. "Okay, well there is not much we can do about parasites. What's the biggest thing on your list?"

"Crocodylus niloticus."

"Sounds like your glitching, Bob," I say. "Or speaking Klingon."

Wes moves quickly toward dry land. "He's not glitching. It's Latin."

The reeds rustle behind me. I spin around. "For what?"

"Crocodile," Wes whispers.

"Correct, Wes. The Nile Crocodile could grow to over five meters."

Wes freezes, looking at the shore. "James." He points at a dozen or more crocodiles sunning themselves in the sand. They lie mixed in with horizontal piles of decaying bamboo, camouflaging them from our direct gaze. Until this moment, we had focused our attention on our destination.

Instinctively, we move away, back into the water. That's when the reeds around us part. I'm hit from behind and fall into the mud. I want to stand, but my legs don't obey me anymore. They are being crushed, compressed by reptile teeth. Before the pain registers, the crocodile drags me backward into the water. I look for my brother and see him fall forward, screaming.

His screams are gone as I'm dragged under the water. It's murky and cold, but as I look down at my attacker, I can see its massive head, jaws big enough to secure both my legs at the thigh. I punch at the scaly skull with no effect, my blood clouding the water as the beast starts its deathroll. Round and round I go until I can't tell which way is up, my body starving for air, and relief.

The correct choice was to take the Red route, head up the city center, keep your head down-don't talk to anybody, like a teen on their smartphone, and board the ship from the front.

Turn to page 121.

Wes slides off his backpack and we squeeze under the Prius. The pavement is hot, grimy, and a line of ants scurry under the wheel well, but it is better than facing the scaly humanoid coming our way. Wes looks like he's about to say something. I hold my finger to my lips as it approaches, and his mouth hangs open, silently. We stay quiet, still, not breathing, as a pair of cowboy boots steps the length of the car.

I hope they will keep on moving. No such luck. They stop by the front tire. I attempt to use the jedi-mind powers I'm pretty sure I don't have. *Keep on walking. This is not the Prius you are looking for. Move along.*

The boots start walking, and for a brief second, I feel the force flowing through me. Then I realize the boots aren't walking away; they are running. The humanoid lizard disappears as small explosions erupt. In my mind's eye there are alien projectiles rocketing through the air above, creating loud impacts on metal and stone.

"What the hell?" Wes says.

More sounds of running come from the store. I look over and catch sight of one of the men in a black suit fire a laser weapon then hustle behind a car. "They're shooting at each other."

"Why're they doing that?" Wes says.

"One of them said something about the other's sister," I say. "How the frak should I know?"

"Because you're the one with the talking information fish in your ear!"

A window explodes in the car next to us, and a chunk of its door clatters to the ground.

"That was close," I say. "We need to get out of here."

Wes's eyes disagree. "Maybe we stay right here and let them kill each other. It's here. It's warm. It's cozy."

Something explodes and vibrates the pavement. Parking lot debris of rock and smoldering metal rolls under the car with us.

"Okay, its less cozy," Wes says. "Which way?"

Wes and I slid out from under the Prius. We rise up on our haunches and peer through the hole blown through the sedan. A man in a black suit stands in front of the Camaro. He fires some kind of laser gun at the leather clad biker lizard leaping through the air. The red laser strikes the lizard's shoulder, dropping him just as another of those turquoise lights rises from the ground into the clouds. This time the human cosplays are construction worker and G.I.

Jeez, who taught them how to dress human? The Village People?

I look back at Wes. "More Sleetaks are coming."

Wes thrusts a thumb behind him. "A few more M.I.B.s just came out of the store."

"This parking lot is getting really crowded."

"Are we still gonna try to get to Bumblebee?" Wes says. "The way is blocked."

"Screw that," I say, as neon-illuminated weapons fire zips overhead. The emerald-green pulsing beams the Reptilians fire might be pretty if it wasn't for the deadly explosions throwing debris and melting metal. "We need to get out of this warzone."

I wave Wes to follow me to the alley. We stay low, move from car to car, hoping no bad guy is camping out, waiting for us to show our stupid faces. We move under the cover of several cars but come to a sudden stop when the alley turns out to be a dead end. A large brick wall with two over-stuffed dumpsters blocks our escape.

"What now, fearless leader?" Wes asks.

I've no idea. But I do have an all-knowing fish thing in my head. "Hey, Bob, we're trapped. Any ideas?"

"My scans are fluctuating. I cannot really see what your situation is, therefore, I am unable to provide an accurate assessment or plan of action. Unless ..."

"Unless what?"

"If you gave me access to your eyes, I could use them to help you formulate a plan."

"You would see through my eyes?"

"Yes. But it stings a lot, and there is a 97.645% chance you will urinate uncontrollably. Or worse."

"Uhm, let's call that plan B."

"What's plan B?" Wes asks.

"Never mind," I say and turn to Wes. "Bob's useless and we can't stay here."

"What's wrong with here? I don't think either of them know where we are."

Impacts explode on the brick wall behind us, and dust falls on our backs.

"It's not safe," I say. "What if one of those space bullets hit this car's gas tank? We'd both blow up *Die Hard* style."

Wes looks at the car. "That won't happen."

"How do you know?" I ask, irritated.

"Because it's an electric car."

I thrust an angry finger at him. "Well, that's ... a very good point."

I look back at the fly-infested dumpsters. "I think those might offer better cover."

"But it's a dead end. If they find us, we have nowhere to run."

"Jeez, why did you pick today to start making spot-on observations," I say in frustration.

Leaning to my side, I peek around the corner of the electric car's back bumper. A body, I can't tell whether human or humanoid lizard, flies across my field of view to the sound of a Wilhelm scream. As it rolls across the pavement with colorful sparks dancing in its wake, I notice the fighting seems to be moving our way. I look over at the dumpster again, thinking it's a better spot than this one.

Wes grabs my shoulder, turns me around, and says, "I have an idea. Follow me."

Go with my little brother's idea, a sibling I used to
affectionately call Turd Blossom.
Turn to page 86.

Retreat to the relative safety of the large industrial dumpsters,
which even at this distance smell like a week's worth of Wookie
farts.
Turn to page 214.

The Hanger 18 confection store seems safe, and hiding amongst sweets sounds a lot better than being out here waiting for the sphere's yellow scanner to ping us. I point out the wide-open back door and tell Wes, "In there. Until this is over."

Wes nods. "You first."

I consider telling Bob what we're about to do, but I'd rather not have him shouting at me. I stay low and check both ways. The space sphere is off to the left, its yellow light passing over the cars. The Hanger 18 employee has her back to us. I think it's a her, but can't see her face. She grunts as she hoists the large trashcan on her shoulder and empties it into the dumpster with a loud thump.

"Now," I whisper. I sprint for the open entrance.

Wes passes me, his speed surprising until I remember he's way more experienced running in sandals. I keep my eyes on the store and pump my arms and legs, my chest on fire. I don't look back.

Wes reaches the entrance a split second before I do, both of us rushing through the small storage room. Wes blasts through the swinging door that leads into the store's main product area, and I'm hot on his tail. My eyes dart around, mesmerized by the colorful alien confections. It's like *Willy Wonka* meets *Close Encounters* in here.

Wes stops suddenly and I slam into him.

I ask him what's his deal, but he doesn't say a word, just points at the bloody body crumpled behind the counter by the cash register. It's a middle-aged employee with a scruffy beard and glasses. Blood flows from his lacerated neck onto the floor, mixing with neon-colored candy UFOs that have fallen from the counter.

"What the frak?" I move toward the body, only to step into another puddle of blood a few feet from the dead guy.

"That's a lot of blood," Wes says. "Do people even have that much blood?"

"Really cool question for another time." I point to the front door. "Exit stage left." We reach the door only to find it locked.

And that's when I notice the *OPEN* sign is facing in. I look for a deadbolt. None. It's a key lock. And we don't have the key. "Shit."

A door slams shut from the storage room, and we both jump.

"Hide," I say, pointing to the large barrels spread around the store.

Wes doesn't hesitate, running to the far corner and ducking behind the barrel of gummy meteors. Or meteorites. Honestly, I've never understood the difference. I hide behind the barrel of mint marshmallow Martians and try to calm my thudding heart, so I can hear what's happening in the storage room.

The employee door swings open, and footsteps clack off the tile. "Uh oh," a young-sounding female says. "Someone's made a mess."

Was that sarcasm? Either she's not looking at all the blood, or she's some kind of sick sadistic serial killer freak. I want to peek above the barrel, but I don't dare.

"Status report," Bob says. "Why are you not at the transport?"

I ignore Bob, wishing there was an interstellar mute button on this thing. The woman is grunting, and I hear something being dragged across the floor. I don't need to look to know it's the dead employee, its remains smearing the puddles of blood.

Wes peeks, gives a little squeak, and ducks back down.

"Don't be shy," she says. "Why don't you two come on out."

I sigh, knowing we're caught.

"Come on. The candy is free today."

Whoever this is, she knows my love language. I stand and realize she also knows murder and how to dispose of a body. She's standing beside the trash can with her back to me, dumping the bearded guy inside. When she turns to smile, I see her true Reptilian self.

"Oh, bless the Old Ones," she says, her Reptilian lips curling into a smile. "I can hardly believe it, after all the training, learning your archaic language, and somehow finding the means to tolerate your warm-blooded stench, I finally catch a break."

"Oh, yeah, how so?" Wes asks, standing behind his barrel.

"I've been deep undercover in this shop on the off chance that Earth's only Star Pilot would take refuge here. When I drew the assignment, I thought, *What are the odds*?" She giggles and points her scaly finger right at me. "And here you are."

"Here *we* are," I echo nervously.

Wes points at the body half-stuffed in the garbage. "If you're looking for my brother, why did you kill ..."

"Which one, the one in the dumpster, or Fred here?" She slaps the bottom of the fat man's shoe, legs sticking up like broken flagpoles.

Wes shrugs. "Either."

She walks toward us. "Let's just say, girls—of any species—don't much like it when the boss pinches their ass."

"I think that's a fair punishment," I say.

Wes nods. "Me too."

I've led us into a trap. I want to run, but where? I wait until she is halfway across the store, then look at Wes. "Back door!" I shout, hoping he understands.

He doesn't need to be told twice, pushing his barrel over and running for the back.

Lizard Lady leaps over the fallen barrel and grabs us by our necks.

Even with both of my hands trying to pry her grip off me, I know she can crush my throat at any second. Looking into her vertical-slit pupils, I can tell she has something else in mind.

She sets us both on our knees in front of the counter. "It would be quite the prize to bring you in alive. Advancement guaranteed, but I've always been more of a scientist than a field agent at heart."

"My dad has always said that doing what you truly love is the key to happiness," I say.

"Smart man." She slides a silver bucket in front of us and reaches in. She pulls out a pink and blue oversized jawbreaker. "Do you know what the major difference between our two species is?"

We both shake our heads.

"Teeth." She grins, showing us hers. "We both have them, of course, but humans employ them oddly. Your kind uses them to crush food into small parts. Chewing, you call it."

"Uh huh," I say, trying to understand where this is going.

"My species is more evolved. We use teeth to grasp and secure our food. Not for tearing or grinding it into smaller pieces. We swallow food whole, like civilized beings."

"Whole?" Wes says.

"Civilized?" I echo.

"Call it a scientific curiosity." Before I know what she's doing, she jams the jawbreaker into my mouth. "No barbaric chewing." She pushes it down my throat, where it lodges in tight. "Swallow!" She quickly withdraws her taloned digits and stuffs one down my brother's throat, then another into my gagging mouth.

Wes is turning blue, his eyes full panic-mode as Ms. Lizard Mengele keeps stuffing us, and shouts, "Swallow!"

I want to beg for mercy, to say something, but she continues stuffing. I grab my throat. I can feel the jawbreakers bulging in my neck. I need air, but there is none. My chest is tight, like my lungs are being squeezed by enormous hands. I'm dizzy, unsteady. My vision narrows, like at the end of a tunnel.

The tunnel collapses, and so do I.

The correct choice was to stick with the plan and jump into Bumblebee's butt!

Turn to page 79.

With all the information we are going to need, according to Bob, strapped to our wrists, Wes and I take off on the Red route. To help us blend in, the ship's matter fabricator, a device capable of synthesizing clothing from pure energy, provided something to wear and shield our bald heads from the sun. It had scanned the attire of the local inhabitants and produced two hooded robes. It even made them look well worn, with a few holes, and some stitching that looks like a hastily made repair by someone who knows as much about sewing as I do about Chinese arithmetic. That kind of detail makes them look pretty authentic.

Wes conceals his backpack underneath his robe. I'm glad Bob suggested it would be the perfect accessory to carry the parts we needed, because I didn't look forward to asking Wes to leave it in the ship. Beyond the medications he carries in it, he's got some sort of deep Linus and his blanket connection with the thing.

For the rest, we flipped our T-shirts inside out, hoping to hide Wes's Lego Star Wars and my Star Pilot designs. Nothing we can do about our cargo shorts. Mom thinks they aren't acceptable in any time, but she wears prosthetic Vulcan ears, so … Our sandals are four thousand years out of place, and I hope their earthy tones will blend in with the locals' footwear. There's only one way to find out.

Walking in the sand isn't as easy as they make it look in the movies. When we climb a dune, Wes sinks and I have to hoist him up. He comes free of the sand, but one sandal doesn't. So, with three sandals between us, we hike across the Egyptian landscape. After a half kilometer, a lot of it uphill, it seems like I should be winded, but I'm not. Maybe it's the fresh, unpolluted air oxygenating my blood like never before, or maybe it's adrenaline from the rising fear that comes when you walk toward an alien spaceship. Whatever it is, I feel energized.

I look back at Wes, who does not seem energized, more like a car about to run out of gas, electricity, and the will to live. "You okay?"

He stands straight and reaches into his backpack. Pulling out his inhaler, he takes a hit. After a few breaths, his color resembles the living again. He still looks like my annoying know-it-all brother, but nobody is perfect. As he puts the inhaler back, he says, "We've got company."

Up ahead, people are moving along a road in the direction we want to go. They are spaced like freeway traffic, some in clumps, while others walk alone. Many are carrying sacks or children, or sacks of children. It's hard to tell. They are too far away for any of them to start a conversation, but I don't want to take any chances. We wait until there's a lengthening gap in the flow of people, then merge, matching pace with those around us. Wes and I exchange glances. I can see we are having the same thought. *So far so good.*

"Status update," Bob says.

"Status update?" Wes says in a hushed tone. "Why don't you say, how's it going?"

"We're fine, so far, Bob," I say. "We're on course and should be at the ship in a few minutes."

I check the map on the small screen attached to my wrist. We aren't exactly on the Red route, but close enough, and we seem to be heading the right way. On the map, I see a structure. I'm not sure why, but it reminds me of a temple constructed to mimic some of the designs and lines on the Greys' ship. I examine the map intently, then realize I'm staring at a device that probably is not too common amongst the locals. I put my arm down just as a figure rushes by us. In their haste, they graze Wes's shoulder.

The figure, a half head taller than Wes, turns back and says, "Excuse me."

He's wearing a similar garment as us, and under his hood, he is bald as well. Even more striking than his lack of hair is his eye make-up. Thick black paint outlines his eyes, making the area around his sockets take on the dark almond shape of the Greys' eyes.

Remembering not to speak, I nod and smile as friendly as I know how.

"May the sky gods favor you," he says, then turns forward and rushes ahead.

Wes says, "Makes sense that they worship them. Didn't Bob say something about this route taking us into the religious center of the area?"

"Yes, I did," Bob answers. "I believe one of the priest's temples is next to the ship."

"Hey, James." Wes points at an area that would be considered the shoulder if we were on a freeway. Huge stone rectangular blocks lined up like train cars are surrounded by people. The slowly moving massive stone blocks remind me of a convoy of semi-trucks.

As we catch up, the sight leaves me utterly speechless. Expecting to find wheeled carts or some other form of ground transport beneath these immense stones, I'm astonished to discover them hovering a meter above the ground. These colossal blocks, each weighing at least a ton, defy gravity. A small group of humans and Reptilians appear to be guiding them rather than pushing them.

Based on the look on Wes's face, he has as many questions as I do. I tell Bob what we're seeing, and he says there were several periods in Earth's history in which the Reptilians lived and worked alongside humans.

"That's fascinating, and not really what I want to know," I say. "How are they making giant stones float?"

"It is very complicated. You wouldn't–"

"Understand," I interrupt. "Can you just dumb it down maybe fifty percent or so?"

"Okay, I'll try. The Greys use natural mechanics. You should see devices attached to the stones or the platform. They tap into the Earth's magnetic field and utilize it to temporarily alter the weight of the stones. A two-ton rock can become lighter than some gasses with the correct calculations."

"Huh," I say, taking in the shoe-box size devices fastened to each side of the stones. "I must be getting smarter because that almost made sense."

"I'm pretty sure that's not happening," Wes says.

"Thanks."

"Just keeping you grounded, big brother."

So captivated by the mesmerizing procession of stone blocks, we are oblivious to our proximity to the Greys' ship. As the convoy veers right, aligning itself with the unfinished third pyramid, we are jolted into awareness. It's a lot to take in at this close distance, and we both stop in the middle of the road and stare. The spaceship is a sleek, cigar-shaped behemoth. Its only apparent connection to the ground is a slender, mechanical tube, more like a mooring line than landing gear. It seems as if the colossal craft, easily the length of a football field and three stories tall, could effortlessly ascend if severed from this solitary anchor.

People move around us as we both stand like petrified trees, barely noticing a slight breeze has blown both our hoods off. I'm sure we're drawing attention to ourselves, so I snap out of it and give Wes a nudge. With the train of floating rocks and the Greys' ship, I'd forgotten about the temple. It lies ten meters away, two stories high, covered in ominous dark limestone, contrasting the bright pyramids, and very noticeably complementing the Greys' menacing ship. I suddenly have a sense of foreboding, but as threatening as it all seems, what causes me the most alarm is the figure waving at us.

It takes me a second to realize it's the guy that had bumped into Wes on the road. He motions us to come to the dark temple's front door.

Wes looks at me. "Why is that guy waving at us?"

"Hey, I know as much as you do."

"That's debatable. Should we go over?"

The bald man with the almond-painted eyes stops waving at us for a moment as another figure approaches him. The figure pulls off his hood, revealing a smooth scalp. He then holds up his hand making a gesture. Three fingers stick straight up, slightly splayed, with the thumb and pinky tucked into the palm. The man who had been waving at us returns the greeting, then pats the other man on the back as he enters the temple. His friend, having passed by, returns to waving at us, calling us over, smiling as if we are friends.

We have obviously caught someone's attention, and I don't know if it's a good or bad thing. I glance over at the stones and see another path. Should we take it?

"Hey Bob," I say. "There is a guy waving us over to the temple. What should we do?"

"You have two objectives; board the ship, and do not draw notice from indigenous lifeforms."

"I'm aware."

"At this juncture, you are failing at both."

"You're not being helpful."

"Is he ever?" Wes says.

Head over to the bald guy with the black almond-painted eyes and hope his smile isn't the kind Jeffrey Dahmer used when inviting young men inside his apartment.
Turn to page 133.

Tuck in between the blocks in the convoy of giant stones and try to disappear in the crowd of workers guiding the blocks to the pyramids.
Turn to page 148.

I have no idea which one of these is the pastforward initiator, so I go with my favorite color light saber and pull the blue switch.

"No, you meatsack!" Bob shouts. "That's the manual override that disengages the onboard destination regulator from the plumpercott time functions. You will back-travel until you run out of—"

Wes looks at me like I'm a moron, his hands white-knuckling the seat's armrests. I want to shout I had no way of knowing, but the Astral Fighter is making a deep rumble, which vibrates through every inch of my body. My world is shaking like I'm in the epicenter of a cosmic earthquake. Everything intensifies, my mind a blur before I black out.

Late Cretaceous Period, the end of the Mesozoic Era (the Age of Reptiles)

"Oh my God," Wes groans, waking me.

I've only been hungover once, and this feels just as bad, my brain not quite firing. My throat burns with every breath, and my teeth feel soft.

"Crap," I mutter, my gaze fixed on the fractured canopy. Through the jagged opening, I see we're suspended high above the ground. Below, alien flowers with enormous petals and broad, unusual leaves cover the surface. Across the landscape, eerie trees with branches like writhing tentacles rise into the twilight, widely spaced and silent. It only takes a moment to realize we are hung up in one of those odd-looking trees. "Where the hell are we?"

"You mean, *when* are we," Wes says. "Hey, do your teeth feel soft?"

"Yeah, and it's hard to breathe." The air is thick, heavy, with the scent of damp earth.

I turn to the console, which is completely black, no readout whatsoever. I look up at the destination readout above us. It's just as black. Frustrated, I smack the side of it. The lights flicker, and numbers appear briefly on the destination indicator. All zeros.

"Zeros," Wes says. "What kind of time destination is that?"

"I have no—"

I'm interrupted by a distant roar.

My blood goes cold. "Was that a lion?"

Wes peers through the crack in the canopy, then shakes his head. "Before we jumped. Bob said something about going back until we run out of—"

Another roar, this time not so distant. I meet my brother's frightened gaze. "So, not a lion?"

"I think we went back further than lions."

"Further than lions?" I swallow hard. "How far?"

Before Wes answers, there's another roar that's followed by thumping vibrations.

"Like *Jurassic Park* far," Wes says.

"No, no," I disagree, and unbuckle my harness. "Maybe we just landed at Universal Studios." I try to stand and discover we're stuck in a downward slope, the ship's nose aimed at the field of large-petaled fauna on the ground. I put my weight on the console to keep upright, but the ship starts to sway. "Bob, are you there?"

"Stop moving around," Wes says. "We could be hanging up here by a thread."

I slide back into my seat, but the ship is still swaying. I don't think I'm causing it. The thumping becomes louder, and the ship teeters with every vibration.

Then the loudest roar I have ever heard. I feel it in my chest. Definitely not a lion.

Whatever it is, it's behind the ship. We sink into our seats, trying to become invisible. The canopy was set on high shield protect, a smart glass mode that prevents visible light, amongst other elements, to pass.

The ship vibrates with every step the beast takes. The branches of the tress rustle and snap as it walks around to the front of the ship. A shadow blankets the Astral fighter. Wes and

I freeze, our breath caught in our throats, our hearts pounding. A low, throaty rumble shudders through the ship's metallic skin.

A monstrous eye, the color of amber with a slitted pupil, peers through the fracture in the canopy. I'm not a dinosaur scientist, but even I can tell it's a T-Rex.

A guttural snarl tears through the air as the beast pulls its massive head back. I know the Astral Fighter is designed to handle impacts from debris fields and small asteroids. Surely it can withstand an attach from a prehistoric carnivore.

Its head thrusts forward. Powerful jaws clamp down on the ship's nose. The Astral fighter groans under the impossible pressure, and a screech of tearing metal rips through the cockpit as the canopy falls away like tin siding in a tornado.

Wes and I scream, trying to hide under the flight console, but it's too late. It's seen us.

The T-Rex's head plunges into the open cockpit. A mouthful of fifteen-centimeter-long teeth grasp the top of my brother. He's still screaming when I hear the crunch. His body is pulled from the cockpit along with half the flight console. My screaming intensifies, realizing I'm covered in my brother's blood.

I turn to run, hoping to find safety deeper in the ship. Before I even get up off the floor, teeth sink into me, dozens of ivory daggers plunging into my body. I'm pulled back and out of the ship. The T-Rex thrusts it jaws upward, using gravity to let my limp body roll into its mouth. I land on a tongue the size of a waterbed, where I see my brother one final time. Or parts of him anyway, before we slide down the gullet, smooth muscle guiding our descent toward a prehistoric digestion.

The correct choice was to pull the Red Switch.
Turn to page 104.

"I'm sorry, but we've got to keep moving. On a stress scale of one to five, I'm at least a seven."

My brother looks at me with desperation, trying to make puppy dog eyes through his Grey makeover. "But my backpack."

"Just FYI, that look doesn't work as an alien. Just looks creepy." I head toward the exit, eighty percent sure he'll follow. "We'll come right back. Promise."

Wes huffs and puffs, but falls in behind me. "We better."

"Have I ever broken a promise to you?"

Wes glowers at me. "You promised to take the heat for the broken coffee table."

"That was before I knew I'd get grounded from video games."

"You promised not to touch my left-over Tommy's."

"It was original Tommy's chili cheese fries. You should have known I was lying. That one's on you."

"You promised not to tell Mom and Dad about my secret crushes."

"Jezz, do you write this stuff down?"

"Yes."

"Okay, well, Linda Hamilton and Helen Mirren are old enough to be your great grandmothers, and Carrie Fischer is dead. Can you blame me? I was worried you'd grow up to be a GILF hunter or something. Or worse."

I glance back, glad to have him along, but hating the fact that I will probably break this promise as well.

Wes's eyes go wide as something blindsides me, bumping into my shoulder and knocking me to the ground.

I jump to my feet and find myself chest to face with two Greys who are wobbling like Bender in *Futurama*, all fueled up.

"Hey, buuuddy," the one on the right says, pointing at me with all three of his fingers, which seems rude. "Watch where you're walking."

"Yeah," the other says. "We are ..." It takes a breath and tries again. "We are sky gods, after all. Show some ... some ..."

"Respect," the other finishes.

"Yeah, some of that, Hew-mons."

I take a step back and bow. "Please forgive us, sky gods."

Wes gasps, and I realize my screw up.

The one on the left pulls a small device from his belt and points it at my face. A bright light flashes, and I'm frozen, unable to move a muscle.

Wes screams, but it's cut short when the Grey spins and fires at him.

I want to beg for mercy, to talk our way out of this, but the only thing I can control is my breath, with my eyes stuck in the on position.

"Looks like we've got ourselves some strange ones, Frank," the shooter says.

The other one, who looks nothing like a Frank, says, "Whatcha want to do with 'em, Trevor?"

Trevor jumps up and down with an excited little squeal. "The new equipment. It arrived yesterday."

Frank's black almond-shaped eyes widen to the size of a walnut. "Does it have the Chrono-Stasis Dissector with 4D Neural Re-Calibrator?"

Trevor nods. "You bet your grey ass it does, and ... and it also has, not yet used on this planet, a Harmonic Resonator with a fully ... fully functioning Viscera and Cranial Deconstructor."

"I thought you needed a level-A rating to operate a Deconstructor?"

"No worries. It comes with in—" Alien belch. "Instructions."

The two Grey execute a poorly timed high three. "Let's beam them straight into one of the lower labs," Frank says.

"I don't ... I don't think we're in any condition to be beaming."

"Good call, Trevor. Safety first."

Trevor tells Frank to go find something to transport the specimens. I assume he means us. When only the three of us are present, Trevor twists our bodies into odd, highly inappropriate positions and starts snapping what must be the alien version of selfies. The Grey stops messing with us only when Frank returns with a metal platform that has raised lips around the edges. It looks like something you might find in a futuristic Costco.

Frank parks the hover cart directly in front of me. I realize what they're going to do with it, and I'm very concerned I might be too heavy for them, especially since they're clearly buzzed.

Two three-fingered hands push my upper back, and I fall face first, no way to brace for the crash landing.

Crunch!

Frak! My nose is broken, blood pooling on the metal.

They guide the cart next to Wes. He slams down next to me, a sickening *thud* when the back of his head smacks down, his grey-painted feet in my peripheral.

I try to will my finger to move, to reach out and touch Wes. To let him know I'm right here. That we'll be okay.

Nothing. I can't even blink and am forced to stare at the platform as they guide us out of the temple and down the stairs, blinded by the sun reflecting off the metal. There's the sound of a hatch releasing before we go up the ramp and into the ship.

Trevor parks the platform right outside a door. It slides open, and he says, "Let's get the big ugly one first."

The Greys stand me up and spin me into the room. "Let's put him here," Trevor says, placing me against the wall so I'm facing what looks a living room, complete with a wall monitor and Grey-size couch.

When they come back with Wes, they roll him into the center of the room, blood dripping down the back of his neck. Neither Grey seems concerned that my brother's eyes are rolled back. He has either passed out or is having one of his seizures. Impossible to tell with our muscles paralyzed.

While Frank grabs drinks from the kitchen, Trevor opens the large box on the table and pulls out a metallic device that looks like a cross between a surgical bone saw and a toilet plunger. "Remove organs and put 'em right back," he says, looking like he just read it off the box.

Frank enters the room with two shot glasses. They cheer and down the drinks, tossing the glasses in the corner.

"Ready to get started?" Trevor asks, powering up the device, the blade whirring.

"Did you read the instructions yet?" Frank pulls papers out of the box.

He shakes his head. "Come on. Their primitive anatomy is not that com ... complicated. They still poop, did you know that?" Looks disgusted. "Animals."

Trevor gazes at the instructions. "Yes, but ... it says you need to an ... an ... anesthetize the specimens first."

"Well, they're paralyzed," Frank says. "That's pretty much the same thing, right?"

"When you're right, you're right, Frank. And you are right."

"Onward!" Frank shouts. "How hard can it be?"

They begin the operation, sawing through Wes's skull and scooping out his brain. Frank hands it to Trevor, who freaks out, screaming, "Gross. It's so slimy."

Frank goes to grab it from him, but it slips out of their grasp and splatters on the floor. Both aliens look at it, then up at me. "Next," Frank says, walking up to me with a smile. "Don't worry. You prob ... probably won't feel a thing."

The correct choice was to cave in to Wes and go back for the backpack.

Turn to page 168.

Wes and I continue to stand in the road, and it's starting to feel uncomfortable. The guy really wants us to come over, and if we continue to ignore him, he might get suspicious. To make our situation even less ideal, two horses pulling a chariot are moving up the road right at us. From its speed, I get the feeling the driver is more accustomed to running people down rather than going around them. I grab Wes's shoulder and nudge him to follow. "Come on."

"We're going toward the weird, grinning guy?"

"He's not so weird," I say as we head over. "And keep in mind, we are the hairless, time-traveling teens from the future with interstellar translating fish in our ears. I'm pretty sure we're the weirdos."

"That's fair."

"My research on impromptu religions spawned by alien contacts is limited in this time period, but I believe they are mostly harmless," Bob says.

"Mostly?" I echo.

"When you go inside, we may lose contact for a while. Our reception is going in and out."

The man stops waving momentarily as two Greys exit the tunnel. As they pass by, the man greets them as if they're old friends. Very social. Not like I imagine someone addressing their gods. And that's when I notice. They are not Greys. They are human.

Their entire bodies, including their bald heads, are painted grey, their heavy black eye makeup mimicking the Greys' black almond-shaped eyes. Around their waist is a garment I don't have words for. Maybe a mini toga, the kind they might wear to the beach.

"What if he wants to chitchat?" Wes asks.

"We'll use our improvising skills," I say, watching the pair of young men wearing ancient Greys' cosplay walk straight to the ship.

"Did we get some of those yet?"

We're in the man's earshot so I lower my voice. "Let's find out."

"Brothers," the man says. Up close, I can see he is close to my age, just a year or two off, up or down. He isn't as tall as me, but he stands up straight as we join him. Before we come to a stop, he motions us inside, so we keep walking. His hand pats my shoulder as he had done with another. As we enter, I glance back at the humans in alien cosplay. A ramp has lowered from the Greys' ship, and the two humans are walking onboard casually as if they belong, like Protestants walking into church.

I don't know what the temperature was outside, but inside the temple it's at least twenty degrees cooler. Do they have air conditioning? The black limestone that covers the outside extends into the temple's interior. The hallway is made of it. The floor is blanketed with tiles of smooth, cool stone that feels eerily like polished glass beneath our feet. Every so often, there is a space in the dark limestone revealing murals, humans worshiping, paying homage to their sky gods. Some of the images remind me of biblical depictions, with minor substitutions. Human heads are replaced with those of jackals and birds of prey, and where a savior might stand, a Grey alien appears with deep black eyes.

The man quickly steps ahead of us to lead the way. Turning back, he looks right at me and says, "I have not seen you at the Holy Sanctum before. Is this your first time?"

I deliver a confident and sincere nod.

"Wonderful, please let me show you to the room of ornaments. My name is Thutmose. How may I address you?"

The only Egyptian name I know is King Tut, and I am pretty sure that's more like a nickname for the boy pharaoh in our time. I gesture to myself. "James."

"Ah," my brother stammers. "Wes."

The man stops walking and turns back to us. "Jhamez and Wahes. Two truly unique names that tell of lands beyond our

Western Necropolis. The sky gods truly do summon us into service from distances both far and wide."

Dude, you have no idea.

"Well, I look forward to hearing all about it." He gestures into a room to our right. "You can disrobe in here."

There are stone benches in the middle of the room. Along the walls are vertical cubbies, kind of like gym lockers without doors. There is a man who has removed his clothing and is hanging his garments up in a cubby. I take a step toward the room, noticing that Wes is stuck. I loop an arm inside his and pull him forward.

"Dude," he says in a hushed tone. "Do you know what disrobe means?"

"Of course I do," I mumble back. "Just go with it."

As we move inside, our impromptu guide says, "Jhamez, Wahes, I have a meeting with the High One, so I will leave you here, but when you're ready, continue down this hallway, take two rights, and you will see the room of anointment. There you will be taken care of."

Wes and I look back, smile and nod like we know what the hell is going on.

"May the sky gods favor you," he says, then disappears down the hall. A moment later, the bald, naked man in the room finishes up and strolls out.

Wes looks at me. "Taken care of?"

I shrug. "I don't know."

"Taken care of," he repeats. "Do you know that in mafia films, *taken care of* means shot in the head."

I sigh. "Does it look like we are in *The Godfather?*"

Wes glowers at me. "Okay, what's the plan?"

"I say we play along. I have a good feeling that this might lead us to where we want to go."

"So, get naked? That's the plan?"

"Why not?"

"I'll tell you why not. Because I'm pretty sure they're going to notice something different about our man parts."

"I'm not sure your junk qualifies as man parts yet," I say, then remember the naked man who had just walked out with a black thicket of hair between his legs. Our recent travel back in time removed ours. "I'm sure it's not a big deal. So we don't have hair down there."

"Oh yeah," Wes said. "That too."

"Why, what were you thinking?"

Wes steps close like someone telling a secret. "In this time, they didn't have a whole lot of Rabbis cutting off the tips of baby boys' penises."

"Oh. Well, who does it now?"

Wes narrows his eyes at me. "Nobody! Seriously, how did you ever learn to tie your shoes?"

I'm about to insult my brother, but Bob interrupts. "Status report."

"Uh, preparing to get naked," I say.

"No, we are not!" Wes says, delivering his counter report.

"Uh, I think I am going to need a little more context," Bob says.

"Sure." I spend a few seconds catching Bob up.

"Naked?" Bob says.

"What do you think it means?" Wes asks, nervously reaching into his backpack.

"Well, ancient humans such as the Mayans in this time preferred that their sacrifices to the sun god be nude."

"Sacrifices!" Wes pulls out his inhaler and takes a hit.

"Dude, why would you say that!" I shout.

"I am sorry. Forget that. I am sure it is not that," Bob says, trying to backpedal. "It is most likely a sex ritual."

"What? That's so much worse!" Wes starts turning fifty shades of panic.

"Nice pivot, Bob," I say as Wes takes more than the doctor-recommended pumps from his inhaler. I reach over to take the medication away before my brother overdoses.

When I'm sure Wes is not going to pass out, I remove my clothes. Wes takes several deep breaths and follows suit. We find two empty cubbies and hang it all up: cloak, shirt, shorts, my pair of sandals, Wes's one sandal.

"What about my backpack?" Wes says.

"Let's put the info units in it and leave it here."

"It has all my meds."

"Dude, you're medicated enough for the next ten panic attacks."

"True."

"Are you ready to do this?"

"No!"

"Me either. But suck in that gut and let's go."

"I'm gonna keep my monitor open as wide as possible in order to help out if I can," Bob says as we step out into the hallway. "When moving covertly, the best posture is to act like you belong. Blend in. Be one with the cantaloupes."

Wes looks at me. I shake my head, both of us unsure if that was a glitch or one of Bob's people's inspirational mantras. But I do wonder if blending in is even possible. We can't communicate other than say our names and gesture like bad mimes, we're a bit overly manscaped, and we're four thousand years out of time.

The cool polished stone feels fragile like we might fall through at any moment, but after a few steps in the passageway, our feet touch down on a hand-woven rug that, if it were around in my time, would hang in the most prestigious museum. The colors are so vibrant, depicting images of a view of Earth I can't imagine the rug maker in this time could possibly have had.

I feel Wes close behind, an extra shadow. I know he is scared. I am too, but if there is any chance of us getting home, we gotta give it our best shot. "Hey," I say over my shoulder, "come walk beside me. It'll look more natural."

"There is nothing natural about this situation," Wes says as he steps up beside me.

"Sure, there is," I say as we turn the last corner. "We are just two dudes from the future in the buff, casually strolling the hallway of an ancient temple in the shadow of an alien spaceship."

"Oh, well, when you put it like that, what could be more natural?"

"That's what I'm saying," I say with a chuckle as soft chatter filters in from up ahead.

There's an entryway to our right, and from the elegant design, I'm pretty sure we're about to arrive at the Room of Anointment. Its elaborate carvings and imagery seem to convey importance.

"Let's just keep on strolling and roll with whatever comes. We are one with the cantaloupes."

"Okay," Wes says. "I'm strolling."

We turn and stop dead in our tracks in the entryway like Roman statues, which I'm almost sure aren't even around yet. The Room of Anointment has a half dozen women inside, all half-dressed. Around their waist are modest coverings, but from the waist up they are as nude as the day they were born.

"Don't freak out," I say. "We've seen boobs before."

"Not in 3D."

The six women, all dark olive skin with hair as black as night, are paired up and spread across several workstations. Each station has an array of jars and equipment that I never imagined existed in this time. The man from the disrobing room is at one of the stations, and two of the women are working on him. One is using an instrument that looks like a graffiti artist's spray gun. It sprays a misty layer of grey color onto his body. They are applying his alien skin.

Wes and I exchange glances. I shrug. "At least it's not a sex thing?"

"You sound disappointed," Wes says.

"Well ..."

Several women in the room have noticed us standing in the entryway as Bob says, "Status report."

"About to get an extreme makeover," I say.

"You have the oddest status reports," Bob says. "Perhaps you are unsure what it means."

The women gesture for us to come to them. Two anointing stations are open, and they smile at us encouragingly.

"After you," I say to Wes.

He shakes his head a little. "Oh no, age before beauty."

"What does that even mean?"

Wes frowns. "It literally means, you go first, and I'm better looking than you. Frak, man, read a book."

I smile and step forward. If Wes has the energy to insult me, then I'm pretty sure he has the energy to keep it together. I hope I've found mine as well. Half the women are of motherly and grandmotherly age. The other half are much younger, closer to our age, and very attractive. I'm hoping that while I'm getting my interstellar makeover nothing pops up. I don't know how many baseball players I can name off in my head, but I'm gonna find out.

Even though I stepped into the room first, Wes arrives at his station before I do. He might be a little more enthusiastic than me. Each station has a spot where it's pretty obvious they want us to stand. Kind of like when you go to the barber, you know exactly where to sit. The spot is a circle, and it's slightly lower, one staircase step, than the rest of the floor, probably so the woman can work on our faces and heads. My brother isn't taller than them, but I definitely am. Wes and I exchange uncertain glances as we step into the spot. That surface is made of smooth polished wood. It reminds me of a trap door. Not in a good way.

The two women at my station smile. One is Mom's age, and the other is maybe a year or two older than me, and very pretty. I try not to look at her, and suck in my gut. I know I can't pull off looking like a Helmsworth. I just don't want to be mistaken for a Hutt.

The older woman holds her arms out like a bird and says, "Like this, Young Master." Her tone is polite and respectful. I glance over at Wes, and they are doing the same thing, but one of the women has a large razor in her hand. It's huge, like serial killer huge. I look back at the young woman at my station. She has one as well.

I tense up for a moment, thinking I have grossly miscalculated the situation, then the machete-sized razor falls to her side.

She looks a little confused and says to her partner. "This one has already done some prepping. His manhood is bare."

"This one as well," comes a soft female voice from Wes's station.

"Maybe they were unaware and just did it themselves," the older woman says. "Young Master," she says to me in a very respectful tone. "Is this your first time to the temple of the sky gods?"

I look at her and smile, then nod.

She returns the smile, warmly, and with a slight curtsy says, "Cleansing your skin of hair is a service we can provide for you. For next time, Young Master."

She turns to the other woman at our stations and, in a completely different tone, says, "Yes, they are but a pair of unfledged youths. I swear they find the most witless young men to perform whatever tasks they undertake upon that sky vessel.

Okay, rude. I look over at Wes, who shrugs.

They put the machete razors down and get to work on us. At my station, the older woman holds out a slender device connected to a long hose. The hose leads to a large jar filled with a grey liquid. Several gears and sprockets are positioned around the base of the jar with a foot pedal attached. She places her bare foot on the pedal and pumps. The grey liquid surges through the hose and emerges from the spray nozzle, spraying paint onto my body.

I feel myself move, turning slightly. The younger woman, the pretty one I am trying very hard not to think about (Babe Ruth, Joe DiMaggio, Jackie Robinson) has her hands on a handle that extends up from the floor. When she moves the handle, I turn slightly. The wood I'm standing on is turning. I'm basically standing on a man-size Lazy Susan.

As we get our Grey makeover, the women continue talking as if we're not here. "Have you noticed the odd shape of their manhood?" one says at Wes's station.

"Yes, it appears they have mutilated themselves."

The one spraying me grey says, "I have heard of this. Men having their tips snipped."

"Why would they cut themselves in this way?"

"Perhaps some of these dullards think it shows a deeper commitment and unity to their sky gods."

"If that is true," comes a voice from Wes's station, "all these simpletons will be doing it soon."

The women all laugh. "Can you imagine if all men did this?"

"If you are wondering," Bob suddenly chimes in, and I jump a little. "They are speaking two different languages."

Ah, that makes sense.

"When they are speaking to you, it's in Egyptian. When they talk amongst themselves, it's in an ancient, well, from your point of view ancient, form of Hebrew. Do not take it personally. They have no idea you have Pisces Converters in your ears.

I nod stupidly, as if Bob can see me.

"Hold still, Young Master," the woman turning my skin grey says. She puts down the nozzle and hose and reaches for a small paint brush dipped in black ooze. "Please close your eyes. I will work as fast as I can."

"I know you can't speak so just listen," Bob says. "I have done some deep digging, and I believe this makeover, as you called it, will be your ticket onto the Greys' ship."

While Bob feeds us info, the women continue their snarky talk. I'm not following their conversation, but they all suddenly stop and laugh at once. I assume someone cracked a good one, most likely at our expense.

"Be quiet, you impetuous cows," says a burly voice from behind us.

It's the man who had introduced himself as Thutmose. He is dressed slightly different, wearing an elaborate robe with crop circle patterns on the chest and sleeves.

The women all cower as if they might be beaten. Several drop to the floor in a fetal position, arms stretched forward.

Thutmose addresses Wes and me. "Do not let the misguided chortles of slaves shake your faith, brothers. You are clearly some of the most committed among us. Once they have completed anointing you properly, please join us on the vessel. There is much work to be done. May the sky gods favor you."

Wes and I nod again.

He turns to leave, then looks back at us. "You do not speak much, do you?"

Oh, frak. We are busted.

I nod and make a lame gesture to my throat, hoping he will think I have whatever they call laryngitis in ancient Egypt.

It does not work. Thutmose looks at me confused. If I had pants on, I'd be on the verge of soiling them.

"I got this," Bob says. "Say exactly what I say."

Bob then says something very slowly. The words in my head zipping in from the other side of the galaxy are completely incomprehensible. I open my mouth but can't remember the word Bob said in the beginning of his sentence. Bob must have detected my hesitation because he repeats the foreign phrase. It just sounds like gobbledygook. I know I'm gonna mangle it, but before I do, Wes speaks.

He confidently repeats what Bob said. He even smiles, which throws me.

"Oh, I should have realized," Thutmose says. He claps his hands twice. "Slaves, please attend them."

A slave from each station quickly steps away.

Thutmose smiles. "I will see you two on board." He then turns and leaves.

"I am brilliant!" Bob screams in our ears. "Do you know how difficult that was. I had to do eight things at once. Berry harvest the phrasing, turn the converter on and off, then back on. Great guava-stalks I am good."

"What did Wes say?" I mumble softly.

"It was either we are very parched," Bob says, "or, we require tacos."

"Well, which one?" I whisper.

"Are they bringing you tacos?" Bob asks.

I spy the women returning with cups in their hands. "No."

"Then it's probably the first one," Bob says.

The women hand us cups of water and we both drink. Turns out I am pretty parched. I look over at Wes. He's hardly recognizable. I know my little, annoying, know-it-all brother is in there somewhere, but under the now grey skin, bald head, and black almond-shaped eye makeup, it's only his height, just an energy drink can taller than an Ewok, that I recognize.

I must look just as strange to my brother. I feel strange. The grey paint dried really fast, and it has some weight to it. Even though I'm buck naked, it doesn't feel that way, especially as the woman wraps a grey garment around my waist. I saw it on the humans in Grey cosplay that went on the ship. I didn't have a word for it then, and I don't now. It's like a skirt, wrap, waist accessory, and the good part is, it covers our manhood. Well, my manhood, and Wes's tiny weenie.

The young woman fastens the garment and smiles. "You are ready, Young Master."

Wes steps off the Lazy Susan and heads my way. We walk out without looking back, which feels weird. Wes must feel it too because he stops at the entryway and turns around facing back in. I do as well.

"It was really hard not to get a ... I had to focus on something else," Wes says.

"Tell me about it. I tried thinking of baseball players, then changed to the sequence of moves to complete the *Star Pilot* final scenario. What did you think about?"

"Legos."

"You would."

"Why aren't we leaving?" Wes says as one of the women waves goodbye to us.

"I don't know. Might have something to do with the room of half-dressed women."

"Status report," Bob says.

"Uh, lingering creepily," I say.

Bob makes that sound that I'm assuming is an annoyed sigh.

"Feels like we should leave a tip or something," Wes says.

"You got your wallet on you?"

"Good point. Let's go."

We turn and head down the hall side by side. Wes looks more relaxed, and I'm feeling like we might actually pull this off. We're both on the same page of this adventure, just two dudes dressed like Greys, ready to sneak onto an alien ship and become thieves four thousand years before we were born. We arrive at a split in the hallway, where one direction leads to the exit, the other goes back to the room with our clothes. I turn one way. Wes turns the other.

"The exit is this way," I say.

"My backpack is this way."

Crap-weasel. We are not on the same page.

Before our luck inevitably runs out, head straight to the Greys'
spaceship and commit a crime.
Turn to page 129.

Cave in to Wes and go back for the backpack and avoid what
will be an unending series of whines and gripes about how I'm
an insensitive bunghole that left his little brother's meds in
ancient Egypt, blah, blah, blah.
Turn to page 168.

The Astral Fighter doesn't look like the one we started with or even the game version. It's got mods and stitched together repairs. I don't know for a fact, but Bob puppet-mastering Earth engineers for the past few decades might have rebuilt the ship, but I question if they did a good enough job to withstand smashing our way through the roof or walls. The open door seems the safest.

"We're going out the front," I tell Wes.

"It feels like that's the way they want us to go."

"Don't be ridiculous," I say, wondering if Wes could be right.

"Maybe we should check back, or behind us for another exit."

The door is open enough to squeeze the Astral Fighter through. I grin. "What was it that Bob said about four thousand years ago."

"I don't—"

"He said, 'Always move forward.'"

Wes turns to me. "I'm pretty sure that was a metaphorical forward, not a literal forward."

"What's the difference? Forward shield to maximum."

Wes spins the dial that operates the shield. "I hope we don't regret this."

Me too. I activate minimal forward thrust. I don't want to explode out the hanger, having no idea what's on the outside. The doors keep opening. Two Astral Fighters could squeeze out now, side by side. We are less than fifty meters from the opening when the soldiers run out of the way. They must not want to get caught in our craft's engine blast, as once I clear the doors, I'm hitting the thrusters.

An alert flashes. I check our scans and see two, no three large vehicles outside. The ship's computer can't identify them. They are not ships. As we near the door, the silhouette of a turret emerges into the hanger.

"Oh, Frak!"

"What is that?" Wes shouts. "Is that a tank?"

A cold realization washes over me. They weren't opening the doors to let us out. They were opening the doors to let an M1A1 Abrams tank ... correction, tanks in.

I put the ship in full reverse, but it's too late. The lead tank fires. Our alien shields can't repel an attack at point-blank range. The 120 mm smoothbore cannon sends an armor-piercing anti-tank round straight at us.

The correct choice was to find another way out.
Turn to page 69.

The bald guy at the dark temple's front door isn't looking. I grab Wes by his cloak and pull him to the side of the road. "Come on, before he spots us," I say as we dart through the small opening between two of the massive stones floating down the road.

"So, we just wait until these pass?" Wes asks. "Then what? We'll be left out in the open."

"No," I say, stepping into the six-foot gap between this stone and the one right behind us. "Just pretend we belong."

Wes goes along with the plan, even though there is little chance of us blending in since all the other workers are walking alongside the rocks and not in between them. No one seems to notice, though, and the closest Reptilian supervisor is three blocks up and totally distracted by the small device in his hand. I'm pretty sure he's streaming something.

We walk at a brisk pace to keep from getting bonked in the back by the stone behind us. The temple and the bald guy get left in the past as we get closer to the pyramid.

Instead of focusing on our surroundings, Wes is mesmerized by the massive rock floating in front of us, the ultimate building block. He points at the small blinking device attached to the middle of it. "Is this really all it needs to float?"

"Shh," I say, hoping he'll remember English won't be heard here for thousands of years. I whisper, "Just leave it alone."

"But how does it manipulate gravity? Bob mentioned the use of natural mechanics and the Earth's magnetic field."

I can see he is already mapping out building instructions in his mind. "Dude, it's not a Lego kit."

"But how do they move it up into place in the pyramid?"

"Don't know, don't care," I say under my breath, looking over my shoulder, hoping we're still unnoticed. "Let's not mess with it."

"It's fine. When's the next time we're going to see this kind of tech?"

Wes has a point, and his finger's way too close to the blinking light. "Hey, no touchy," I tell him.

He touches it.

The rock slams down and crushes the front half of my feet, every bone shattered.

I can't move, can't stop screaming, can barely register Wes doing the same.

I whip my head around, hoping they managed to pause the rock behind us, but we're just inches away from being crushed, Death Star trash compactor-style. The wall of stone crashes into my butt and back, shoving me into the unmoving rock, pressing all the air from me, smashing my skull. My brother and I are about to be the width of a thin crust pizza, with red sauce spilling everywhere.

The correct choice was to head over to the bald guy with the black almond-painted eyes and hope his smile isn't the kind Jeffrey Dahmer used when inviting young men inside his apartment.

Turn to page 133.

Although Gold Leader was very adamant when he said stay on target, I also remember what happened to him.

I look at Wes. "Isn't that what got him killed? He wouldn't zig or zag, and Darth Vader blew him and his Y-Wing into rebel space dust."

Wes rubs his grey chin. "Oh yeah."

"I think we need to keep our plans flexible. Taking the shorter route seems like a good flex."

"I don't think you're using that right," Wes says.

"Probably not, but Bob thinks you can do it. Right, Bob?"

"Uhm," Bob says.

"Uhm?" I echo.

"My analysis says there is a 63.9% chance Wes can retrieve the parts without raising suspicion."

"Pretty good odds," I say.

"Oh, and this is good news. There is an 89.373% chance that the ship will not blow up during the process."

"Even better," I say.

Wes glares at me. "Which way, Bob?"

"I'm sending the new path to your info units."

I check mine. The new path is already displayed, and the Greys' main engine room is a few dozen meters away. Before we take a step on the new path, there's a familiar sound. "Is that a cow?" I move in the direction of the *moo*.

"Wait, where are you going?" Wes says.

"We just heard cows on an alien spaceship. Aren't you curious?"

Wes grabs my arm. "It's been well documented that aliens have taken and mutilated cattle all over the world."

"Mutilate. Why?" I say as I keep walking.

"Why do they make crop circles, experiment on humans, check their prostate? Nobody knows."

"I just want a quick look."

"This is the kind of dumb thing white people do in horror movies," Wes says as he steps behind me.

"Status report," Bob chimes in.

"James is doing a stupid white people thing."

Bob makes that annoyed sound again. "Did the new path info not come through?"

"Yes, it did, Bob," Wes says.

"Then why do your images on my scope have you moving in a different direction?"

I see a doorway and move toward it. "I'm just checking something out."

We hear the *moos* again, but this time it's not just one cow but many. I look back at Wes and see his curiosity has finally risen. He tucks in closer behind me, and we peek into the room.

The source of the mooing is the first thing we see. They don't appear like cows I'm familiar with. Their hides are earthy colors, and they have long dangerous-looking horns. But just like the cows I know, they seem as oblivious to whatever's going on, including their fate. It's a small herd, maybe thirty give or take a hoof, and they have devices secured to their backs by prongs, embedded in their hides. They look exactly like the devices attached to the pyramid stones outside, but smaller. The animals are corralled in a large, open area. A soft, blue glow emanates from the chamber's ceiling, cascading down over the cattle. It must have some holding power because even though there is a lot of space in the room we're looking in, the bovine seem to stay inside the light. The room itself feels cold and impersonal, probably a stark contrast to the natural world from which the cattle were taken.

Just beyond the herd, a massive, circular platform functions as a surgical theater. It's outfitted with an assortment of bizarre, alien medical devices that hum softly. Behind the theater, several large tanks overflow with a pinkish liquid. Inside, objects resembling organs—cow organs, I desperately hope—float listlessly, like dead fish.

"Have you seen enough?" Wes asks.

"Most definitely."

"Can we get back on track?" Bob asks. "We are trying to alter the course of an entire galaxy here, not indulge in your bipedal bovine curiosity."

Bovine Curiosity. "Cool band name, Bob. No worries, we're back on track." I check my info unit. The passage we're in dead-ends at our destination. As we approach, the vibration through my bare feet intensifies. Same for the hum that makes the hair on the back of my neck tingle through painted-over skin.

There is no doorway or opening to the Greys' transdimensional engine room. Our passage just becomes a part of the room. The space is cavernous, bathed in an eerie, otherworldly glow. The air is thick with the howl of machinery unlike anything I could have imagined. Bob said that the Astral Fighter I piloted was designed not only for the game *Star Pilot*, but to make me comfortable, with controls and indicators I could understand. This room is the opposite of that. I don't understand or feel comfortable with anything going on in here.

The walls, the floor, even the ceiling, which is difficult to take in with all the flaring lights, doesn't seem to be made of metal or manufactured material. Some areas are translucent, making a neural network of vein-like connections pulse. It feels organic. Alive.

"I don't want to sound negative," Wes says, "but am I going to take out a few parts or conduct surgery?"

"Ya, I feel you, little brother. Hey, Bob, are you sure we can do this? This room looks like the inside of a space whale a la H.R. Giger."

"Statistically, you should be able to do this," Bob says, "As long as you do not stand at the entryway drawing attention to yourself, which you appear to be doing."

We hear Bob, but still don't move, and the engine room, for all its fantasticalness, is not empty. Many Greys are visible working on several upper levels. There's at least one Reptilian working with several Grey-cosplaying humans working on ground level about twenty meters away. They don't seem to notice us, but the Reptilian does.

Stupid non-binocular vision.

Wes and I start walking. I try to strut like I belong here and know where I'm going, neither of which is true. I glance back at Wes. He struts like someone trying not to faint or hurl. Super cool.

The Reptilian is still watching us, but not as suspiciously. That is an assumption on my part. I have no idea what a suspicious expression on a Reptilian looks like, but he's not showing his teeth, which I count as a plus.

"Do you see the main kumquat insulation situator?" Bob asks.

I roll my eyes. "Doesn't everybody?"

"Stop acting like a brainless meatsack and look for a raised platform, oval shaped, possibly toward the center of the room!"

"Super mean," Wes says. "Oh, there." He points straight ahead.

I see it as well.

Bob directs Wes over to an area around the structure's backside. He kneels and goes to work, communicating back and forth with Bob. There are a ton of fruit and vegetable glitches, but Wes seems to understand what he's saying. Maybe all the Lego time really has made Wes mechanically inclined. I do my best to tune them out because my role in this is to keep watch. While Wes toils, my eyes scan our surroundings like a well-trained hawk. Or a scared, grey-painted teen on the verge of pissing his sparkly garment he doesn't have a name for.

The Reptilian that eyed us when we came in is far enough away that, should he look our way, he probably wouldn't see us unless they have some vision that sees around corners. I'm on my third or fourth scan of our surroundings when Wes says, "Got it."

He's precariously holding three potato-sized alien engine parts. I grab one to help out. It feels cold on one side and warm on the other, like something that hasn't been in the microwave long enough.

"Get moving," Bob says.

"Wait," I say. "Look, we can't walk around, let alone out of the ship's door, with these things in our hands. Might draw attention."

"Frak, you're right," Wes says.

I'm glad he agrees because I have an idea he may not like. "Let's try to stick them in the backpack. We'll have to take a few things out."

Wes groans, but he kneels and sets the parts down. He opens his backpack and removes our three sandals. It's not going to be enough room. Wes tries anyway, but can't zip it up.

"Bob, do we need all three of these things? I mean two of them look practically the same." I know what Bob's answer is going to be, but I want to help Wes out.

"Yes, we need all three. Each has a unique carotene matrix harvesting the citrus that—"

"Okay, okay," I interrupt. I didn't know Bob would say that exactly, but I guessed the gist.

Wes reaches in and takes out the limited-edition collectors Lego box set, then zips up the backpack.

I hold out my hand, "Let me carry it. My body is bigger. I've got a better chance of concealing it."

My brother eyes me suspiciously.

"I'll take care of your Lego box."

"With your life?"

I tilt my head. "Be real. You know I'd be lying if I say yes."

Wes contemplates. With an uncertain scowl, he hands it over.

"I'll take care of your box." I try to give him a reassuring brotherly smile, but we both know if it comes to it, I'll huck it first chance I get if it means saving our butts.

We turn to go but stop dead in our tracks. While we were sorting out the backpack situation, our lookout, aka me, dropped the ball. The Reptilian that eyed us suspiciously before has not only walked over to investigate, but has brought a friend. Standing beside him is a cosplaying human, a bit taller than me, with a matching sparkly grey form-fitting diaper.

"What are you doing in this section?" the human asks.

I shrug and hold my hands out, hoping the confused gesture means the same thing in this time as it does four thousand years in the future.

The Reptilian steps forward and looks at the area Wes was working on. "They have taken pollen-cells from the kumquat manifold."

"Maybe Bob can do what he did last time," Wes whispers.

"Ah, Bob. A little help."

"I was not ready," Bob says. "Can you have him repeat what he said?"

"Are you serious?" I say.

They can hear us talking, and it's obvious they don't have a clue what we are saying, which is not good. The Reptilian looks angry. Hard to tell with no eyebrows, but definitely ten percent more hostile.

"What language do you speak?" the human asks.

"Oh Booobbbb," I say, my voice shaking.

The Reptilian, in his ten percent more hostile voice, turns to his human companion and says, "Something is not right. Alert the Masters!"

"Time to go to plan B," Bob says.

"What the frak is plan B?" Wes says.

"Run!"

Wes and I exchange looks of terror. My heart hammers against my ribs, and in that moment of sheer panic, only one course of action comes to mind: to channel the Three Stooges.

Stepping forward, I feign astonishment, thrust a finger toward some unseen target behind our discoverers, and shout, "Great googly moogly, look at that!"

A very confused Reptilian and grey-painted human look over their shoulders. Wes, having not watched quite as much Stooges as me with our dad, gets the hint. He takes off a heartbeat before I do.

We sprint past them, heading for the door as fast as our grey-painted bare feet can take us. Neither of us look back, but if we did, no doubt something would be chasing us. When we clear the engine room, we don't stop moving. It's going to be a footrace to the exit, and I don't need Bob to tell me the odds to conclude that we can't win. No way can a sedentary gamer and his asthmatic little brother outrun hardworking ancient people who probably don't rest until bedtime. We're better off hiding somewhere until we can find a way out. Then I hear the cows, and I have a thought.

"This way," I shout at Wes.

As he slows, Wes points in the direction he was running. "But this is the way out."

"We'll never make it." I wave with the Lego box for him to follow. "I have a plan."

He follows and we run toward the cattle room. It's a turn to the left and then straight another ten meters. I duck inside, and Wes arrives a few heartbeats later. It was just a short run from the kumquat machine thingy to here, but Wes is clearly winded. He bends over and puts his hands on his knees. After a few deep breaths, he stands and says, "Okay, what's your plan."

"I thought we'd come in here," I say proudly.

"That's not a plan," Wes says, shaking his head. "That's barely a thought!"

"Keep your voice down." I put my arm around him and usher him further into the cattle room. "There's more to my plan."

Wes stops and puts a hand on his hip. "Okay."

"Let's be real. We were never going to make it all the way to the exit with those guys on our butts. And since no one has burst in here looking for us, I gotta assume they think we're running to the exit."

"So?"

"So, that gives us some time to figure out our next move."

"That's the plan?" Wes shouts. "To take some time to figure out a plan."

"Well, when you say it like that, it sounds stupid."

"It is stupid!"

I move deeper into the room. "Look, maybe we can find something in here, like a weapon or something, to help us."

"We're never getting out of here. We're never going home. We're gonna get dissected like these cows. Or worse."

"Status report," Bob says.

"Wallowing in self-pity," Wes says.

"Why are you back in the cattle exploratory chamber? The exit is the other way."

"And so are the people and non-people chasing us," I say. "Shaking them off our tail was my plan."

"He doesn't have a plan," Wes says. "I don't even think he can spell the word *plan*. Bob, can you help us, please?"

"Do you know anything about this room, Bob?" I say, "Is there anything we could use as weapons?"

"Well, there are surgical lasers for dissection, but they are only effective at close range. I do not believe wielding weapons is a good idea. That's why I did not let you take any hand weapons from the Astral Fighter."

"Wait," I say. "We have guns back at the ship?"

"Yes, there is a small armory for ground combat, but without training, you are statistically more likely to shoot yourselves or each other. And considering the way you two bicker, I am not certain it would be an accident."

Wes and I both nod. "That's fair," I say.

"You do not have any weapons, but there are many alternatives to fighting."

"Thanks, Obi Wan," I say while walking around the cows. They're big, and as I circle the four-legged beasts, I realize there are more than I initially thought. "Hey, Wes, how many cows do you think are in here?"

Wes walks over. "I don't know, maybe three dozen."

"My scans say forty-two," Bob says.

"Forty-two," I repeat. The number is familiar for several reasons, but one rises to the top. I smile. "I think I know an alternative to fighting."

"What?" Wes says.

"Chaos."

"Hey, Bob, remember Level 42 in *Star Pilot*?"

"Of course. I created the game."

"The Star Pilots have just entered a new sector where they are vastly outnumbered, but–"

"Oh my God," Wes interrupts. "Don't tell me the whole stupid video game scenario. Just get to the fraking point."

I'm a little bummed Wes won't let me finish the whole scenario because it's pretty lit, but he's stressed, and lizards and naked aliens with big heads are chasing us. "Fine. Using tractor beams, we gathered asteroids and flung them into a fleet of enemy ships. It created enough chaos for the Star Pilot, aka me, to slip by the defenses and make my escape."

"We don't have asteroids," Wes says.

"No, but we have forty-two cows."

"They are Hamitic Longhorns," Bob adds.

I roll my eyes. "Thanks, Bob, that's helpful." I look at Wes. "We send out the longhorns, we tuck in behind them, and escape in the chaos."

Wes sighs, then slowly brings a hand to his chin. "Huh, a stampede a la Fiesta de San Fermin. Like in *The Sun Also Rises*, turn the Greys' ship into Pamplona. Could work."

"Yeah, I didn't understand a thing you just said, but I'm sensing you're in."

"Jeez, read a book. And, yes, I'm in."

"Okay, Bob," I say. "We need to get these longhorns moving, but there's this blue light that shines down over them. I think it hypnotizes them to stay put."

"You are not completely wrong," Bob says.

"That's a first," Wes chimes in.

I glower at Wes. "Can you insult my intelligence later?"

"You can count on it."

"Meatsacks! Will you focus?" Bob yells inside our heads, and it hurts a little. Not the meatsacks thing—getting used to that—but the actual yelling.

"Okay," I say. "What do you got?"

"The blue light is a pleasure center stimulator. They stay there because it feels good. We need to change it to red."

"How do we do that?" I ask, but Wes is already moving toward a control panel. It's a little low for me, but not if you're a Grey. Wes steps up to it and places a hand over it like he can sense the controls.

"Look for a dial, something that moves in a circular motion. It might not be a physical dial, more like a light source."

I'm amazed, but Wes seems to know exactly what he's doing. His hand glides over a spherical gold light that rises from the console. I'm not sure if it's my imagination, but the 3D image it projects looks a lot like Stonehenge. As he moves his hand, the image rotates. The light changes; the blue fading, replaced by green. The cows begin to stir. Some are bumping into one another. No, that's not correct, they're rubbing on one another.

"They are moving a little now, Bob."

"Is the light red?"

"No, green," I say.

"Get it off green."

"What's wrong with green?"

"Nothing, if you want to see them start mating."

"Off green, off green!" I shout.

"I heard him." Wes moves the Stonehenge-shaped dial. The light fades from green into a burgundy hue. The cows continue to bump one another, but no longer in a *hey, how-you-doin',* kind of way. It's now more aggressive, more hostile. I notice that some of the devices attached to their hides are lighting up, but more importantly, I notice that I'm standing between them and the exit.

"I think they went this way," someone says down the hall.

I hustle over to Wes. "I think we're about to have company."

"Working on it," Wes says, continuing to move his hand over the control. The light is becoming less burgundy and more red. The cows are extremely agitated but still standing in place.

"We need to get them moving," I say.

"Okay, I got an idea." Wes steps from the control panel and moves behind the herd. He holds out his right arm, then with a flick of his hands, says, "Shoo."

"Are you joking?"

Wes flicks his hand faster. "Shoo, shoo."

"Uh, for frak sakes."

Over 42 sets of horns, I see two Greys and a human enter. The painted-grey human shouts, "There they are!"

I try to remember how they get cattle moving in all the westerns I've seen. My mind goes completely blank as I realize I don't watch westerns. Frak. But I did see several episodes of a new show called *Yellowstone* with that old *Field of Dreams* guy.

I got this. I move in close behind one of the cows and scream, "Yee hah!"

A cow looks back at me with one curious eye, but none move. The red light is causing them pain, but they're too stupid to move. I try again, but this time I slap the cow with the Lego box. The cow reacts to the impact as the Lego pieces move around like a maraca. I yell, "Yee hah," louder than before and shake the box.

With a suddenness that makes me step back, the herd rushes forward. Two full breaths later, Wes and I stand alone, the deafening thunder of hoofbeats and the screams of humans and aliens ringing in our ears. We don't hear the sickening crunch of bones, but as the herd surges out of the chamber, the gruesome spectacle becomes clear. Grey heads explode like balloons filled with colorful whipped cream. The bodies are a horrific mass of Grey and human flesh, so mangled it's impossible to tell where one ends and the other begins.

"Nasty," Wes says.

"Better them than us," I say. "Come on."

We run around the alien Rorschach splatter and follow the longhorns. As they collide with one another, more of the devices on them light up, causing them to slow. When they do, I shake the Lego box a little and they are off again. To my surprise and delight, they are not staying together. The passages branch off and the cows separate, creating chaos in all directions. I can hear beings shrieking, running, crashing, and long pointy horns gouging walls and anything in their path. It's chaos, and it's wonderful. I grin as we trot behind them.

"Okay, admit it," I say.

"What?"

"My plan to come up with a plan was a pretty good plan, huh?"

"Shut up. Just go easy on my Lego box."

"There is no pleasing you, dude."

"It's not over yet."

True, but it feels like the odds have tilted in our favor. There's an explosion way behind us, and like the odds, the ship starts to tilt. Wes and I careen into a wall and stand a minute to take a breath. Another explosion. An alarm sounds.

"That can't be good," Wes says.

I shake my head. "The more chaos the better." I look behind us. Lights flicker like dying fluorescent bulbs. Could be flames or something else. Hard to tell, but it doesn't matter. "Okay, let's get moving again, but no more running."

"Why?"

"Two humans running for the exit will draw attention. Let's just blend in with the chaos and look like we belong."

Wes nods, and we start strolling, calmly. I'm surprised at how we're moving unnoticed, but as the commotion behind us gets louder with mini explosions, yelling, screaming, and I want to say even weapon's fire, I understand. The chaos we left in our wake is working far better than we'd hoped. But as we're about to step into the area we entered the ship, our luck runs out.

Thutmose and the Grey from outside are standing at the end of our corridor. I assume it is the same Grey; not to be racist, but honestly, they all look alike. I mean, wear a hat or something. They stand next to the flying platform, which hovers a half meter off the floor, idling like a car sitting in a handicap spot outside a Starbucks. We hunker down at the end of the passage, staying out of sight, and as I gaze at the hovering vehicle, I get a risky, possibly dumb, idea.

"I bet we could steal that thing," I say.

Wes points at the platform. "You want to try and carjack the flying balcony?"

"With my Star Pilot skills and your natural mechanical whatevers, we could fly it right back to our ship."

"Jeez, talk about delusions of grandeur. Your skills come from a video game and my mechanical whatevers are fostered by Legos."

"You're so negative. Think about what we've done so far. You've removed parts from an alien ship, and I've already been in a dogfight and took out ... Hey, Bob, how many Reptilian ships did I take out?"

Bob doesn't answer.

"Hey, Bob, status report?" I say mockingly.

Still no answer.

"Yo, Bob. Ancient Earth to Bob." I tap my ear like that will help. "Are you in there?"

"I bet some of these explosions are interfering with communication," Wes says.

"You see, right there." I point at Wes. "That's your mechanical whatevers kicking in. I wouldn't have thought of that."

"You don't think of a lot of things."

"True, and mean, but I really think we can do this."

"Even if we could manage to steal the flying thing, and that's a big *if*, the door is not open. What're we gonna do after that? Fly around and look for an open window."

"I'll try the password again. Nanu nanu."

"Oh my God, that was a coincidence," Wes says. "You really think the password to an alien ship's door is from a seventies' TV show?"

I'm confused. "It's from a TV show? I saw it in a meme."

Wes slaps his forehead. "We're gonna die."

I chuckle. "Probably already have."

"What?"

"Never mind. Look, it's about twenty meters to where the hatch is. We jet over to the platform, you jump on, figure out how it works, and I'll slow down Tutface and the Grey."

The Greys look mean, but from what I've seen so far, their bodies are frail. I'm gonna kick him hard in the chest and punch Tutface. I took two years of Krav Maga, and I know exactly where to hit him. I'll try not to feel bad about hitting Tutguy. He was nice to us when we needed him to be, and what will he get for it? A punch in the face. No good deed and all.

"There they are!" a voice shouts behind us.

There's a detail of very angry Greys walking fast in our direction. A human with that degree of anger on their face would be running at us with purpose, but I guess their frail Grey bodies can only muster a brisk and stern walk. Frail or not, neither of us wants to be here when they arrive.

Before we have time to react to the wave of Greys walking briskly, the hatch we hoped to escape through begins to open.

Attempt to carjack, or flying-platform-jack, the hovering vehicle and try to zip out the opening hatch before the power-walking Greys grab us.
Turn to page 223.

Use our current resources, ingenuity, and ability to move faster than an alien power walker to dash straight for the opening hatch and freedom—for as long as it lasts.
Turn to page 42.

Every time my mom told me something was dangerous, she was right. I learned this mostly because I don't listen. Electric outlet, got shocked. Skateboarding, broke my wrist. Stilts, got a concussion. The *Lost* TV show. Okay, technically not dangerous, but Mom said it had a very unsatisfying ending, and she was right! Now she's saying that Bob, a being that put a fish in my ear and has been as fun as sticking a finger in a light socket, is the bad guy.

"Are we going?" Wes asks.

Feels like I should ask another question, but ... I look back at the room transforming into what, I have no idea. Screw this. Plan Nine can kiss by butt. "Let's go."

All Wes needed was my go ahead. He flies up the stairs.

I run after him, knees pumping, eyes aimed up at the light pouring in from the top. I'm getting tired, dizzy. I don't remember this many steps on the way down. Why in the frak would a supposedly advanced species, like whatever Bob is, even have stairs? They don't have elevators on his side of the galaxy?

"We're coming!" Wes screams.

"Hurry, boys. This thing you're in is getting ready to leave."

Wes looks back at me. "Is fish guy still trying to take us?"

I don't know, but it does feel like someone's trying to abduct us. "Keep going." I wave him on.

Wes reaches the trunk interior and looks back for me. I join him just as a yellow light hits us from above. It's warm and tingles, like being in a vat of warm soda. Something latches onto my entire skeleton and lifts me up. It's happening to Wes as well. In seconds, we are outside the Camaro, flying over it.

"What's happening?" Wes shouts.

"No clue!" I look up, attempting to follow the light to its source. When I find it, my heart skips a beat. The alien sphere is rising toward the clouds with us in its wake, trapped in a yellow tractor beam.

"Boys, you're okay," the Mom-imposter says. "These superior beings have volunteered to rescue you. We'll be together soon."

"I don't think that's Mom," Wes says.

"Really? Ya' think?"

"Bob," I shout. "We made a mistake."

"What's he saying?" Wes says.

"Bob," I repeat.

The sphere zips over Roswell, three hundred meters above the town. Then it flies erratically, moving from side to side. We tumble around in the light like fish in a Ziplock bag. I try to see what's happening and notice blasts of light rising from Roswell. "I think someone is shooting at the flying ball."

Wes tumbles over my head and smacks me with his foot. "It's the Men in Black. They're trying to shoot it down."

I bounce off the edge of our yellow light prison like a rubber ball. "What happens to us if they do?"

Before Wes answers, the Sphere is stuck hard. It jolts violently. A massive crack runs up its length, and the yellow light flickers. An instant later, the light is gone, and so is the sensation of weightlessness. Gravity takes hold, and we fall.

We both scream as the town of Roswell rushes toward us.

"Status report."

"Bob, where've you been?"

"Something was blocking our connection. Were you in a–"

"Never mind! We're falling." I reach over and grab my brother's hand. We hold on tight to one another.

"I concur. You are falling. You will reach terminal velocity in three seconds."

"Can you help?"

Wes points below. "Look, a spaceship!"

There's a metallic conical shape on the surface directly underneath us. "I see it!" I say, hoping it's Bob, or a friend of Bob, or an enemy of Bob, coming to help us.

"Oh, frak me!" Wes says. "It's just the McDonalds!"

A wave of disappointment consumes me. "This McSuuuuuuucks!"

The correct choice was to investigate a bit more before abandoning Bob and his bizarre take on galactic history.
Turn to page 179.

Although Wes's backpack will clash with our current alien makeover, I decide to make it work. Wes's whining when separated from his backpack can be intense. Reminds me of a toddler and his binkie. I hope he gets over it before he goes to college. We are about to turn to the dressing room when I see two Greys lingering down the passageway that goes to the exit. They stagger a bit, like old men coming out of a bar. We wait for them to shamble on.

One points a digit from his three-fingered hand at his companion and says, "Let's just grab one or ... or two. And, we'll just remove a few organs and put 'em right back. Easy peasy, human squeezy."

The other one responds, but I don't catch it. Something about cleaning up their mess this time.

They shamble on as Wes and I head to the dressing room. "Hey, Bob, do Greys get drunk?"

"Drunk, stoned, melon-faced, you name it. On the tip of the Sagittarius arm of our galaxy they have twelve planets dedicated to rehabilitation. Each planet is a step."

"Yikes."

"Yeah, total doucheberries," Bob says.

When we arrive, Wes heads straight for his backpack. As he snags it, I get an idea. "Is there enough room in there for our clothes? I don't want to walk around in this grey, sparkly, skirt diaper for the rest of this adventure."

"Are you kidding?" Wes says. "If we make it back to Roswell dressed like this, no one would look at us twice."

"True, but let's take them anyway." Wes opens the backpack. It's gonna be a tight squeeze. "There'd be more room in there if you tossed the box of Legos."

"No way," Wes says. "If we end up stranded in ancient Egypt, I'm gonna need something to play with." He looks at me. "You are not that entertaining."

"Okay, mean."

We roll our clothes tight and Wes squeezes them in, careful not to damage his collectable Lego set. There's just enough room left for three sandals, a fourth would have kept it from zipping up. Thank you, deep sand.

Wes is being unusually reasonable for my anxiety-riddled little brother. Makes me want to compliment him. Which is also unusual. "Hey, nice job saying the strange words Bob had you say. You saved our newly colored grey butts back there."

"Thanks," he says, slipping the backpack on.

"How'd you do that anyway?"

"It helps to speak more than one language."

"More than one?" I question, then realize what he means. "Oh my God, Klingon is not a real language."

Wes heads to the exit. "Says you."

"Nerd."

"Dork." Wes turns down the passageway. He stays in front of me, and I stay close behind, hoping my body will conceal the backpack a little. I have no idea if it will work, but if we do get caught, at least Wes will have his inhaler. I'm pretty sure whatever the Greys will do to us will induce a panic attack.

Outside, the sun is warm, a sudden change from the air conditioning-like atmosphere in the temple. Remembering the spot I saw the other cosplaying humans board the ship, we move in that direction. There was a ramp that came down as they approached, and as we near the same spot, the ramp hasn't emerged. Maybe we need a password or something.

The traffic of people hasn't changed, and we are kind of lost in the activity. No one is looking at us twice. As we get closer to the ship, there is only us. I hoped when we were out of people traffic, the ramp would start coming down like it had for the others, but no luck.

What are we doing wrong?

"Hey, Bob," I say. "We're at the ship."

"See." Bob sounds excited. "Now, that is a status report."

"Stop being a dick. Listen, the ramp isn't coming down."

"Are you sure you are in the right spot?"

I look around and then at Wes. He nods in agreement. "Pretty sure."

"I'll check the records and see if I can come up with something," Bob says.

"In the meantime, should we walk around or stand here like desperate hitchhikers?" Wes asks.

"There's gotta be something I'm missing," I say. "Did you see the two painted-up Grey-humans get on the ship when we were going into the temple?"

"No, I didn't. Did they do something to get the ship to open?"

"Maybe. Let me think for a second."

"Frak," Wes says. "Think fast 'cause we're about to have company."

I can feel Wes's anxiety as I follow his gaze. At the opposite end of the colossal space vessel, a Grey stands on a hovering platform. Despite the distance, I can see its large, black, almond-shaped eyes boring into us. The platform itself is a sleek, minimalist design with a thin railing on two sides and a raised control panel in the center. The alien's stare intensifies with a suddenness that causes a chill to move up my spine even in the hot sun. The chill turns to frost bite as the platform begins to glide toward us.

Frak me. Panic starts to set in but then it hits me. "I remember!"

"What?"

"The hand signal. I saw the guy who went in the temple flash it at Tut-moose."

"Thutmose," Wes corrects.

"Whatever. The two that went on the ship started to hold up their hands, but I looked away before they did whatever they did."

"What did the guy at the temple do?"

I hold up my right hand shoulder-high. "It was kind of like this." I start with a boy scout salute, three fingers straight up, then splay them. "I think this is it."

Wes quickly mimicks my hand gesture. "It's kind of lazy, straight up West Side."

"What?"

"I'm a bit more street than you are," Wes says.

"Sure you are, Lego-boy." I look up at the ship, desperate to see it open. Sweat is beading on my forehead. The Grey on the platform is nearly here.

"Is there something else?" Wes says. "A cool wave or password."

I shake my head and say the first thing that pops into my mind. "Nanu nanu."

"Seriously? I can't believe we're related." Wes's glare, displaying his dismay at our shared genetics, quickly fades as the ship opens. Shafts of yellow light escape the interior of the hull as the ramp descends to earth at our feet.

Our eyes widen, and Wes says, "I take it back. You're my favorite brother."

"I'm your only brother."

"Same thing."

Stepping up on the ramp, I try not to look over at the approaching Grey on the hovering platform. Doing so would seem suspicious, but I can't help myself, and the result is kind of a good news bad news thing. The Grey isn't heading our way anymore. Good news. But he isn't turning around and going back to whatever Grey thing he was doing. Bad news. It watches us go up the ramp, big black peepers locked onto us like a wolf eyes a meal.

We hustle up, and before we reach the top, the ramp is already closing. By the time we step into the ship, the ramp closes behind us with a noise I can only imagine is what it sounds like being sealed inside a Tupperware container, our freshness preserved for later.

The chamber we're standing in is massive. I'm sure it's my imagination, but it looks bigger inside. There are structures, like a city, buildings for lack of a better word, rising from the floor, the walls, and even the ceiling, reaching outward toward the center. It's very disorientating, so I try to stare straight ahead.

Wes removes our info units from his backpack and hands one to me. The small screens come alive as soon as I secure it to my wrist. It displays a schematic of the ship's interior and a very helpful green dot, which delivers that very useful message like on a mall map: *You Are Here.*

"I think it's located the parts," Wes says. "Looks far."

With a quick tap, I expand the schematic and can see what Wes means. A path is displayed, and it looks like we have to traverse pretty deep into the ship. "Well, we better get going, before someone realizes we're stowaways."

We move in the direction the info unit advises. We're about to enter a corridor when I hear that weird sealing sound from when the ramp closed, but kind of in reverse. I glance back and notice the ramp is down again. A second later, the Grey riding the platform emerges, and Thutmose is with him, holding onto the thin railing.

We quickly duck into the corridor. "Think they're looking for us?" Wes says.

"Let's not hang around and find out." When we entered the corridor, we were jogging a little. I touch Wes's arm and gesture for him to slow down. We need to look like we're supposed to be here, on our way to where we're supposed to be. Anything less would raise suspicion. Wes understands, and we ease into a nice, casual, strolling around an alien spaceship pace.

The corridor is not empty. Greys move about their business, not paying us much mind. Gives me a minute to take them in. Up close, they are just as alien looking as they are from far away, but when their big eyes blink, it makes a soft sound. Hard to describe, kind of like the sound your hand makes brushing crumbs off a table. Hard to notice unless you're listening for it.

Most of the Greys are about an Xbox controller taller than Wes. The tops of their roundish, Grey skulls come up to my nose. Unlike the Reptilians, I can't detect any sex, male or female. Strutting about barefoot and nude, they don't look physically tough, with their spindly arms and thin torsos. I'm pretty sure my asthmatic brother could kick the star dust out of one in a fair fight, but they have an arrogance about them when they walk, like they think they're all that and a bag of Takis. I guess going from world to world being treated like gods gives even intelligent aliens delusions of grandeur.

We pass several humans dressed like us in the corridor. They seem to be working on something, their hands deep inside an open panel. Looks like they're doing maintenance. They look at us as we stroll by. I try not to make eye contact but fail. One of the humans looks at us perplexed. Hard to tell exactly through the Grey-worshiping makeover, but I detect he has questions. Thinking fast, I point down the corridor and nod at him, hopefully delivering the message, *"Uh, hi guys. We'd stop and chat, but we've been summoned to do this other very important thing this way."*

When we move out of earshot, Wes says, "Very smooth."

"Well, I might not be a street as you, but I get by."

"Not sure it was smooth enough," Wes says, glancing back. "They stopped doing whatever it was they were doing, and they're talking to each other."

"Are they watching us?"

Wes looks back again. "Yep."

"Well, frak. Let's turn up here and get out of this passage."

The new passage is half the size and deserted. We keep walking and glance back a few times to make sure we are not being followed. When it's clear no one is on our tail, we slow down a little. I wasn't even aware we had quickened our step, until we slowed. My pounding heart must have been in control.

"Status report," Bob says, his voice booming through the Pisces Converter. "You are off course. Is something wrong?"

"Some humans were eyeing us, and James's ancient Egyptian street skills made us turn out of their sight."

I sigh. "Nothing's wrong. We're all right."

"You are heading toward the ship's transdimensional propulsion."

"Is that like the engine room?" Wes says.

"One of them," Bob says. "I am going to search for a path to put you back on course."

"We can just backtrack," I say.

"Always move forward," Bob says. "Oh, that is interesting."

"What?" Wes says.

"My situational banana-com has an interesting idea."

I roll my eyes. "What does the banana-com say?"

"It is suggesting an alternative plan, but it appears dangerous."

"More dangerous than what we're already doing?" Wes asks.

"Good point," Bob says. "Our original plan was to remove new parts from the Greys' inventory in the main storage section of the ship, still a good hike away."

"We know that," I say.

"But we could remove parts already in use just a short distance from your present location."

"That sounds a little different than taking parts off of a storage shelf," I say. "Removing parts from an alien engine seems way complicated."

"I can walk you through the procedure, assuming my manuals are relevant, and with Wes's natural mechanical instincts and dexterity, there is a decent chance it could work."

"How far away are we from the parts we need in storage?" I ask.

"You are almost halfway there," Bob says. "The original plan has less technical risks, but more opportunities to run into someone that will blow the turnip on you."

"Well, we don't want that. What do you think, Wes?"

Even through this makeup, I can see Wes is uneasy. I don't know that he is turning pale, but I assume he is.

He looks up at me and says, "Remember what Gold Leader said?"

His reference is uber nerdy, but I get his meaning. Gold Leader had said, *"Stay on Target."*

Disregard Gold Leader's command and choose the new plan to harvest parts from the ship's transdimensional thingy-ma-bob.
Turn to page 150.

Stay with the original plan; continue to the storage area and harvest new parts, relying on our Egyptian and alien street smarts to help navigate any interaction with ancient humans or aliens.
Turn to page 191.

As I spin the ship, I mentally prepare myself for hand-to-hand combat. I have two years Krav Maga under my belt, and I've seen every action movie ever made. I take a deep breath and summon my inner Steven Segal. Not the current fat one—the kick-ass *Under Siege* and *Hard to Kill* one. Best part, I've already defeated Broken Neck once. I can do it again. Sequel!

After the third dizzying 360 rollover, I level us off. Behind me, Broken Neck slams into the deck, his frail form rolling over the motionless Grey bodies. I activate the environmental stabilizers and hit the autopilot, feeling the ship steadying. I snatch the spatula from my lap, undo my safety harness, and spring from my seat.

"What are you doing," Wes asks, wiping vomit from his chin.

I want to say something cool, but I don't have time to workshop it, and it comes out, "It's time to take out the trash."

"What?"

The Grey rises onto its three-fingered hands and knobby knees. He reaches for his spatula, so I drop a swift Hammer Fist onto the top of its head. I expect a bone-jarring impact, but the bottom of my fist slams into something unexpectedly soft. It's like hitting an enormous, squishy stress ball.

The Grey drops to the floor but manages to grab its spatula. It rises as my adrenaline propels me forward, and I target what I believe is a weak spot. Last time I hit its neck, that was an accident; this time, I aim purposefully. Throat Strike! My hand connects with its medical neck brace, which proves sturdier than its squishy head. Pain rockets up my arm. I may have broken some knuckles.

I step back, cradling my broken bones. The Grey grins. It raises its spatula, and I instinctively swing mine. Our spatulas connect between us, and electric sparks flash, sending a shock into our bodies. The force throws us both back into opposite walls.

Stunned, the Grey looks up at me, its almond-shaped eyes growing to the size of coconuts. "Are you insane?" it says. "You will kill us all."

I know it won't understand, but I'm too pumped not to reply. "Yes, I'm loco, bro. Insane in the membrane! Come get some!" Again, didn't have time to workshop it.

"You want to fight like barbarians?" The Grey jumps to its feet. "So be it, Hew-mon." The Grey activates something on his spatula, and it transforms like an expandable baton. It the blink of an eye, his weapon became twice as big as mine.

Wes points. "His grew!"

"I can see that." I push away from the wall and hope there's some universal truth to the phrase *size doesn't matter.*

We both charge, the shorter Grey with a rapier-sized spatula and me with a spatula the size of a Bowie knife. Our weapons meet with a resounding clank. Purple sparks shoot from both ends of each spatula, and I nearly lose mine. I pull back, but Broken Neck charges again, his movements surprisingly swift. I raise my spatula, preparing to parry his next strike.

"Status report," Bob says.

"James is in kind of a lightsaber fight at the moment," Wes answers.

"What?" Bob says. "How is he doing?"

"Uhm ..."

I deflect blow after blow, backing up with each powerful strike. Soon, the wall presses against my back. I lunge forward, driving a forceful palm strike directly into his broad forehead. His Grey body slams against the bulkhead, the impact echoing loudly in the confined space. He regains his footing, readying his next attack. His gaze shifts to Wes, who now stands by his seat. Broken Neck grins at me, and then aims his weapon squarely at my brother.

"No!" I scream, but it's too late.

A shimmering beam of light erupts from the tip of his giant spatula and strikes my brother in the chest. For a few horrifying moments, the beam suspends his body in the air. Then, a sickening sucking sound as his body goes limp. Wes flops to the floor, a grotesque human puddle. It's as if Broken Neck surgically removed my brother's skeleton. What poured onto the floor was everything else: organs, muscle, wrapped inside a sack of painted grey flesh. Worse yet, he's still alive. I watch his eyes, wide with horror, desperately attempt to blink.

I turn to the Grey. All I can see is red. I want to murder him so hard. "You de-boned my brother, you alien asshole!" I spring forward, spatula arcing for the alien's head. Broken Neck brings his weapon up, both hands gripping its ends, to block my attack. I hammer on him, blow after blow, hoping my strength will eventually break through. The alien parries each assault. I barely notice the subtle shift as he twists one end of his weapon. With a sharp, metallic *clink*, he detaches the handle section.

My anger's unbalancing me, but I don't care, and that's when Broken Neck seizes his chance. He thrusts the handle section upward, a swift movement that slices into my midsection. His black eyes narrow as he depresses a button on the handle. A searing, blue heat surges through me, instantly and agonizingly separating every atom in my body.

The correct choice was to bet big on Wes's natural mechanical instincts and hand him the Spatula. Tell him to wipe the vomit off his chin and figure this out before the Grey finds his weapon.

Turn to page 22.

"Come on," Wes says. "Let's go."

"Hold on. Hey, Mom, one more question."

"Okay, hun, but hurry it up."

"Who is the best Starfleet Captain?"

"What?"

"On *Star Trek*, who is the best Captain? You know, your favorite?"

"Oh." There's a suspicious pause. "Captain Picard of course."

Wes's eyes go wide. "For a number of reasons, that is the wrong answer."

For our mom's age group, that is a pretty good guess, but my mom is unique. Her Captain is Kirk.

Wes backs away from the stairs. "That's not Mom."

"Clearly." I turn away. "Hey, Bob, we got a voice sounding like our mom coming down and telling us to go back up."

"Well, do not do that! It is not your mom."

"We figured that out, but now what?"

"I will conclude the transformation while you strap in."

"You want me to get in the chair?"

"It will be difficult to pilot the ship in your bi-pedal standing position," Bob says.

"What's he saying?" Wes asks.

I step to the pilot's seat. "He's being insulting, or sarcastic. It's hard to tell which."

The space continues to come together around us. As I reach for the chair, the staircase dissolves into thin air, replaced by a sleek access tube leading deeper into the vessel. Recognition washes over me, a strange sensation to have in this new, bizarre reality.

I sit down and Wes steps over. "What should I do?"

I put on the shoulder harness and ask Bob, "What about Wes?"

"Give me a moment. I need to reconfigure. I failed to anticipate a co-pilot."

A low, mechanical whine sounds behind me. I glance back to find the floor parting, and a second chair ascends through the opening. It resembles the one I am seated in, though smaller in scale. "I'm guessing that's your seat."

The new chair glides forward, locking into place next to me with a faint hiss as the floor seamlessly closes behind it. The environment around us continues its metamorphosis, shedding its room-like appearance and morphing into a sleek, tear-shaped space reminiscent of an Astral Fighter's cockpit—the ship I've been flying in the game *Final Star Pilot*.

As Wes straps in, I look down at the controls. The cockpit layout, though alien, holds a chilling familiarity. I mentally map the controls. It is uncanny—although on a much larger scale and spread across a command console, the design mirrors a modern video game controller. The Right Stick Button likely activates thrust and controls direction. The right and left bumpers, no doubt, will serve as shields. The right and left triggers, weapons. The left stick will likely activate the weapons inventory, while the D-pad will alter focus, allowing the pilot to shift between targeting modes and external views.

"This isn't a coincidence," I say to Bob. "I know how to pilot this ship."

"Your remedial game controller was designed to be an interface with one of the most advanced transports in the galaxy. Now put your helmets on."

I look around but do not see any helmets.

It's not a controller function, but I remember in the game's opening vid-clips, the pilot manipulating a control on their armrest. My gaze falls upon my own left arm, and there it is, a matching control. I press the gold button on its outer edge. Two sleek helmets materialize from the ceiling and descend silently towards us.

"Ah, what's happening?" Wes asks as the helmet comes down over his head.

"Don't worry," I say. "I know almost exactly what I'm doing."

"Which is?"

"Preparing to launch."

"Forward screens opening," Bob says.

A crystal-clear canopy materializes before us, reflecting familiar instrument readings. Beyond it, the sleek nose of the Astral Fighter, a breathtaking sight. And then, the launch tube itself—a cavernous expanse illuminated by a mesmerizing display of pulsing lights.

I check my helmet. It's a perfect fit, almost as if it were made for me.

"I am routing the Pisces Converter into your helmet," Bob says. "Can you hear me alright?"

"I can," I say.

"Me too," Wes says.

I turn to Wes. "You hear him?"

He nods. "Hi, Bob. I guess you're real."

"You did not think I was?"

"Well, if your questionably intelligent brother said there was a voice in his head talking through a tiny space fish, wouldn't you be a little skeptical?"

"Excellent point," Bob says.

"Questionably intelligent?" I say.

Wes looks at me. "You didn't learn the truth about Santa Claus until middle school."

I frown. "I'm still mad at you about that."

"You're my older brother. It was embarrassing."

A light flashes over my head, causing me to look up. The scene above is a stark contrast to the familiar piloting controls. This console is an alien monstrosity, a bizarre hybrid of jet fighter and antique steamboat. Banks of buttons, marked with indecipherable symbols, line the surface. Two digital displays, strangely familiar with their Earth-based numerals, flicker to life. Looming over it all are two colossal switches, their clunky design reminiscent of props from a low-budget sci-fi film. One is a vibrant blue, the other an ominous red. They seem important, especially when I realize that the digits on one of the screens is today's date.

"Ready to launch in ten," Bob says. "Stay sharp. I am sure they will be waiting for you."

"Hey, Bob, what's this stuff up here?"

"Don't touch any of that unless I say. Especially the Plumpercott Melon Matrix."

"None of those words made sense," Wes says.

"Pisces is glitching. There are no words in your language for the tech, so it's trying to extrapolate," Bob says. "Launching in five."

Still looking up, I say, "One screen has today's date. What's the other screen for?"

"It is for the other date."

"What date?"

"The destination."

"Destination?"

Wes looks like he's about to explode with joy. "Are we in a time machine?"

"Two, one, launch," Bob says.

"Ahhhhh!" Wes screams so loud I can barely hear someone else screaming. Me.

One moment we are looking down the narrow vertical shaft of the launch tube, the next we erupt into the vast blue canvas above Roswell, New Mexico. My rear screen fills with the shrinking scene: the parking lot we'd blasted out of; then the surrounding buildings turning into a toy town; and finally, the entire sprawl of Roswell dwarfs beneath our rapidly ascending Astral Fighter.

"Stop screaming!" Bob shouts.

I close my mouth and catch my breath. "Okay, okay, I got this," I say more to myself than anyone else. I seize the controls. "Okay, we're okay."

"You need to level off," Bob says. "We don't need you leaving the atmosphere."

"Don't leave the atmosphere," I repeat.

"Yes, please," Wes adds, "no leaving the atmosphere."

"You have done this before," Bob says. "Cut the thrust, maintain altitude."

My heart is pounding through my chest, but as I go through the motions, reducing thrust, checking the altitude, I take a deep breath. "Okay, and for the record, I've never done this."

"You executed a terrestrial launch in an Astral Fighter one thousand, seven hundred and one times in the Star Pilot simulator."

"Simulator. That is a just game," I say. "I never felt acceleration like that."

"And you did not feel any this time. You are in a completely motion-stabilizing environment. Best in the galaxy."

"Are you kidding?" Wes says. "It felt like an elephant was sitting on my chest."

"My brother's right. Must have been 4 or 5 Gs. I think I peed a little."

"No, it can't ... Oh wait," Bob says.

"What?"

"I forgot to engage the environmental stabilizers."

"Seriously?"

"Yeah, that must have been rough on your youthful biology. I do apologize."

"You're sorry?" Wes says. "Maybe we should have gone back up the stairs."

"Again, my apologies. We have never made it this far before. Switching on internal stabilization."

Somewhere in the back of my mind I register that Bob said something odd, but I don't have time to think about it as the suddenness of a new sensation envelops us, demanding my attention. Other than what I see on my screen and in the surrounding view screens, I can no longer tell we are moving. If I close my eyes, I could almost convince myself I am back home, perched in my Lifezeal gaming chair.

I glance at Wes. He looks relaxed. Well, not relaxed exactly, but he no longer looks like he's gonna spew again. Before we get to enjoy the sensation or lack thereof, the sensors go off.

"You have got incoming," Bob says.

I see it, approaching fast from below on the starboard side. "It's the sphere from Roswell."

"It's Reptilian," Bob says. "They will be in firing range in eight seconds."

"Firing range?" Wes says. "Aren't they gonna try and capture us? You know, give us a stern talking to?"

"Should I activate weapons?" I ask, moving my hand in that direction.

"Negative, Pilot. Evade, until I am ready."

"Ready to what?"

"To make the jump," Bob says. "I did not anticipate your brother's presence. You have never brought him before, and I need to recalculate, adjusting for the added mass."

"I object to being referred to as 'added mass,'" Wes says.

There are several things Bob said in the last six seconds that give me pause, and I really want to raise my hand and ask a question, but ...

"Star Pilot, evade!" Bob shouts.

My instincts take over. I drop us down, executing a sharp arc, and hit the thrusters. The sky vanishes from the viewscreen, replaced by a panorama of Earth. In an F-18, my brother and I would be plastered against our seats, but here, nothing like that happens. No sensation of movement, no pressure against our bodies. It is as if we are perfectly still, playing a video game as the world spins beneath us.

The maneuver takes the Reptilian sphere by surprise. For a brief second, the nose of the Astral Fight is aimed at my opponent before it breaks right. I check behind and watch in amazement as the craft changes direction so fast it doesn't even seem like a turn, more like a magic trick.

"Bob, we can't outmaneuver that craft, can we?"

"Not for long, no."

"It's coming back around," Wes says

"Bob, if I can't outmaneuver it, and you won't let me shoot it, what do you want me to do."

"Come on, Pilot, what is the Astral Fighter?"

I grin. "Speed."

"Punch it, kid," Bob says.

"Yeah." I hit the thrusters and watch the reading go from 535 kilometers an hour to 3,200.

The sphere falls away, and we see the Earth 3,000 meters below, moving like a rushing river.

"I think we lost it, Bob," I say.

"Maintain trajectory and altitude. At this speed, terrestrial obstructions can appear quite suddenly."

I understand, having skimmed the surface of alien planets at even faster velocities on a dozen or more alien worlds. The exhilaration of this real-life gaming moment is overwhelming, but nagging questions push through. I still don't know why this is happening. "Bob," I take a deep breath. "Can I ask you a question?"

"I am engaged in fifteen different computations at once, but go ahead."

"The game, *Star Pilot*, I've been playing it for the past two years. That's why I'm here?"

"Yes. I designed and placed that simulation in a dozen worlds where adolescents of a multitude of species have attempted to do what you did."

"Which is?"

"Finish the game."

"What does it mean?"

"It means you have the skills that give us the best chance of altering the course of galactic history."

"Galactic history?"

"Well, history to me, future to you," Bob says. "Remember the Progenitors' plan I informed you about?"

"The number nine thing, taking the galaxy over from the inside plan?"

"Yes, well they did it. They pulled it off. In my time, the only species that exist besides the Reptilians are slaves, living a life of misery and oppression."

"Even your kind?" Wes says.

"No, my species was fortunate. The Reptilians are aware of us, but my kind's ability to exist in bi-locations and access time has kept us safe. We exist just out of their reach, for now."

"What is it you need me to do?"

"I need you to jump back to your year 1997 and disrupt an event that took place over North American airspace."

"Okay ..." I shake my head, not feeling real good about the time travel aspect of Bob's plan. "Let's put a pin in that for a minute." I look around the ship. "This Astral Fighter is slightly different from the one I used in the game. Why is that?"

"All you needed to see in your simulated Astral Fighter was the piloting and fighting features of the ship. The simulator allowed me to assess your combat skills, which is what you will require if we are to be successful."

"Successful?" I say, feeling several veins in my head pulsing. "Look, Bob, I didn't agree to any of this."

"Yes, you did."

"I did not!"

"When you activated the game, you signed the Terms and Conditions. A legal custom on your planet, I believe."

"No, the custom is we don't read those!"

"They get you every time," Wes says.

"The terms say, and I quote, 'By engaging in this simulation, you agree to possible involuntary recruitment to defend the galaxy in all timelines against the Progenitor Armada—"

"Oh, for frak's sake, I was just playing a game!"

"Star Pilot, please relax. I am detecting elevated blood flow. All that is required of you is to continue to use the skills we know you possess. From my location, I can control many of the craft's functions, life support, energy distribution, and most important, the temporal honeymelon fluxseed. The piloting and the fighting are in your primitive but capable hands."

"I think the fish is glitching a bit, but I think I follow," I say. "If I'm being honest, I'm not super comfortable with the time travel thing."

"No need to concern yourself. I will coordinate the jump through the Nectar-fusion huckleberry-interface."

I shake my head. "Jeez, I hope that was glitch-inspired, 'cause it sounded like nonsense. Maybe I'd feel better if you explained a little how time travel works."

"You simply won't understand," Bob says. "I do not wish to sound impertinent, but I've seen your S.A.T. scores."

"That tracks," Wes chimes in.

"Wow, both of you. Hurtful."

"Look. Vegas," Wes says.

"What?"

"I think we're near Las Vegas."

I check the monitors, and even though we're moving 3,000 kilometers an hour, I can see the strange desert pyramid and surrounding city.

"Did you say Vegas?" Bob sounds surprised.

"Is that bad?" I say.

"Your line of flight takes you toward Area 51, restricted airspace," Bob says.

I check the monitor. A pair of F-22s from Edwards Air Force Base going Mach two are on an intercept course. "Bob's right," I say.

"The Earth planes are not the biggest problem at the moment. There is a Reptilian stronghold on the north end of Vegas. I'm sure they have detected you by now."

"I don't see any ..."

"James!" Wes shouts while pointing at the canopy on his side.

A horde of Reptilian spheres descend from above, firing on us before I can even react. We feel the first impact just as I activate forward shields. With the environmental stabilizers engaged, it's impossible to gauge how bad they hit us. The shields absorb the remaining enemy fire as the spheres zip by us on all sides like a swarm of enraged wasps.

"They're coming back," Wes says.

"I see 'em. Bob, how much longer to do that jumping away from here thing?"

"I need a little more time for precise calculations."

"Bob, can we skip the calculations and just hit the leave now button?"

"Time travel isn't like gaming, James. Without precise calculations, you could fly right through a star or bounce too close to a supernova, and that would end the trip real quick."

"Is he paraphrasing *Star Wars*?" Wes asks.

I stop listening to Bob and Wes as the damage report flashes on the screen. We've lost 40% of our thrust. My heart sinks realizing we can no longer outrun them. I activate weapons. "Bob, I'm gonna have to engage."

"Engage?" Wes says.

"Launching seeker mines, full spread," I shout as I release a barrage of enemy-hunting aerial bombs. The Reptilian crafts are approaching in two battle lines, each with a full squadron of fifty spheres. The forward line breaks apart, evading the bombs. The second line isn't so lucky. Explosions light up my monitor. Two years of experience acquiring battle tactics are now kicking in. I change direction diving toward the Earth. The closer I am to the surface, the better chance of confusing their sensors. As the ground fills the canopy, they fire.

Our shields are on full power, which means they must be manually adjusted during the battle. Something I didn't have to do a lot in the game. "Wes, I need your help."

Wes looks at me, eyes wide. "What?"

I point to a dial in between us. I grab it and move the shields to deflect the Reptilian's attack. "You have to rotate the shields around the ship."

Wes nods, puts his hands on the dial. "It's like Video Pong."

God bless Wes's love of vintage old-timey video games. "Yes," I say. "Like a very deadly, unfriendly version of Pong."

Wes spins the dial, deflecting the shots one after the other. With Wes on defense, I go back to offence. I have twice the amount of forward weapons than rear ones, so I turn the fighter around. "I'm taking it to them," I say to Wes as he moves our shield forward.

An impact slams the stern of our ship. "Sorry," Wes says. "One got through."

"That's okay," I say. "I think."

Another damage report flashes in front of me. One of Bob's interfaces is down, and I hope he doesn't need it as I open up the forward guns. A blinding wall of laser fire lights up the sky ahead of us, creating a path of exploding Reptilian spheres. Sweat rolls down my forehead as we emerge on the other side of what's left of the Reptilian ships.

"That was impressive," Wes says.

"I know, right?"

"I got some bad news," Bob says.

"Don't be a buzzkill, Bob."

"The temporal interface is down. I'll need you to manually engage the pastward plumpercott matrix."

"The pastward plumper? What the hell is that?"

"It's not in the game?" Wes asks.

I shake my head as something colossal descends from the clouds a mile above us. It is monstrous, triangular-shaped, with pulsating lights marking each corner. Between these points of light, a void of immense darkness seems to devour all sunlight.

"You need to pull the initiation switch above you," Bob says. "Then hold on."

Remembering the two huge switches over my head, I look up. Which one?

Before I ask, dozens of spheres emerge from the dark void above. No, hundreds.

"Which one, Bob? The blue or the red?"

"The pastforward initiator!" Bob screams.

"I don't know which one that is?"

"It is the one closest to the temporal flux-seeds. On the gluten side."

"Stupid glitching-fish. Are you serious, right now?"

"Yelling at the Pisces Convertor will only make it more flustered."

"James!" Wes screams. "They're firing."

So many projectiles are headed toward us, our screens can't track them all. We have seconds to live.

"Bob," I say. "The blue one or the red one?"

"Pull the condensed-flux. Look at persimmon pearberry!"

My screen flashes in terrifying letters, *IMPACT IN THREE SECONDS*.

I reach toward the switches. The blue one is closest to me, and the red one is nearer to Wes.

"Pull it now, you bi-pedal meatsack!" Bob shouts.

Pull the Blue Switch. Turn to page 126.

Pull the Red Switch. Turn to page 104.

"Gold Leader's command ended in his death," I remind Wes.

"True, but the advice was solid. Stay on target," he says. "That is how Luke eventually destroyed the Death Star."

"Ahhh. I hate it when you use *Star Wars* logic against me. Okay, Bob, we're going with the original plan. Harvest new parts."

"Understood, Star Pilot."

Wes looks relieved as we return to our original path and get back on track. Everything's smooth sailing until we pass a trio of Grey cosplayers doing maintenance on a section of the wall. Two of them are having a heated discussion about where to put which thingy where, when a very busty female Reptilian approaches them and barks some instructions. I'm trying not to look as we pass by, but I can't help myself, and the Reptilian catches my eye.

I look away, and we continue down the passage while I fight the urge to suspiciously pick up my pace.

Wes looks back. "I think she's following us."

I look back. Frak! Wes is right.

"What do we do?"

"This way." We take an abrupt turn down a corridor, half the size of the main passage we were in, and completely void of humans or aliens. It's so empty we can hear our bare feet slapping on the smooth floor. The sound echoes as we increase to power-walking speed, hoping to put distance between us and Lizard Lady. "Bob, we're taking a detour."

No response from Bob as we hurry in the new direction.

"Are you there, Bob?" Wes says.

I glance back and feel a wave of relief. She isn't behind us. My relief evaporates in an instant, as I collide with something both soft and scaly. Lizard Lady knew a short cut and got in front of us.

I bounce back from her, but she reaches out and grabs my shoulders. She is my height, and looks into my eyes. "Hey there," she says. "Message received."

I shake my head, hoping that's a universal gesture that means, *What the hell are you talking about?*

"You know, with the look," she says. "I could see it in your eyes. You're curious."

I step back and put my hands up between us.

She steps forward, putting her breasts up against my open palms. Shocked, my hands linger before I react.

"Status report," Bob says.

"James is having an unwanted close encounter," Wes whispers.

She looks over at my brother, then back at me. "Tell the little one to give us a moment." She waves a hand at Wes.

I look back at him and nod, indicating he should step back a little.

As Wes backs up, he whispers, "Bob, where do you keep going? Do you have other universes you're saving at the moment?"

I lower my hands further. She grabs my wrists and guides my hands to her hips. I don't have much choice. She is incredibly strong.

"I can't be with you every second. I am running multiple simulations and factoring actions against the melon co-germinator."

"I'll be straight with you," Lizard Lady says. "I am two days away from my hibernation cycle, and I have unfertilized eggs. My mate and I are ... we're not in a good place to fertilize, if you know what I mean."

I have no idea what she means, but I nod.

She pulls my waist against her, the ridges on her pelvis bones grinding into me. "What I'm saying is that I'm open to a little cross species fertilization before my mate and I go into the long sleep."

"Did she say cross species fertilization?" Bob asks.

"Yes," Wes says, no longer whispering.

"That is a terrible idea, James."

"It's not really his idea," Wes replies for me.

She presses up against my body and growls. Her lips part, displaying jagged teeth that are as alluring as a crocodile's, with breath to match.

"James, mating with a Reptilian could result in a violent death, or worse."

I don't need a disembodied voice from the other side of the galaxy to tell me that. I can see that in the forked tongue that slides out and licks the sweat off my cheek.

"GorNia!" comes a shout from behind me.

Lizard Lady looks startled and takes several steps back. Her vertical-slit-pupiled eyes widen.

Heavy footfalls sound from behind me, and before I turn to look, a huge male Reptilian is standing next to us. "You have been warned GorNia."

Her surprise fades and she turns her affections away from me and to the male. She steps in front of him and puts her hands on his chest. "Grig, Honey. Don't be mad."

"I have warned you. The sky gods have warned you. If they catch you again, you will be de-scaled. Do you want to be de-scaled?"

"Of course not. It's just that we enter hibernation in less than two days, and you know I love it when we make the beast with two tails, but I just need to spice things up a little. Add a little pink skin into the mix."

"I admire the dedication to spice things up, but remember what happened last time? There wasn't enough of that poor human left to make a decent eunuch to serve the Pharaohs."

She turns around, and for some stupid reason, I'm still standing there, a deer caught in the headlights. She slaps a clawed hand on my shoulder. "But this one seems strong. I think it could take it. It might even survive."

"Nonsense," Grig says, shoving my chest.

I'm only a meter from the wall, but my feet leave the floor. I slap into the surface behind me, and something cracks. As I collapse, I attempt to put my hands out to brace the fall, but they don't obey. A second later, my point of view is sideways and from the floor up. I see scaly feet around me.

"You broke him," GorNia says.

"You see, my love. They're as fragile as the Grey."

Wes runs to my side, kneeling. "Bob, James is down."

Down is right. I can't feel anything below my shoulders. My neck is broken.

"I am sorry, Grig."

A heavy sigh drifts down from above. "Okay. I'll take the bodies to the incinerator. If you promise this is the last time."

"Bodies?" Wes says. "Incinerator?"

"Run!" Bob shouts.

"It is the last time," GorNia says. "No more pink skin delight. Promise."

Wes jumps up, but he doesn't get far. His feet levitate off the floor. I can hear him choking. After a horrific crack, Wes is silent. Grig bends down, grabs me with his other hand, and throws me over his massive shoulder.

"Why don't I believe you?" Grig says. "My mother might have been right. She said I'd made a mistake when I selected yours from all the other talons in the aquarium."

"Oh, Grigy. My sweet Scaley-buns."

Grig turns away. "I'll see you in the hibernation chamber. Bring your own slumber cocoon. I don't know if I want to share mine." He moves down the passage dragging my brother's limp body like a droid with a dead motivator.

"Grig, please don't do this," GorNia says. "I'll let you do that thing you've always wanted to ..."

The correct choice was to disregard Gold Leader's command and choose the new plan.

Turn to page 150.

I move over to the control panel, stepping over Wes, who is lying on the floor trying to get the final kumquat into place.

"What are you doing?" Wes says.

"I'm readying a probe for launch."

"Who are we probing?"

"Hopefully no one. But just in case," I say. "How much longer?"

Wes sighs. "Well, based on all the times I've done this before, I'd have to say, I have *no* idea."

"He is doing fine," Bob says. "We should be back on course to 1997 in just a few minutes."

I activate a probe and set it to standby. "Yeah, about that. What exactly am I supposed to do?"

"In 1997, in the skies over a province you call Arizona, Plan 9 will take its initial steps for phase two."

"Phase two?" I say. "What was phase one?"

"Jeez," Wes says. "Phase one was to spread the Progenitors' Reptilian genetic code throughout the galaxy. Pay attention."

"I pay attention." I really don't.

"Phase two is to reestablish links with the Reptilians that have evolved on their respective planets," Bob says. "It all starts on Earth, in Arizona, in 1997. What happens there creates the template they use for reestablishing contact with their genetic creations."

Wes sits up. "Holy Close Encounters! The Phoenix Lights."

"What are you going on about?" I ask as I double check the probe's armaments.

"It's only one of the biggest UFO sightings in alien history. In 1997, lights appeared over the Phoenix area for hours. There were hundreds of witnesses."

"Fascinating," I say, not at all fascinated. I wave the spatula where Wes is working. "Look, less geeking out about alien folklore and more kumquat attaching. I want to get out of here."

I watch the monitor as the probe arrives at its launch bay, then I move back over to our slightly open hatch. "So, I'm supposed to party crash this reunion of Reptilians?"

"Yes," Bob says.

"And this will stop their Plan 9."

"Prognostication analysis via axel blonebeeries says not completely, but it will set them back."

"For how long?"

"For nearly two Earth centuries."

I shrug. "That's long enough for me."

Wes sits back up. "So we're just kicking this problem down the road for a few centuries?"

I glance back out the open hatch and catch sight of one of the platforms, and it seems to be heading our way. "We'll be long dead. It'll be someone else's problem."

"I'd like to have a family one day," Wes says. "Kids, and they might have kids."

I turn to Wes. "You know that family making involves talking to girls, right?"

Wes gets up. "I talk to girls."

"Our cousins don't count. Are you done? Can we go?"

"It's going to take a few moments for the kumquat alignment," Bob says. "The hummus matrix needs to adjust to the Greys' tech."

I shake my head. "I hate hummus."

"Bob," Wes says. "Isn't there a more permanent solution to the Reptilians trying to take over the galaxy? Pushing them back a few hundred years seems so pointless."

"Nothing in this universe is permanent, Wes," Bob says. "But I do understand. We have considered longer term solutions, but the applications are abhorrently immoral."

"More immoral than enslaving the galaxy?" Wes counters.

As Bob and Wes keep debating, the platform I had thought might be heading for us is now definitely heading for us. They're still sweeping and scanning, so they must not see us yet, but their speed has increased, and at least two other flying balconies have joined them.

"Hey, Bob," I say, interrupting their debate. "How long for the adjustment?"

"One kumquat aligned, two to go."

"Not what I asked." I slap the control that closes the hatch, then move to the pilot seat. "Strap in, Wes. We need to move as soon as we're able." I look up at the time controls, which I have no idea how to set. "How much longer, Bob?"

"Two kumquats aligned."

"Again, not what I asked, Bob!"

"Do not power the engines yet," Bob says.

"They'll detect us?"

"Correct."

"Just buckling in. Wes, get your helmet on. It's gonna be a fast takeoff."

"Still detecting explosions on the main ship," Bob says. "The chaos you created caused considerable damage."

"Just like level 42."

"Yes, but I think it made the Greys highly motivated to locate you."

"You mean they're pissed."

"That is what I said."

"I'm gonna open the external view. One monitor shouldn't be detectable."

"I concur. The final kumquat is almost aligned."

One monitor flickers to life at my left. "Is it my imagination, or is the final kumquat taking longer than the others?"

"It is, but it must root to the other two stalks via a peel-seed connection."

"Of course it does," I say, and reach for the alien spatula I'd taken from the Grey ship. "Hey, Bob, any idea what this is?"

"Can't see it. Let me access the cabin cameras." After a beat, Bob shouts, "Put that down!"

"Frak, okay." I set it back down on the control panel. "Is it dangerous?"

"In the hands of a primitive biped, yes!"

"Stop yelling. Is it a weapon?"

"It's a lot of things. An eviscerator, an atomizer, a tech disruptor, nero paralyzer—"

"Okay, okay," I say. "You had me at eviscerator. How does it work?"

"Leave it alone. You are more likely to liquify your brother's insides than do anything productive with it."

Wes shoots me a horrified glance.

"Fine," I say. Never mind that I've been playing with the thing like an eight-year-old fondles a fidget spinner for the last twenty minutes. Doesn't seem all that dangerous to me. But there are a few nobs I haven't fiddled with yet.

"They're almost on us," Wes says, gazing at the view screen. He's right, and there is something else bothersome. The Grey piloting the lead hovering platform has a device around his skinny neck. If I were to make a guess, I'd say it's a medical brace to support his neck and head. And if I were to make another guess, I would say someone punched him in the throat and broke his neck. Might explain the look of bloodthirsty vengeance in his already black eyes.

"Bob, we really need to go," I say.

"James," Wes says. "I think they found us."

One of the platforms veers towards us. It's accelerating, and the other two craft follow.

"The alignment needs just a few more seconds," Bob says.

We don't have a few more seconds. The lead platform reveals what is clearly a weapon. It rises up from the platform to the Grey's waist level and looks like a cross between a child's seesaw and a harpoon gun. A Grey moves over to operate it, and as we are an unmoving target, I suspect he doesn't need to be an exceptional marksman to destroy us.

With a closed fist, I hit the control panel and launch the probe, making sure it's armed and ready to fire the moment it takes flight. As soon as it's airborne, I fire its pulsar cannons. I didn't wait to aim; I really just wanted to draw their attention. Which it does.

The Greys return fire, swiftly disabling the probe with a surprisingly brilliant explosion. Before it crashes, I launch another. The probe distraction tactic is working, but it's not a long-term solution.

"Wes, remember how to rotate the shields?" I ask as I power up the engines and activate external shielding.

"Yes."

The second probe sustains damage but remains in the air. I quickly maneuver it, adjusting its turret and this time, take aim before firing. Lasers strike the lead platform, causing it to list heavily. Metallic debris cascades from the platform as two of the three Greys are ejected, plummeting into the sand below.

I smile, watching them both head plant into the ancient Egyptian soil. The remaining Grey rights himself, or itself—it's difficult to guess their pronouns—and takes control of the harpoon-like weapon. He fires.

I brace for the impact, but Wes is on it. He rotates the shields and somehow adjusts the deflection to maximum. The shot hits its target and rocks the ship. I wish I could return fire. The Astral Fighter's weapons are too close to the sand to be usable.

"Bob, can I get a status report on our kumquats?"

"We have alignment!" Bob shouts.

"Bout fracking time." I ignite the engines. "Let's blow this taco stand."

We ascend fast and rough, but the environmental stabilizers maintain a sense of stillness within the cockpit. I check the rear view, and surprise-surprise, the hovering balconies are in pursuit. I engage the Astral Fighter's weapon systems, but before they are fully armed, the Greys abruptly break off the chase and vanish from sight.

"Incoming!" Bob shouts.

Even before I see the energy missiles on my screen, I know what has happened. The moment I powered the engines, the main ship found us and fired. I abruptly alter course, abandoning our ascent, and level off at two hundred meters. I check the missiles' trajectory.

Frak. They change their course to intercept us.

"Okay, let's see if they can do this." As the missiles close in on us, I wait for them to get near enough and hope that my years of gaming have been worth it. When the moment is right, I try a Herbst Maneuver, a rapid 180 degree turn while maintaining altitude. The first fifty times I tried this in *World of Warplanes*, I crashed my P-40 Warhawk spectacularly. This is the first time I'll try it in an Astral Fighter, and in real life. When the missiles are at .25 kilometers, I execute.

I know the stabilizers are on, but in my mind and gut I can feel the turn like a rollercoaster car that has left the track. I grip the controls, trying to will the ship back onto the rails. We're losing altitude. Not a good sign.

Wes can sense I may have made a huge mistake, or maybe he's just reading the panic on my face. "Anything I can do?"

I want to say, *Pray*, but neither of us know how.

My hands move faster than my brain, and I barely register what I'm doing. The undercarriage thrusters fire, leveling the Astral Fighter. I cut the thrust as the ship makes a 180 turn. In the monitor, missiles zip by, one on either side of us. They don't seem to be following, but I know that's temporary. They have seen their prey, and they won't relent until they exhaust their fuel or hit something.

"Hey, Bob. I take it they've locked onto us."

"Affirmative. They are coming back around."

"Can I outrun them?"

"Not in the atmosphere," Bob says.

I knew that. I just needed confirmation from a time-traveling space fern. I've got a choice to make and not much time to make it.

Remaining in the atmosphere causes too much drag on the ship, making the more aerodynamic energy missiles much faster, but if I aim the nose of the ship toward the heavens and hit the thrusters, there is a chance we can make it to space, where our superior engines can outrun them.
Turn to page 211.

Pilot the Astral Fighter back toward Earth and look for an alternative target for the missiles.
Turn to page 205.

Wes has the right idea about getting out of the ship, but as a big brother, I'm not allowed to make anything easy for him. Even if we are over 4,500 years away from being born.

Wes and his shiny bald dome wait in front of the exit door. I set my helmet on the console and say, "So, you're just going to ignore the all-knowing fish-thing in my ear's suggestions?"

Wes faces me. "Who says he's all-knowing?"

"Well, he does, mostly." I join him at the door. His missing eyebrows are creeping me out. A good reminder for me not to look in any reflective surfaces. "It'll be nice to move around a bit."

"Let's do it," he says, his hand hovering over the button.

I panic and grab his wrist. "Hold on. What about the air? Can we breathe it?"

"We're still on Earth, so yeah."

"Well, is there oxygen on all the lands of Earth. You know, back then?"

Wes looks at me confused. "Sometimes you say things, and it just hurts my head." He presses the button. The door slides open, and a small ramp descends to the sand.

"Just messing with you. I know there's oxygen all over Earth." I'm like ninety percent sure. We step out into the past, which is way hotter than it needs to be. I ask, "Can you hear that?"

Wes freezes at the bottom the ramp, looks all around. "What?"

"Chill," I say, waving him on.

"Well, what is it? What'd you hear?"

"Mom yelling at us to put on sunscreen."

He groans and heads up the small hill toward a bush.

"Where you going? No one's around."

He unzips and steps closer to the bush. "I do me, and you do you."

"Fair enough." I do a quick calculation and take hold of myself, surprised at just how damn smooth I am. It's been four hours and a Big Gulp since I've pissed. I unleash a healthy stream to carve a wavy W, the E a little less bold. I'm finishing the S and look up, startled by the sand rippling a few feet behind Wes.

I cut off my peeing mid-stream, soaking my shorts, but I don't care because something is slithering up on my brother. "Wes!"

He shrugs me off, looking down like he's still mourning his missing pubes.

I run up the hill, tripping, scrambling, getting back up. The snake is firehose thick, jet black, and parks right behind Wes, well within striking range. I stop a few feet back and toss a handful of sand at it, which feels like firing a squirt gun at a mountain lion.

The cobra aggressively twists, flaring its menacing hood. Its face hovers two feet off the ground, and its body, fully unraveled, stretches at least as long as I am.

I freeze, not a muscle moving except my heart, threatening to explode out of my chest. "Wes," I say, as serious as a funeral. "Do not move."

The cobra keeps its eyes on me, swaying.

Wes doesn't move his feet, just his hand. *Zip.*

The cobra whips around to strike Wes, but I snatch its body like one of those pro hunters I've seen on YouTube. Unlike the pro hunters I've seen on YouTube, I have no idea what I'm doing, and I grabbed it way too fraking close to its head. It darts down, its fangs burying into my forearm.

I scream and release my grip, but the cobra hangs on, the venom burning in my veins.

Wes knocks it off me and into the bush.

I keep screaming and fall to my knees, holding my hand over the bite like it can make it go away.

"Status report," Bob says.

It takes all I have to say, "Snake."

"What kind?" Bob asks

"C-cobra," I manage.

Wes screams, "We need anti-venom!"

Bob is telling me the same thing but using way more words.

Wes can't hear what Bob's saying, and I can't say much more than a word, each breath harder to take. "Hold on. There must be some in the ship," he says, running for the Astral Fighter.

"The Egyptian cobra's venom can kill prey in seconds and large enemies within fifteen minutes," Bob says.

Wes runs out of the ship, helmet on. "I'm afraid James is more of a medium-sized prey," he tells Bob as he bear crawls up the hill.

"Then let's say you have a solid six minutes or so to get your brother back into the ship. Just don't let him get bit ag—"

"Owww!" I scream as fangs puncture my calf.

As my vision blurs, I see Wes kick sand at the cobra. Unfazed by the sand, the snake turns and strikes, sinking its fangs into the top of my brother's foot. He screams and falls back, as I close my eyes.

The correct choice was to stay inside and give Bob a minute.

Turn to page 8.

An explosion in the direction of the pyramids catches my attention. The Greys' ship is in serious distress, and it gives me an idea. I bank hard and head straight for it.

"What're you doing?" Wes asks. "You're going toward the aliens that are trying to kill us?"

"I'm gonna return these missiles to sender," I announce, thinking that was a pretty darn clever thing to say.

"I don't know what that means," Wes says.

"Figures." I take the fighter down, hugging the terrain; what jet pilots call nap-of-the-earth flying. "Hey, Bob, any idea of the distance between the Greys' hull and the ground when they are docked on an alien planet."

"I would have to research that."

"Can you just eyeball it for me? My scans and line of sight are blocked by the dunes."

"Why are we so low?" Wes shouts.

"We're not that low. Trust me."

"I think I just saw a snake!"

I bank hard, skimming a massive dune. "Bob!"

"Given the uneven terrain, and the listing of the ship, I'd say less than three-point-five meters."

"And if I remember the Astral Fighter specs, it's three-point-eight meters wide."

"Yes," Bob says.

I grin. "Perfect."

"What?" Wes says. "That is not how measurements work, at all."

"I have good news," Bob says. "That last maneuver took out one of the missiles. It exploded into the dunes, upsetting a tribe of nomads on the other side."

"Well, everybody has problems today." I check my readings. "Time to the Greys' ship—ten seconds."

"The missile will catch you in eight," Bob says.

"Not a problem," I say.

"No, big problem," Wes says. "Your math is terrible!"

I just need a few extra seconds, and I know how to get them. I head straight at the next dune, full throttle. It's the size of a Vegas casino, and I wait until the Astral Fighter is over its parking lot before I pull the stick back. The missile has more velocity, but it can't maneuver as sharp. We race up the wall of the dune and dive back down when it crests. In the rearview screen, the missile tries to adjust to follow, but slams into the top of the sand mound. Right into the penthouse. Unfortunately, it doesn't explode, but emerges through the other side. I hope the collision gave us the few extra seconds I need. No time to check.

We zip up the causeway so close to the ground, ancient pedestrians are diving out of the way. The edge of the fighter is meters away from the procession of future pyramid blocks as the Greys' massive ship comes into view. From this angle, I can see the gap under the ship, and it's not a constant. The vessel is listing to port about twenty degrees, making the gap I need to thread a bit wider on one side. But to keep things interesting, blue flames explode from the ship's undercarriage through breaches in the hull. The side with the wide gap is full of blue flames.

"If you get me killed, I'm telling Mom!"

"Shut up, Wesley."

The Astral Fighter streaks under the colossal vessel. A storm of blue flames envelops our ship. I stop breathing and hold our course. After a moment that feels like a lifetime, we emerge from the plasma fire. My console flashes, telling me there is damage, but I don't have time to deal with it. A massive limestone-covered pyramid fills my viewscreen.

Wes points ahead. "Look out, pyramid!"

"I see it!" I bank hard, and the fighter scrapes against the pyramid's smooth, limestone skin.

"Another pyramid!"

"I see it." I turn again, ridiculously sharp, to avoid the collision.

Wes points at the viewscreen. "Cows!"

Levitating bovine stampede across our flight path. Instinctively, I dive. Hooves run over the Astral Fighter's roof. Just as we clear the herd, Wes screams again. "Look out for the—"

A proximity alarm drowns Wes out as a colorful structure fills my view.

"Oh, Frak!" I don't believe I thought about rolling the ship; I just did it. The view flips forty-five degrees. The maneuver gives us enough clearance to minimize a collision but not avoid it. We both feel it like an asteroid to the hull. "Hell, what was that?"

We both gaze at the rear screen and are mesmerized as the Sphinx's nose tumbles to the earth. The damage alert snaps me back. We've got hull damage, and one of the atmospheric stabilizers is way out of alignment, but we can stay airborne.

"Hey, Bob. I'm ready to leave this time zone."

"I am downloading the instructions into the Honeyflux-seeds. I may need you to activate the plumpercott melon matrix. If you can manage not to crash into any more ego structures, we should be ready to jump in a minute."

I'll be damned, but I think I'm starting to understand the fruit-infused glitches. I could do without Bob's sarcasm, though.

"I told you to look out," Wes says. "How could you not see the Sphinx?"

"Do you have any idea how fast we were moving? Stop side-seat piloting."

I find a nice cruising altitude and switch off all the alarms. The lights on my console stop flashing, and I look over at Wes. His arms are folded. Being strapped into his seat doesn't allow him to slouch in anger, but I can tell he wants to. Before I ask, a light flashes.

Proximity alert.

I just turned that off.

Then our shields start to go down.

"Are you messing with the shields?"

Wes unfolds his arms just enough to show me his hands. "No."

There's the sound of metal on metal above us. I activate an external view. A hovering platform has just landed on the roof.

"Ah, crap on a cracker." I spin the ship, hoping to throw them off.

Wes sits forward, eyeing the monitor. "They're still there."

"I see 'em, Let's see if they can rodeo."

"What?" Wes says.

I throw the ship into a chaotic dance, plunging and twisting in a desperate attempt to dislodge the clinging aliens.

Wes slaps a hand over his mouth. "I'm gonna be sick."

"Close your eyes. Don't look at the view screen."

"Hey, my sensors indicate the ship has unaccounted for weight," Bob says. "You may have intruders."

"Thanks, Bob. I'll check on that," I say, taking us lower.

My plan is to roll the ship as we skim over a dune and give our uninvited passengers a massive headache. In the moonlight, I see a dune that fits the bill: high, massive, and directly ahead. I get ready to roll the ship, and we hear it again, that metal on metal sound. Another of the Greys' flying balconies has found us.

"Our problems are multiplying," Wes says.

"The more the merrier," I say, and spin the ship like a top.

I gotta hand it to the Greys. They can rodeo. Of the four Greys on the outside of the ship, two on each platform, only one flew off, leaving Broken Neck flying solo.

At least they are on the outside, unless ...

"Bob, can they get inside?"

"They are an intelligent and advanced species," Bob says. "Of course they can get in!"

"Well, they couldn't navigate Legos, so it's a legit question."

A bright blue light from behind us flashes like a slow strobe.

"They're in!" Wes screams, looking behind us.

I turn slightly, just enough to see three Greys in the rear section. They have us dead to rights. Broken Neck even brought a spatula of his own. My bet is he knows how to use it. A stupid idea pops in my head, and I've got seconds to see how stupid it is.

"Bob, shut down the environmental stabilizers."

"What?"

"Now, Bob," I shout as a Grey aims his spatula.

A wave of nausea moves through me as the full effects of moving at nearly 200 kilometers an hour at a 35-degree angle hit me. I push through the nausea. "Now, let's rodeo."

I reduce speed and invert the ship. Three loud thuds sound behind us as the Greys, with superior intelligence, suffer the full impacts of not wearing a seatbelt.

The sound of Wes throwing up is slightly audible over the Greys tumbling on our ceiling. I bank back and forth, hearing them slam into the walls. The spatula I had set on the console rolls into my lap. I place a hand on it and look over my shoulder. I'm pretty sure two Greys are unconscious or dead. Neither try to resist the twists and turns, tumbling around like damp clothes in the dryer. The third, Broken Neck, is still trying to right himself. Perhaps the device on his neck is giving him a leg up on his interstellar comrades.

Broken Neck is crawling for a spatula weapon two meters away.

Frak!

I roll the ship and hit the thrusters. "Bob, how much longer till we jump out of here."

"The ship's weight is way off. I have to adjust."

"That wasn't my question."

"A minute," Bob says. "Do you remember which plumpercott to pull on the melon matrix?"

"Jesus! Yes."

I look back at the Grey inching toward the weapon. There are two possible courses of action, and if I'm being perfectly honest, I'm not enthusiastic about either of them.

Give the ship one more dangerous spin, sending the Grey flying. Put the ship on autopilot, and go take on the Grey hand-to-hand. I bested him once. Maybe I can do it again.

Turn to page 176.

Bet big on Wes's natural mechanical instincts and hand him the Spatula. Tell him to wipe the vomit off his chin and figure this out before the Grey finds his weapon.

Turn to page 22.

"We can't outrun them in the atmosphere," I say to Wes.

"Bob just said that. So what do we do?"

"Try to outrun them."

"Yeah, but that would mean ..."

I tilt the Astral Fighter's nose to aim at the heavens. Earth leaves our view screens, and all we see are stars.

"You're taking us into space," Wes says.

"We're in a spaceship. It was bound to happen eventually." I put the truster to full.

Wes scrunches in his seat. "I just assumed it would be later rather than sooner. I don't know if I'm ready for space."

"Dude, you've time traveled, snuck aboard a Grey's spaceship, stolen engine parts, and reinstalled them in another spaceship."

"Yeah, well I wasn't ready for any of that either."

"Missiles closing," Bob says.

A vertical accent is the hardest on the engines, fuel, power, and everything else we need to survive, but it's also the shortest distance to leaving the atmosphere. I check our speed, and it's not giving me joy. I know we're fighting the full force of gravity, but at maximum power, we should be going faster and accelerating.

"Bob, I think something is wrong with the engines."

"I don't think the auto-flush was complete. Did you do it manually?"

"What're you talking about?"

"After a rough landing, the engines need a few moments to flush out terrestrial matter before demanding peak performance. It is covered in the basic Star Pilot e-manual."

"Oh, that."

"Star Pilot, you did read it thoroughly?"

"I skimmed it. Honestly, if there wasn't schematics or pictures I—"

"You skimmed it?" Wes shouts.

"Frak," I say as the port engine begins to stall. I divert power to compensate. "The manual was really long. Besides, flushing engines never came up in the game."

"What do you mean, 'it never came up'?" Wes says.

"I'm too good a pilot to crash. I blew up a few times, but I never crashed."

"Oh, great," Wes says. "We're going to die because of your gaming hubris and poor reading habits."

"We're not going to die." I check the missiles' trajectory. My blood runs cold. The missiles are closing in fast. Another engine sputters. A warning light flashes—*Impact in ten seconds*. Okay, we might die.

"You are losing speed, Star Pilot."

"I'm aware." I wasn't, but ... Okay, new plan. Cut engines. The ship's heat signature will go cold. We go into a power dive, head straight into the barrage, use stabilizing thrusters to maneuver. They don't create much heat, and we should be able to dodge the missiles like asteroids. Really fast moving, explosive asteroids. I can do this.

At just under seventy kilometers above the Earth, I execute. I cut the remaining engines, and just like a stunt plane, the Astral Fighter goes into a Hammerhead Turn. When the nose is down, I move both hands over the stabilizing thrusters. I need full concentration.

Impact in seven seconds.

"We are diving *at* the missiles?" Wes shouts.

"Yep."

"Please just tell me, is this a strategy or suicide? Either way, I need to prepare."

It's a good question. "It's just like dodgeball."

Impact in four seconds.

"I hate dodgeball," Wes whimpers.

"Star Pilot," Bob says, "the odds of this strategy being successful—"

"Never tell me the odds!" I shout.

Impact in two seconds.

I take a breath and engage port thrusters. The ship flips 180 degrees. I can almost feel the missile as it whips by, skimming our undercarriage. I engage dual thrusters, sending us back as two more missiles zip by, close enough to read their manufacturer's serial numbers.

Three down, four to go. I might pull this off. I check the sensors. Three missiles have maneuvered into a triangle configuration. I don't know if the gap is big enough. I don't have time to think. I fire the starboard stabilizers and spin the ship like a whirligig. All three projectiles pass us by.

One more.

Where is number seven? It's getting harder to see. Sensors are flickering, and there are flames. Why are their flames?

"Are we on fire?" Wes asks.

"Aerodynamic Heating," Bob says. "The outside of the craft is heating up like a capsule on reentry."

"Dammit," I shout, realizing my mistake.

"Do you think it locks on heat?" Wes says.

There is no time to answer.

Boom.

The correct choice was to pilot the Astral Fighter back toward Earth and look for an alternative target for the missiles.

Turn to page 205.

This is probably the prettiest light show I've ever seen, but unfortunately, there's no doubt it's the deadliest. With all these laser beams and energy blasts, there's no way we're making it back to the store. If we're lucky, we'll just get abducted. There must be another way.

The smell of the closest dumpster draws my attention again. It looks super durable and strong enough to protect us.

I point it out to Wes. "Let's wait this out in that thing."

Wes, courageous as a kitten, is already on his feet, running for it.

No one's looking, so I chase after him. The smell increases exponentially the closer we get. I'm not looking forward to the intensity of the smell at ground-zero, but we're too close to turn back. We're side by side when we leap for the top of the dumpster, the horrific aroma hitting us like a wave.

Wes thumps against the side with a loud *oomph,* while I pretend I'm a parkour pro and vault over the lip, flying in feet first. My eyes go hazy, and my involuntary gags take on a life of their own at the rotting sea salty stench of what it must be like to fall headfirst into a whale's anus. But the smell is nothing compared to the immense pain in my stomach, like the worst gut punch in the history of gut punches.

The sharp metal tip of a table-top umbrella angled up has pierced my belly. The pole doesn't give, but my flesh does. Momentum sends me forward, driving down the pole. It bursts out my mid-back, but misses severing my spine because, holy fraking hell, I feel every bit of pain, my screams amplified with the echo.

"What?" Wes asks as he lowers himself down, not letting go of the lip until his toes can touch. With both hands over his nose, he faces me and gags. One hand drops to cover his mouth as he gags again.

I try to push myself up using the aluminum pole that skewered me. My hands are too bloody, and I can't get a grip. I slide back down. Wes gags again, and I meet his eyes. "Does it look bad?"

Wes lowers a hand, to say something, but all that comes out is vomit. The warm stream splatters the side of my head and neck and really enhances the dumpster's aroma, like adding rotten eggs to spoiled milk. I puke but mine is full of blood.

I know I'm dying, but at least I don't have to breathe dumpster stench anymore.

The correct choice was to go with my little brother's idea, a sibling I used to affectionately call Turd Blossom.

Turn to page 86.

"This sucks," I shout, turning to Uncle Bob. "You said this place was better than Six Flags. I want to go home."

The MP stops moving, and for a second, the only sound is the grind of the elevator.

"I mean where's all the cool stuff, Unk?" I continue. "All we've seen is some boring old army dudes, some stupid labs, and nothing that looks like a flying saucer. You said we might see a spaceship! A real fracken spaceship."

Uncle Bob's mouth opens, and I'm sure the time traveling fern is as stunned as the MPs are.

I point at Uncle Bob. "Mom says you're a loser, you've always been a loser, and she hates inviting you for Thanksgiving. She only does it because she promised Grandma she would, so you won't be alone for the holidays." I look back at Wes with a *come on, join in* grin.

Wes smirks and points to me. "Dumbass is right. This is so lame. It's worse than the camping trip you took me on. Take us home, or I'll tell Mom that secret I'm supposed to keep. You know the one."

My eyes go wide. *What the frak, Wes?*

Just then, the elevator jolts to a halt. Mechanical gears lock in place, and the door slides open. The MP shoulders his rifle. The other one looks at Uncle Bob and salutes. "We'll let you get back to it, Lieutenant."

Uncle Bob returns the salute and mumbles, "Thank you, Corporal."

We stand still as they exit. When we're alone in the huge elevator, Bob says, "What was that about?"

I smile and hold my hand up in the air toward Wes. "That is our new and improved improvising skills," I say as Wes gives me a high five. "That was great, Wes. You went dark. Camping secret?"

"Yeah, I figured our fictional Uncle Kevin let me have a beer on a camping trip. Mom would hate that." Wes looks at me curiously. "Why, what were you thinking?"

I nod my head. "The beer thing. That was it."

* * *

After we leave the elevator, Uncle Bob moves fast. We tuck in behind him and match his steps. I try to look at what we're moving past because I'm sure it's all top secret, but Bob doesn't give us any time to sightsee.

We slip through an unmarked door that is clearly not a front entrance and emerge into the dry evening air, not unlike Egypt four thousand years ago. Searchlights sweep across the compound as we zigzag through a motor pool filled with vehicles in various states of disrepair. Many look like they haven't moved in years.

Uncle Bob stops at a jeep old enough for General Patton to have driven. He crouches down and points to a hangar about twenty meters away. "The Astral Fighter is in there."

"What about the hull damage?" I ask.

Uncle Bob grins, then explains he has spent the past fifty years borrowing Area 51 engineers and steadily guiding them with the repairs. Step by step, he allowed them to believe they were innovative, coming up with amazing scientific leaps in order to conduct the restoration. He even used a synthetic version of my DNA to allow them to access and temporarily power the ship, giving them the hope that one day they might be able to fly it.

"I had to make use of what we had here on Earth," Bob says, "so it may look a little patched together. I even used the bottom of the Greys' hovering platform to seal a breach in the hull. It's not pretty, but it will fly."

Uncle Bob takes a duplicate security key from his shirt pocket and hands it to me. "Randle's code is 108-387."

"You're not coming?"

"I'm going to take Lt. Randle's body to a safe place and release him, then reconnect with you via the Pisces Converters."

"So, you'll be in our heads again?" Wes says.

"Unfortunately. Being in your heads is very limiting."

I ask, "Is that an intelligence crack?"

"In your heads, I'm blind and don't have a real sense of what is going on. I must depend on your status reports, which are very lacking, to say the least."

"Is Uncle Kevin gonna be okay?" I ask.

"He will be disorientated, but otherwise unharmed."

"That is not what I mean. How much trouble is he in?"

"A considerable amount. They will link his codes to your escape, and he will be taken into custody. His inability to recall anything will work in his favor, as there have been a rash of engineers reporting memory lapses. He will avoid the stockade, but he will be dishonorably discharged."

"Is there anything we can do to avoid that?" Wes asks.

"No. Now get going." Without another word, Uncle Bob stands, turns, and jogs back the way we came.

"Bob's cold," Wes says.

"Have you ever met a warm plant?"

"Good point."

I scan the open ground we must cross to reach the ship. Every few seconds, a searchlight beam sweeps across the area, but there are definitely enough gaps that two teenagers, lost-in-time, could slip through.

I turn to Wes. "You ready to finish this adventure?"

"I swear to God, if we make it back alive, I'm never leaving home again."

I nod. "Right there with you. Come on."

We move across the sparsely lit area, pausing twice to let searchlights pass us by. Reaching the adjacent building, we press ourselves against the exterior wall. It feels like metal, perhaps aluminum. I manage to open the side door using Uncle Kevin's duplicated keycard and code, and enter the hangar. It's vast, easily large enough to house several commercial airliners, but only one craft sits inside. In the center of this colossal space rests the Astral Fighter.

It sits alone, like an endangered species in a vast enclosure built for its protection. Even from this distance, I can see it's different. The exterior is a patchwork of colors, representing the skill level of the scientists Bob borrowed. I hope they did their best and focused on function because they clearly were not concerned with looks.

I glance at Wes. His expression reminds me of the one Princess Leia had right before she said to Han Solo, "You came in that thing?"

We're standing in plain sight like a couple of morons. I grab Wes's wrist and pull him behind a piece of large, slightly dusty equipment that provides decent cover. We peek around it, scanning for anyone we need to avoid—which is, essentially, everyone. Half a dozen uniformed soldiers mill around the enormous hangar doors, which look like they could accommodate a blimp. Currently, they're open just wide enough for a golf cart. I don't see anyone else nearby, and I think we can make it to the ship at a full run before they can react, *if* they even notice us. Right now, they're mostly focused on something outside the doors, into the night. One even appears to be talking to someone just beyond the doorway.

"Alright," I say. "We walk straight to the ship. Don't run until they see us."

"And when they do?"

"Haul ass."

"What if it's locked?" Wes says.

"Can't be." I hold up my hand. "DNA key."

Wes rolls his eyes. "Sorry, I forgot. You're the *one*."

"And don't you forget it." I stand, then motion for Wes to follow me to the ship.

We're halfway across the vast hangar when one of the soldiers turns our way. A split second later, they all turn our way, shouting. I can't hear what they're saying over my voice shouting, "Run!"

The soldiers sprint toward us, moving much faster than us. Apparently, trained soldiers are in significantly better sprinting condition than American teenagers. But it doesn't matter. We're at the ship. The hatch controls look slightly different, but I place my palm on the hull, and the ship instantly recognizes me. The door opens, and we duck inside.

I'm about to close the hatch when we hear gunfire. Bullets ricochet off the hull. I need to get this door shut *now*, before bullets bounce around inside. I slap the door controls and dive for cover as sparks erupt within the ship. Wes and I huddle on the floor as the door slides closed.

Finally, it shuts, and we hear the hiss as air pressure is equalized, securing us inside. I ask Wes if he's hit.

He shakes his head. "You?"

"If I am, there is nothing we can do about it now." I jump to my feet and pull him up. "We're outta here."

Bullets continue to hit the outside of the ship. I'm pretty sure they can't shoot their way inside, but the sooner we get the shields up and get this thing in the air, the better.

We jump in our seats, and I deploy the helmets. Just before we get them on, I hear a voice.

"Status report."

It's been a while since I've had Bob's voice in my head, fifty years to be exact, and even though I should be used to it, the sudden sound startles me.

"James, Wes, status report," Bob says.

"Status?" I say. "There is an annoying plant-person shouting in my head. Can you turn the volume down?"

"My apologies. I thought you couldn't hear me."

"We hear you," Wes says.

I gesture to the shield dial, and Wes is on it. He rotates the shield to cover where the bullets are hitting. Their ricocheting sound muffles as if they are bouncing off a giant, impenetrable pillow.

I power up the ship. "Did you get Uncle Kevin's body to safety?"

"Your bi-pedal family friend is fine. Worry about our situation."

Uncle Kevin is a nice guy, and I feel bad knowing what we've done to him. "Excuse me for caring. It just seems like we've effed up his life a bit, don't you think?"

"He will be fine."

"Are you kidding? In our time he's a Trekkie nerd, who dresses like a Klingon, and lives with his mom."

"My research suggests the phrase *Trekkie nerd* is redundant. Furthermore, did you even know the one you call Uncle Kevin?"

"Well, sure." I shrug. "I mean, a little."

"Your superficial assessment of him is accurate, but if you had dug a little deeper, you would know that he invented a security application that he sold for twenty-two million dollars, and now he spends all his time on the things he loves, which includes *Star Trek*. And yes, he does live with his female parent—in a five-million-dollar mansion on the beach in Santa Barbara."

"Good for Uncle Kevin," Wes says, strapping into his seat.

"Wow," I say. "You really can't judge a book by its Klingon cover."

"James, they stopped firing at us."

Wes is right. I give the ship some thrust, just enough to lift us off the ground. We hover at about two meters as the soldiers open the doors to the hanger.

"Why're they opening the doors?" Wes says. "We're stealing their ship."

"Bob, I think they're letting us go," I say.

"Then what are you waiting for? Our rendezvous with the Reptilian Progenitors is in less than twenty Earth minutes."

It feels odd. I rotate the ship, bringing the bow around to face the hangar doors, hoping to get a better look at what they're doing. Beyond the doors lies only darkness. We can make out figures moving, but nothing more. When the door opens wide enough for the Astral Fighter to pass through, I know I have to make a decision. It shouldn't, but it feels like one of those life-or-death choices. Each incorrect decision brings me closer to brain damage. My least favorite kind of damage.

Hit the thrusters and escape through the open hanger door.
Turn to page 146.

Just like Cloud City, an open door can be an invitation, or a trap. Find another way out.
Turn to page 69.

There's no time for hesitation. Go big or go home. The greater the risk and all that. "Screw it," I tell Wes. "We're hijacking their hover car."

"You'll take out those two?" he asks, nodding at Tutface and the Grey, who are talking beside it.

"Consider it done," I say, hoping to fool both of us into believing it.

Like two badly trained ninjas, we scramble to the platform. The odds of this plan working are probably about one in ten, but it's already in motion and all we've got. I give up the stealth act and sprint full speed for them.

The Grey, whose back is to me, begins to turn my way when I'm less than two meters away.

I leap and fly foot first into his lower back, screaming my best Bruce Lee, "Kiai!"

My sensei would've shaken his head and said my technique was sloppy, but it does the job, slamming the Grey's head so hard into Tutface's shoulder that its forehead splits in two, pink goo dribbling on the floor while his body twitches like it's touching a live wire.

Stunned, Tutface wipes goo off his face as he stares at the dead Grey. To hell with a fair fight: a distracted enemy is an easy target. I recover from the kick and throw a karate chop to his Adam's apple. Both of his hands clutch his throat, and he falls to the floor, gasping for air.

I jump on the hover car, feeling like the bastard son of John Wick and Princess Leia.

Wes steps away from the console. "What took you so long?"

I check behind, see the Grey power walkers are almost to us. "Hold on tight," I say, giving Wes time to grab the railing before I hit what I hope is the turbo button.

We shoot forward way faster than I expected, and jerk to a stop even sooner, my body slamming into the console, flying through the air, and crashing to the floor.

Everything hurts, both my thighs snapped in half. Wes lies a few feet away, but he's not moving, his neck bent at unnatural angle.

The Greys power walk past the hover car that I only now see is tethered to a parking stall. They circle around us, glaring with angry eyes. Tutface walks over and presses a button on his device, opening a hatch in the wall, a red glow and heat pouring out of it.

There's a low beeping sound as the Greys move out of the way for the large robot sweeper. It bumps into Wes and directs him toward the open hatch, maneuvering back and forth until Wes tumbles down into the incinerator.

It turns to me. Game over.

The correct choice was to use your current resources, ingenuity, and ability to move faster than an alien power walker to dash straight for the opening hatch and freedom - for as long as it lasts.

Turn to page 42.

"Something weird is going on," I tell Wes. "I swear I just saw you outside that window."

"Are you taking your anxiety meds?"

"I don't take anxiety meds."

"Maybe you should start."

"I'm not crazy."

"Debatable."

I know what I saw. That was Wes, or some unknown twin. Maybe his twin isn't such a dweeb.

"I'll be right back," I say, heading for the door.

The door closes behind me, and I'm back in the blazing heat. Nothing like New Mexico in summer. My eyes take a few seconds to adjust to the brightness. There's no one out here that looks like Wes, just a trio of old ladies heading into a bakery called Mothership Muffins, and a pair of large men in black suits standing outside their black SUV parked across the street. They look like bodyguards, or government stooges, who seem to use the same unimaginative barber and share a single personality.

The taller one on the right notices me. I didn't think his eyes could squint any more than they already were, but they do as he looks me up and down. He brings his wrists up to his mouth and speaks into his cufflink.

"There's something you don't see every day," I mumble to myself.

He moves into the street, heading my way, as his partner gets in the driver's seat, turns on the car. He walks straight at me, aggressively. Part of me wants to hold my ground, deal with whatever his problem is right here in the street. Another part of me wants to duck into the Mothership bakery and hide behind their muffins.

When he's close enough, I ask, "Is there something wrong?"

He stops in front of me. "I was going to ask you the same thing?"

I smile. "I'm good. Just hanging in Roswell, looking for aliens and waiting to get abducted."

"In that case," he says, "it's your lucky day."

The SUV pulls up to the curb, and before it stops, the back door flies open. The guy in front of me grabs my shoulders and hurls me into the vehicle. It happens so fast, I don't even get a chance to yell.

There's another black suit in the back. Female, ponytail, no smile, syringe in hand.

The guy holds me so my neck's exposed, while less-friendly Nurse Ratchet stabs me in the neck with the needle.

I swear, just a second ago, the guy said this was my lucky day. None of this feels lucky!

I try to ask why they're doing this, but my ability to talk is gone, everything moving slow-motion, and not in a fun recreational way. I sink into the soft leather, barely aware we're moving.

The woman turns my head, so I'm staring at the door, and sticks something in my ear.

"Empty," she says, turning me the other way, her chest just inches from my face. Again, with the ear thing, but this time deep, like way deep. Tickle my brain deep. "Very empty."

She sits back in her seat and speaks into her cufflink. "We have secured Artifact One, but the temporal communication devise is not present."

"Must be with the other Artifact," a disembodied voice says. "Have agents Baker and Martin move in and secure number two. Any sign of hostiles?"

I see hostiles, I try to scream. They've abducted me, drugged me, and have been very intimate with both of my ears! But I can't move, let alone scream.

"Negative," she says. "But I have no doubt they are on site."

"The human artifacts cannot fall into their hands. You have the green light to terminate."

Terminate? That better be code for tell him to have a nice day and let him go.

She looks at me, and I see something in her eyes. A moment of emotion. "I didn't think they would look so young," she says.

"If your clearance were higher, you wouldn't think that. We don't even know how long the artifacts have been on Earth."

What the frak are they talking about? I've been on Earth eighteen long, boring years.

"Understood." The woman pulls out a strange device, her finger on its trigger. She holds the end of it to my forehead and tells me to close my eyes. "I don't know what your mission was, but it is over now."

The correct choice was to stay inside, ponder the situation, continue browsing and maybe insult Wes some more.
Turn to page 34.

We can't just wait here for the aliens to capture us. "We've got to listen to the fish-guy," I whisper, pointing at my ear.

"Why?" Wes says.

"It's just a gut feeling."

"Yesterday your gut told you to hit on that girl at the truck stop. How'd that work out?"

"Anyone can make that mistake. And *he* was very understanding. C'mon, we're making a run for Bumblebee."

Wes nods.

There's no way around the leather-clad alien closest to the Camaro. He just changed his search pattern, and he'll see us the second we get close. But right now he's got his back to us.

"You run until you get to that car," I say. "Don't stop."

Wes says okay, and I make a break for it, running right at the alien biker, planning on knocking him to the ground. I've had two years of Krav Maga, mostly online, and have seen every Jason Statham movie. Twice. I got this.

"Hey, Larry," the cowboy lizard says. "Behind you!"

The biker spins around in time to grab me by the throat.

I don't got this.

His human hand turns into a scaly taloned thing, claws digging into my neck.

He draws a clawed fist back and drives it into my stomach, his hand disappearing beneath my view.

The pain is tremendous, like nothing I've ever experienced, combined with an incredible pressure in my stomach. It feels like something is about to burst out, like a Xenomorph, but not as cute.

I glance over. Wes reaches the Camaro and runs around it, frantically checking each of the doors. He screams when he turns toward me, unaware of the cowboy lizard walking up behind him.

The one who's fist-deep inside me, says. "Hey, Larry."

The cowboy lizard who just grabbed Wes by his throat and lifted him off the ground looks our way.

The biker pulls his hand out of me, bringing with it huge strands of spaghetti-like pasta as big as intestines. Oh, shit, those are intestines. Mine!

With my innards wrapped around his wrist, he raises his arm and pulls out an unwinding tangle—a magician doing the endless handkerchief trick. "Look, they've got a fun-filled inside."

Try again. Turn to page 57.

"Okay, Bob," I say, "we're going with the baby killing plan."

"The what?"

"Please don't call it that," Wes says.

"The killing baby Hitler plan. Dark Blossom," I say.

"You mean Death Blossom."

I break off from my rendezvous with Red-Four. "Whatever. Tell me what I need to know."

"Red-Five, where are you going?"

I switch off the comms.

"Are you sure about this?" Bob asks. "Temporal fussion-melons estimate there is a—"

"I don't want to know the odds. Let's just do this."

"As you wish, Star Pilot. The temporal bomb is low yield, so you will have to detonate from inside the Cruiser."

"Inside?" Wes says.

"There's a handy bit of information we didn't have before." I throttle back and rotate the Astral Fighter, plotting a course for the Talon Cruiser's launch bay located at the very center of the ship where the massive hull sections converge. We roar toward the cruiser as a hail of anti-aircraft fire streaks toward us.

"Wes, all shields forward."

"I hope you know what you're doing."

"You and me both."

The cruiser looms, a monstrous behemoth against the backdrop of Earth. The Astral Fighter rockets toward the massive doors of the launch bay. To my surprise, they're partially open. I fire with every weapon still online. The hangar doors and the surrounding area erupt in explosions as we fly directly into the heart of the chaos.

The hangar deck rushes up to meet us, and I decelerate as best I can. The Astral Fighter lands hard—hard enough that the environmental stabilizers can't mask the impact. We feel the collision like a car crash and come to a stop with a thud.

"Status report," Bob says.

"We're inside the hanger, and I'm sure they know we're here. What's next?"

"Death Blossom is ready. I just need a minute to calibrate the time-quake to your ship."

A loud thud echoes in the cabin. Something strong is pounding on the outside.

"I'm not sure how much time we have, Bob."

"It might speed things up if you program the destination into the temporal Honeyflux-seed."

I look up at the console. "The honey-flux thingy is around here somewhere."

Wes sits up and reaches for the overhead display. "I'm on it."

I'm about to ask if he knows what he's doing when I hear metal tearing behind me. In the aft section of the ship, where the sidewall connects to the bulkhead, something is ripping open a section of the ship. The bottom of the Greys' hovering platform Bob's borrowed scientist used to seal a breach in our hull is being pulled away from the outside.

Through the slowly widening gap, I see a face so hideous it makes the Sleestaks back on Earth look like cuddly Cabbage Patch dolls. Three scaly, clawed appendages—I want to call them hands, but that feels wrong—force their way into the opening, pulling and tearing.

The extremely strong and pissed off Reptilian Progenitor is only seconds away from ripping the Greys' platform from our ship, when I feel a beam of heat to my side. I look at Wes aiming his sonic spatula at the creature.

A horrific, blood curdling shriek echoes, and the alien vanishes.

"You're getting pretty handy with that thing," I say.

"Glad you brought me?" Wes says while returning the weapon no fourteen-year-old in the universe should have to his backpack.

"Don't push it. Bob, we have a breach in the ship. Is that going to be a problem?"

"Helmets on," he says. "The countdown has begun."

I'm keenly aware Bob did not answer my question, and I try not to think about the reason why. The heads-up display shows the countdown. We have eight seconds. I glance at the destination display that Wes punched in. It shows the day, month, and year we left Roswell, and I know it's just a bunch of cold numbers on a display screen, but it feels like home.

"This is gonna work, right, Bob?"

Four seconds.

"If it does not, it has been an honor trying to save the galaxy with you, Star Pilot."

Two seconds.

"Not really the response I was shopping for, Bob!"

One second.

"Booobbbbbb!"

August 19, 2019, Roswell, New Mexico

I open my eyes just as the familiar sensation of my very being reestablishing itself in place and time dissipates. I take a deep breath and sit up in the cockpit for what I hope is the last time. I have a few aches and pains but nothing a Tylenol can't handle. Either I'm getting used to time travel, or the shorter jaunt through history is just easier on the human body. At least I hope it was shorter.

I check the display. *8-19-2019. Home.*

"Hey, meatsacks," Bob says. "You need to vacate the ship; it is set to move into another reality."

I look over at Wes, who already has his helmet off. We both unbuckle and stand just as the seats disappear. Wes scoops up his backpack as the ship's controls turn transparent. A second later, they vanish. The cockpit is changing rapidly. Each layer we saw stripped away a few days ago is rematerializing. In moments, we're standing in a minimalist compartment with metallic walls, resembling nothing that would suggest a spaceship.

"Stairs," Wes says.

I turn and see the spiral staircase we'd come down. Wes slips into the straps of his backpack, and we head up. We're about halfway up when I look back at Wes. He looks as tired as I feel, but we can't stop. The stairs are disappearing behind him. I don't know if Bob's controlling that, or if it's on auto-disappear. Either way, I don't want to find out.

We reach the top and don't hesitate. I touch my hand to the ceiling, and the key that is my DNA pops the roof open. I peek outside and see people walking by. Some glance at my brother and me, but no one stops for a closer look. After all, this is Roswell; the sight of two teens climbing out of the trunk of a vintage Chevy Camaro isn't the strangest thing they've seen.

We step out onto the sidewalk. Our Astral Fighter has folded back into a reality in which it is a yellow Camaro, now parked across the street from the Invasion Station. I smile when I see my dad's SUV resting in front of the store.

"I wonder if we're still inside?" I say.

"One way to find out," Wes says. We cross the street and step into a tiny alley in between the gift shop building and the I Want To Believe deli. Wes moves around to the store window and peeks inside. "Hey, I see us. Oh, man."

"What?"

"Why didn't you tell me my head was so big."

"I thought you knew."

"Frak," Wes says and quickly ducks down, then moves away from the window. "I think you saw me. I mean not you-you, yesterday you."

"Oh," I say, remembering. "I did see you. But I think I decided it was just your clone."

Wes shakes his head. "I'll never understand how your brain works."

I shrug. "Me either."

The sound of a car approaching fast catches my attention. I glance over and see the sedan that chased us, or rather will chase us, speeding up the street. I grab Wes and pull him into the alley as the vehicle screeches to a halt. Two familiar M.I.B. agents step from the car, leaving it idling in the middle of the street. I recognize them as the two that grabbed Mom and Dad, or are about to grab Mom and Dad.

"Bob, why is this still happening?" I say as the agents run into the gift shop. "Why is M.I.B. here? I thought we fixed everything."

"You did, Star Pilot, but this must still occur or nothing will change. M.I.B. has been looking for you since your escape from Area 51. They have set up facial recognition scanners in key areas where alien activity has occurred around the globe, hoping to locate you. The moment you stepped into Roswell, they found you."

"Well, how did the Reptilians find us?" Wes asks.

"I suspect as M.I.B. is their main obstacle to global dominance, the Reptilians monitor their movements. They went after you because M.I.B. wanted you. They may not have even known why, or maybe they did. It does not matter now."

"What does matter?" I ask in frustration.

"Mom and Dad," Wes says.

"Of course they matter," I say.

"No," Wes says, pointing at the store's window. "Mom and Dad. They're taking them."

"Bob, what should we do."

"Nothing," Bob says.

"Nothing," I repeat, as I look inside and see our other selves duck into the back storeroom.

"The timelines are rerouting and will take a little while to establish new roots. The galaxy is massive, but you should experience the effects of the blossemberry fertilization soon. Just relax."

"Screw that," Wes says, unslinging his backpack.

The M.I.B. agents escort Mom and Dad from the building. They both appear scared, and Mom looks back inside, I assume for us. One of the agents speaks into his sleeve. "Artifacts are not secure, but we have isolated their travel companions. Send reinforcements."

Before I can stop him, Wes pulls the sonic spatula from his backpack and steps in front of the agents. With a quick flash from the Greys' weapon, the agents and our parents stop moving.

I quickly run up to Wes. "What'd you do?"

"Just stunned. Come on, get Dad's keys."

I get the keys from Dad's pocket, and we each grab our parents' hands. We pull them toward the car. They move like zombies but don't resist. Wes opens the rear door, and we hastily deposit them in the backseat. I jump behind the wheel and start the engine.

Pulling away from the curb, I glance back at the M.I.B. agents, who seem to be moving a little, like two bears slowly coming out of hibernation. Dad's SUV doesn't have the acceleration of an Astral Fighter, but I gun the engine as if it did.

* * *

A few minutes later, we are at the convention hotel. Mom and Dad didn't remember wanting to take a nap and letting me drive the rest of the way to the hotel, but since there was no other logical explanation as to why they woke up in the back seat already at the hotel, they had little choice but to try and accept it. They've let me drive on long family trips before, so the story wasn't too crazy, but I'm sure they'd have questions.

I tell them we will hang back and get the luggage while they check in. Mom looks at us both, and for a second, I think she's gonna ask one of those questions that is clearly racing through her mind. Instead, she puts her hand on my head, rustles my hair, and says, "You both need haircuts."

I let out a sigh of relief and watch as our parents walk into the hotel lobby. Wes steps next to me. I want to put my arm around him, a celebratory gesture to commemorate all we've been through. Things only he and I will remember, but the gesture seems weird, so I just chuck him on the shoulder. "Can you believe what we've done?"

Wes shakes his head. "I can't believe we didn't die, like several times."

That we know of. Which reminds me to have Bob check on something. "Hey, Bob?"

"Your parents are going to be alright," Bob says. "The world around them and you is starting to react to the new melon balls in the timeline."

"That's fascinating, but not what I was going to ask."

"What is it, Star Pilot?"

"With all the resets, I mean, did they do any ..." I tap a finger to my temple. "Is my brain good?"

"I've run several med scans, and you are no smarter or dumber than you were before."

"That is both good and sad at the same time," Wes says.

I glower at Wes. "Hey, Bob, not that I'm eager to say goodbye or anything, but how do we get these fish out of our heads?"

"The Pisces Converters will not cause either of you any noticeable long-term harm, but if you really want them out, you'll need an aquarium, some soy sauce, and a peacock feather."

"How in the world—"

"I'll send you a YouTube tutorial," Bob interrupts. "Please listen. The timelines I am connected to are changing, and when they are complete, we will lose contact for quite some time, and I need to tell you something."

"We're listening," Wes says.

"Our actions may have been successful, but we might have tweaked your planet's future a bit. Remember the Greys' platform piece?"

"Yeah."

"During the Astral Fighter's reentry into 2019, it dislodged completely and fell off. It crashed into a facility in China."

I ask if anybody was hurt.

"No. Well, not immediately, but according to my future-cast data ... it did ..." There's a popping sound like an old radio station losing its signal, and some of Bob's words are lost. "You need to prepare."

"Prepare for what? Whatever happened, China is on the other side of our planet."

Wes and I stand still, waiting for Bob to say something.

"Bob, are you there?" Wes says.

With another staticky pop, Bob's voice comes back very faint. "... damaged a lab in Wuhan, Chi ... prepare. When you get home, have your parents secure canned food ... and lots of toilet paper ..."

"What?" I say.

After several silent beats, Wes says. "I think we lost him."

"Did he say toilet paper?"

"Most likely another glitch."

"Probably right."

Wes sticks his finger in his ear. "Where're we gonna find peacock feathers?"

I shrug. "A very generous peacock?"

My brother looks at me sideways. "You *are* a meatsack."

"Right back at you."

THE END

Note from the Publisher

I don't recall our first meeting—probably at a Horror Writers Association table at the Los Angeles Times Festival of Books, Midsummer Scream, or some Southern California con—but Kevin David Anderson has been a fixture ever since: always promoting the organization, other authors and the genre, never just himself, and always ready with a laugh.

After devouring Kevin's horror-comedy collection *Midnight Men*, I asked him to write a *Try Not to Die* entry. I worried a little when he said he wanted a sci-fi adventure because I'd left my childhood love of spaceships behind, but the first draft erased every doubt. Kevin's characters, his pace, and his absurd, gleeful brutality had me laughing out loud. This is Kevin's book through and through; I simply had the honor of helping shape the language, format, and glorious deaths. I'll admit it: I helped deliver this bloody little bastard.

Working on this gave me the courage to write my own horror comedy, *Try Not to Die: With Satan Inside*, coming this Christmas, and Kevin's contributing to the tie-in anthology *Who's Satan Inside*. Keep an eye out.

Finally: the two flash-fiction pieces that follow were auctioned for the Books & Brews II fundraiser and dedicated to Jordan Triplett and Jessica Vance. Enjoy their spectacularly grim demises.

Mark Tullius

Publishing Ups and Downs

Mark Tullius

The hotel elevator opens at the top floor and we get off. I show Jake the way and he runs ahead, waiting for me at the stairwell that leads to the roof.

"Whatcha waiting for?" I say, heading up. I open the door with the "Staff Only" sign and step into the bright afternoon.

Jake stops in the doorway. "You're sure this is okay? Feels wrong."

"It's all good. Remember, this whole thing is about testing ourselves." That doesn't ease his anxiety, so I add, "Cleared it with the manager. Gave him a twenty-dollar tip as a thank you."

He nods and follows me to the corner of the roof where there's a picnic table with an umbrella. A row of neatly-trimmed knee-high bushes runs all along the ledge of the building.

My fear of heights has improved tremendously over the past year, but my heart gets going when I'm nearing the table, a good eight feet from the ledge. I take a deep breath and blow it out.

"Come on," Jake says, walking over to the bushes. "Look how small everyone is down there."

"Hey, hey, hey," I say, hating to see him get so close. "How about you sit on this side?"

He humors me and takes a seat at the table. "So who are we meeting?"

"Jordan. I met her last year at Books & Brews. I don't think you were at the table when we talked though."

"What's the meeting for?"

"Well, I was supposed to write a death scene including her, but I've been having a really hard time being creative. And who the hell wants to kill people they like?"

"You."

I ruffle his hair. "That's my boy."

"You've probably killed everyone you've ever known."

"Yeah, but I'm sure I was super sad about it inside."

"So, if you're not going to kill her, what's this about?"

"Her passion is helping indie authors. It's the reason she runs a blog and book club. Even put out an anthology. I wanted to talk publishing with her, see if we can help each other."

He pulls out his phone. "Sounds boring."

Everything's boring to a 12-year-old, and Jake doesn't give two shits about my books even though we're writing one together. I check the time on my phone and Jordan doesn't disappoint, walking out the door a few seconds before noon.

"Oh wow. This is so cool," she says, walking right up to the ledge, no fear of heights, just as promised.

"Before we get started, we have a gift from Jake."

He pulls the long thin box out of his back pocket and holds it out to her.

"Oh my gosh," she says, inspecting it. "A Harry Potter wand box."

"Open it," Jake says with a big smile.

Jordan pulls the top off the box and out jump the dozens of spiders we had packed inside, harmless little things flying everywhere. Her scream rocks me and I take a step back the same time she does. She throws the box and swats at her face, falls backward when her legs smash into the bushes.

I try to grab her, but she's already falling, her scream ending with a splat.

V is for Violence

Mark Tullius

My favorite time of day has always been the dead of night. The crunch of each step on the dirt path, the breeze blowing through the pines. Everything is asleep except predators, yet there's nothing for me to fear. I've been working these woods for the last five years. The gun, taser, and bear spray on my belt, are just for looks. They keep the campers feeling safe. Secure.

After all, there's absolutely no need for any animal to mess with me since I've ensured that every carnivore nearby is well fed and cared for. Like my good friend, Big Black, the old bear who's gotten fat and slow from everything I've left him. Same for Oliver the owl, who lost his eye because of a stupid kid throwing rocks.

I've nearly finished clearing out this section of the campgrounds, alerting everyone to the danger that only another human could cause. I can still see the shock on Janice's face when I showed them the kind of danger they were in. All that's left is this tent to the left and the RV around the bend.

I shine my flashlight on my clipboard. There are two campers registered for this spot under one last name, the V in Vance my favorite letter, the way it ends in such a sharp point. The blood splatter obscured one of the first names, but I can clearly make out Jay. The other person must be Jay's spouse or kid.

There's no way of knowing if the Vances have a weapon, so I announce myself a dozen yards from the tent. "Ranger Fallbrook here," I say, shining my light on the dirt in front of its entrance. I keep my voice calm like I imagine Fallbrook would if he were in my shoes and not face down in the ravine behind the shower building with a dozen stab wounds. "Sorry to wake you, but there's an emergency."

"One second," a tired voice calls from inside.

"It's two in the goddamn morning," a man grumbles, sounding like he's speaking to the other person and not running his mouth to me. "What the hell?"

I cut the distance in half, only about six feet between me and the lowering zipper. I keep the light on the ground between us so it appears I'm trying to help him, but I'm really keeping him from getting a good look at my face.

Mr. Vance crawls out from the tent still grumbling. "This better be good. I don't smell a fire," he says, standing up, a good half a head taller than me. The woman crawls out behind him, asking him to please keep calm.

"I completely understand," I say, slipping out the knife from my back pocket. "I'd be upset as well."

"So what is it?" he barks.

I shine the light in his face, knowing he would raise his hands and expose that beautiful belly. I bury my blade, ripping it up until I strike ribs, then out.

His wife screams but I cut it short, the blade slicing through her throat. They're not dead yet, but they will be soon, no one left to find them but the animals. Just one more stop and my work for the night is done.

About the Authors

Kevin David Anderson

Kevin David Anderson burst onto the scene with *Night of the Living Trekkies*, a laugh-out-loud zombie romp set at a Star Trek convention, praised by *Publishers Weekly* and named one of the best zombie novels of 2010 by *The Washington Post*. His follow-up, *Night of the ZomBEEs*, and dozens of short stories have been enjoyed worldwide in anthologies, magazines, and hit podcasts like *The No Sleep Podcast* and *Pseudopod*.

When he's not writing horror, comedy, or a twisted mix of both, Anderson is usually cracking nerdy dad jokes with his son. Together they created *The Geektastic Joke Book for Kids*, *Star Wars: The Jokes Awaken* (a top 10 Star Wars gift for kids), and *Jurassic Jokes*. A proud member of the Horror Writers Association, he lives in Southern California, where he teaches special education and keeps dreaming up new ways to make readers scream—and laugh.

Visit Kevin's Website at KevinDavidAnderson.com

Mark Tullius

My writing covers a wide range, with fiction being my favorite to create, twenty or so titles under my belt. There are 20 titles in my interactive *Try Not to Die* series and 30 more in the works. I also have two nonfiction titles, both inspired by a reckless lifestyle, playing Ivy League football, and battering my brain as an unsuccessful MMA fighter and boxer. *Unlocking the Cage* is the largest sociological study of MMA fighters to date and *TBI or CTE* aims to spread awareness and hope to others that suffer with traumatic brain injury symptoms.

I live in sunny California with my wife, two kids, five cats, and one demon. Derek the Demon pops in whenever he's bored and makes special appearances on my social media.

You can also get your first set of free stories by signing up to my newsletter. This letter is only for the brave, or at least those brave enough to deal with bad dad jokes, a crude sense of humor, and loads and loads of unhappy endings. Derek and I would love to have you join us!

Visit Mark's Website at MarkTullius.Com

Download Your Free Copy

Includes the first two chapters and one or two death scenes from each of the first 14 books in the Try Not to Die series.

Download for free.

For More Fun-Filled Deaths

please check out the rest of the *Try Not to Die* series.

Out Now:

At Grandma's House
In Brightside
In the Pandemic
In the Wizard's Tower
In the Wild West
At Ghostland
At Dethfest
Back at Grandma's House
On Slashtag
In a Dark Fairy Tale
At the Meadow Spire Mall
The Shadowlands
In This Damned House
In Arcranium
Escaping the Cult
Super High
In Brownsville
In the UK
By Your Own Hand
In Roswell and Beyond

In the Works:

With Satan Inside
At Desperation House
On Werewolf Island
In Slattery Falls
In the Tournament of Mortem
In Hollow 2
In a Video Game
With No Way Out
With many more soon to be announced.

Try Not to Die Merchandise

For the latest *Try Not to Die* hoodies, shirts, puzzles, blankets, and signed copies, visit Mark's store:

Your Free Books are Waiting

Think You Can Survive? Prove It.

The *Try Not to Die* series is just getting started — and you can be the first to experience each deadly new chapter.
Sign up for Mark Tullius's free newsletter and you'll receive:

- Three FREE ebooks: *TNTD: At Grandma's House, Morsels of Mayhem & Somber Stroll*
- Early access to upcoming Try Not to Die releases
- Exclusive content you won't find anywhere else

Survive the books. Enjoy the perks.
Join now — if you dare.